Praise for

'So surprising and charming it would be hard not to feel uplifted'
Observer

'Energetic, confident and compassionate ... He is one to watch'
Scotland on Sunday

'Beautifully observed and hilariously uncomfortable'
Guardian

'The book is funny, fascinating and perfectly realised ... comparisons with *The Curious Incident of The Dog in the Night Time* are already coming thick and fast, and the book merits them'
Irish Independent

'Funny, poignant, rude, life-affirming'
Bookseller

'Brave'
Daily Mail

'A very human story of relationships and loyalty'
Irish Examiner

'Bittersweet'
Daily Express

BRIAN CONAGHAN

BLOOMSBURY
LONDON OXFORD NEW YORK NEW DELHI SYDNEY

Bloomsbury Publishing, London, Oxford, New York, New Delhi and Sydney

First published in Great Britain in April 2016 by Bloomsbury Publishing Plc
50 Bedford Square, London WC1B 3DP

www.bloomsbury.com

BLOOMSBURY is a registered trademark of Bloomsbury Publishing Plc

A CIP catalogue record for this book is available from the British Library

Hardback ISBN 978 1 4088 5574 4
Export ISBN 978 1 4088 7841 5

Typeset by RefineCatch Limited, Bungay, Suffolk
Printed and bound in Great Britain by CPI Group (UK) Ltd, Croydon CR0 4YY

1 3 5 7 9 10 8 6 4 2

For Rosie

1
Under the Covers

It was hard to remain silent. I tried. I really did, but my breathing kept getting louder as I gasped for clean air. My body was trembling, adding noise to the silence. Mum pulled me closer to her, holding tight. Dad cuddled us both. Three spoons under one duvet. With the summer heat and us huddled together the smell wasn't amusing. I shifted about.

'Shhh,' Dad whispered. 'Try not to make a sound.'

Mum kissed the back of my neck. Her wheezing chest blew out little puffs of air on to my head. 'It's OK, Charlie, everything's going to be all right,' she said.

'Promise?' I said.

'Promise,' Mum said.

'Shhh,' Dad said again, firmer, like an annoyed school-teacher.

‘Mum, I’m really scared.’

‘I know you are, sweetheart, I know you are.’ Mum squeezed my bones.

‘We’re all scared, Charlie,’ Dad said. ‘But we need to hold it together. It’ll be over soon.’

Dad was scared, which increased my own terror levels. Dads aren’t meant to get scared. Dads protect. Dads make things better. But I guess there are some things in life even dads can’t affect. Bombs, for one.

The first pangs of nerves had begun as soon as the newsreader on the television stared out at us: *We expect this criminal act to be catastrophic for some of our residents.* The poor guy had looked stricken.

In Little Town, where I live, people know that something dreadful might happen to them one day; they realise that our Regime has infuriated some other Government, and that Government – specifically, the one over the border in Old Country – don’t like how certain things are done here: the way of life, the beliefs, the strangleholding … They think it’s all wrong, undemocratic. Inhumane. Pot and kettle springs to mind! Let’s call a spade a spade: Old Country’s Government thinks Little Town is just plain bad. Funny thing is we’ve heard that things over there aren’t much better (they don’t exactly welcome people speaking out either), but no one really knows for sure, because no one ventures across the border. Ever! In school everyone is told that many moons ago Little Town belonged to Old Country and that it was inevitable that they'd come knocking – or bombing – to demand it back. But who knows for sure? What we do know, however, is that *our* Regime isn't liked, even by us.

I know Little Town isn't exactly a barrel of laughs, and we did expect some repercussions for various disagreements, but not this. Never this.

We were under that duvet for a whole twenty minutes before the first explosion. It was far away yet made my entire insides bounce. Mum's body tensed. I heard Dad's teeth grind together.

There was another crack; it seemed closer. A third quickly followed. It *was* closer. BOOM! The house rattled. I heard screams and cries from outside. Curfew breakers? People who hadn't seen the news? Who hadn't heeded the warnings?

These bombs sounded like a fireworks and thunder combination; human squeals echoed, cries became howls. Another bomb.

Then another.

And another.

'I don't want to die. I don't want to die.' I turned to face my parents. No duvet could save us. What was Dad thinking when he said, *Well, I suppose we best do something about these bloody bombs then*? Why didn't he have a bunker or a shelter? What good was a duvet?

'I'm not ready to die,' I cried.

'We're not going to die, Charlie.' Dad's voice sounded unconvincing, wavering a bit. I fought for air. Mum wheezed. Here we were, the Law family, waiting for the ceiling to cave in on us. Waiting for the great leap into the unknown. These bombs that had brought the Law family together were about to blast us apart.

I glanced at my watch. Six minutes of relentless bombing.

A declaration of war? No army as such existed in Little Town – just some Rascals running around in military boots – so what was the point?

It's funny the things you think about when you're frozen with fear. I kept hoping that our shed wouldn't be damaged. I had big plans for that shed. But the main thing, I suppose, was at least we weren't dead.

Well, not yet anyway.

2
Our Education

In school when we're being told all this stuff about Old Country my mind wanders a touch. Now, I'm not usually a mind-wanderer but sometimes, just sometimes, I think about schools over there in Old Country. I wonder if pupils there are being educated about Little Town.

No doubt.

THINGS WE ARE TAUGHT ABOUT OLD COUNTRY

- They have buckets of money.
- Their army has tanks, wagons, helicopters, flying bombers, a trillion guns and loads of soldiers.
- Boys AND girls have to do Old Country Service in the army.
- Old Country Government wear silly military gear.

- You can't exactly vote for who you want this Government to be.
- It's not easy to enter or exit Old Country.
- Everything is big over there. EVERYTHING.
- If people don't conform, well …
- They despise all things Little Town.
- They despise me.

THINGS I IMAGINE ARE BEING TAUGHT ABOUT LITTLE TOWN

- Little Town is filthy.
- They are totally and completely skint.
- People can't wander the streets willy-nilly.
- It's hard to find jobs in Little Town.
- Their society is full of murky, backhanded, dirty, double-dealing thugs.
- Little Town's Regime couldn't run a raffle in a three-man tent.
- A bunch of raggle-taggle Rascals run the place.
- If people speak out, well …
- Little Towners despise all things Old Country.
- There will not be a Little Town much longer.

Once I told my history teacher that I wouldn't mind spending a few days in an Old Country school – like, for a sociology spying mission – just to try and *understand the similarities and differences, sir.*

'There are no similarities, Law,' he said, eyes bulging and steam seeping out of his nostrils. 'None at all!'

I guess not!

3
The Rules

It breaks my heart to see what's happened to this place. Before the bombs came Mum would say this at least once a week, no joking. Sometimes three times. When I came home from school without any homework to do, she'd say it. When I had to walk three miles to the only chemist in Little Town who sold her asthma inhaler, she'd say it. When I returned from the shops with an incomplete list of supplies, she'd say it. I got used to hearing this phrase.

Dad directed his annoyance towards the newspapers and television, scoffing and mocking all the stories of the day. This was *so far removed from the balanced, non-prejudiced news* that he wrote *back in the day* when he was *taking chances, being brave, standing up for honesty and transparency.* It was funny seeing Dad shout at rival newspapers.

'You know you can get an inhaler any day of the week in Old Country,' I informed Mum one time, as she had only three puff days remaining until I had to go and get her another. Dad flipped his lid, flashing his eyes above his paper and locking them on me.

'Does that school of yours not teach you anything, son?' I didn't want to rhyme off what we actually learnt in school so I let him go off on one of his flips. 'Old Country is out of bounds for us; you need papers to go over the border, a passport, a specific reason. We don't have any of those things, so why bloody mention it?'

'But I was just –'

'OK, Charlie?' Dad dropped his paper to his knees. 'Are we clear about that?'

'Crystal,' I said.

Dad could be very sensitive about the political situation. He wanted nothing more than for everyone to come and go as they pleased, to live in perfect harmony and all that. But at the same time he didn't want to attract trouble; he wanted to do his job without any hassles. That's why he kept his mouth shut.

Another time I mentioned to Mum that I'd heard about a place in Little Town where we could get quality supplies any day of the week. A bit like a warehouse where, if you knew the right people – or password, I don't know – you'd get in. I'd heard on the QT that if you paid a little bit more than shop prices you could get your hands on just about anything. Even inhalers. If you knew any of the top brass who ran these places then even better. I actually thought Mum would've been happy with this news. Shows what I know!

'I can get all the details at school, from Norman, if you want,' I told her. Some people at school knew the score; they had their ears to the ground. Norman would definitely spill the beans if you got him talking.

When Mum gets angry her breathing becomes heavier, like she's trying to suck in huge volumes of air so her tirade can be more powerful.

'Now, you listen to me, Charlie Law, and listen good: if I ever catch you going to any of those places it'll be school, home, room, bed for you for the next year.'

'But I was just –'

'Are we clear about that?'

'Crystal.'

I was certain that Dad knew about these warehouses because I'd heard him mutter things behind his newspaper like, *An embarrassment to call themselves officials* AND *Who voted for this lot, eh?* AND *Bloody shower of gangsters if you ask me* AND *Who do they think they actually represent? Not me, that's who!*

It did seem a bit unfair that people living in Old Country could get whatever they wanted whenever they wanted and we couldn't. I bet teenagers over there didn't have to wait ages until their parents saved enough money to buy them a new pair of swanky trainers or a denim jacket or books. I bet teenagers over there sneaked out to late nightclubs and maybe, just maybe, they did get to stay out after dark without feeling terrified. I'm betting, of course, but truth is I didn't know for sure.

Whenever I got them all worried, Mum and Dad sat me down to tell me (once again) the dos and don'ts of Little Town. As I got older more stuff was added to the list. After the whole thing about getting inhalers from Old Country and black-market warehouses in Little Town, we had one major parental powwow. Afterwards I formulated and constructed my own list and stuck it on the inside of one of my books.

CHARLIE LAW'S TEN LAWS OF LITTLE TOWN

1. Respect the dark curfew. No going out after dark in groups of three or more, unless you can prove that you are with family members. *(Easy to get around: walk somewhere separately)*
2. No ball games in public places. *(Parks … I know)*
3. No pets. *(One word: disease)*
4. No boozing in the streets. *(House boozing* OK, *though)*
5. No shouting in the streets. *(Not even in jest = public order crime)*
6. No giving cheek to the lawmakers. *(Unless you want a clout around the lughole)*

7. No dodging school unless you have one of the verified illnesses on the list or you've been asked to carry out lawmaker work. *(Only a sudden limb amputation would've prevented me from attending school, and even then it would depend which limb)*
8. No tomfoolery in public places. *(Which I took to mean, don't enjoy yourself … ever!)*
9. NO STEALING. *(A biggie!)*
10. Instruction to beat ALL instructions: never draw attention to yourself, and WHATEVER YOU DO, DON'T GET CAUGHT.

4
A Perfect Union

The beginning of that summer, before the bombs came, was utterly dull. For teenagers, the summer holidays in Little Town equalled mind-melting boredom. They do in most places, I suppose.

– *Hey, what do you want to do tonight?*
– *Nothing.*
– *Brilliant, let's do nothing then.*
– *Excellent.*
– Cool.
– *Shall we contact the others?*
– *Don't care.*
– *Excellent.*
– Cool.

But as I was about to turn fifteen, my chops got rattled good and hard, BOOM! Everything and everyone changed. And not always for the better.

Pav and his family arrived a few weeks before the bombs came. How unlucky is that? All the way to Little Town for a new life, a new start, and this happens to them. Bad luck just seems to follow some people around. They moved into our block, on the same floor as us, directly across in fact. Dad quickly got in there and spoke to them, getting all their vital stats.

Main stat: they came from Old Country.

Old Country!

I know, right?

Pav was around the same age as me and due to attend my school after the summer holidays. By all accounts (well, Dad's) his father was some sort of mega mind back in Old Country, but in Little Town he would be cleaning floors and walls in our run-down hospital. His mother also had a big-brain job back where they came from, but now she was going to be cooking, shopping and mending clothes at home. The same as my mum. Pav had an older sister who chose not to come to Little Town. No reason why; maybe she's one of those independent girls who knows her own mind.

Dad said that the whole family looked as if they needed a good scrub and some fine grub inside them.

'There's not a pick on that boy,' he always said about Pav.

My first meeting with Pav was like no other *first meeting* I'd ever had. For starters he didn't speak the lingo. Well, he did, but in a funny sort of way. Whoever taught him it badly needed to re-hit the books themselves.

Mum called me from our shared backyard (which nobody ever used for social or fun things). Usually Mum would pop her head out of the window, open her lungs and scream her instructions, but this time she actually came all the way down to the back door. Trying to make an impression, wanting to be seen as all posh and uncommon.

'Charlie,' Mum said.

'What?'

'Could you come here, please?'

'I haven't done anything.'

'I know you haven't. Just come here.' Her tone eased my fear. I de-tensed my shoulders.

'But I'm doing stuff,' I said. By *stuff* I meant I was nose deep in a book, taking breaks to occasionally look at bees nibbling on flowers. I'm not sure everyone would've agreed that reading and nature-watching constituted *doing stuff*. Fact: some folk didn't like people who read. Thankfully Mum and Dad were OK about it.

'Come here, I've someone I want you to meet,' Mum said.

For a moment I thought that Erin F was going to appear

from behind Mum like a vision of beauty exiting melted ice. We could have looked at the bees together.

– I'm here for you, Charlie.
– Erin F!
– I want you to be the one, Charlie.
– You'll only break my heart, Erin F.
– I won't, promise.

If only.

'Who?' I asked.

'Just come here and see, Charlie.'

I put my book inside my trousers in the same way cowboys do with their guns. If anyone gives me shit I'm going to *read* their arses into next week. *Come any closer, punk, and I swear I'll open this beast up on page thirty-four and spray these words right into your gut.*

I walked towards Mum.

'OK, I'm here,' I said, standing ten paces in front of her.

'Come on, he's here,' Mum said, turning around, gesturing to whoever was hidden behind her. Then he slowly appeared.

Head first.

Army-short hair.

Fair.

His T-shirt and shorts arrangement drowned him; the clothes made his bare legs seem like two scrawny twigs. My index finger and thumb would've definitely fitted round his ankles, in case I wanted to try. A genuine stickman. His eyes were the colour of the sky. Now, I'd never seen a rabbit in the headlights as we didn't have a car but the look on his face was how I'd imagined a frightened rabbit to look. A hearty fish and chips wouldn't have gone amiss on his bones. Or some lemons. He neither smiled nor growled.

'Charlie, this is Pavel. He's our new neighbour.' Mum put her two hands on Pavel's shoulders, as only a mum would.

I advanced five paces. Halfway.

'Hi, Pavel. I'm Charlie. Charlie Law.' I extended my hand.

Mum pushed him towards me with a little encouraging shove. He had no choice other than to place his hand inside mine. I was careful not to squeeze too hard in case I crushed his twig fingers. Our shake went up and down three times.

'Pavel Duda I is,' he said.

'Pleased to meet you, Pavel Duda,' I said.

'Please to meet, yes.'

'Pavel? That's not a Little Town name, is it?' I asked him.

'No Little Town name.'

'Old Country, right?' My voice sounded high pitched. I felt embarrassed by it. Perhaps not everyone in Old Country hated us. I knew that some Old Country folk were being kicked out or leaving because they didn't agree with their own Government, but still.

'Yes, I from Old Country.' Pavel nodded his head.

'I'll leave you two boys to get to know each other then,' Mum said.

Before I could say NO! PLEASE DON'T LEAVE ME WITH HIM she'd made a beeline back up the stairs. Escaped.

We looked at each other. Sussing? I don't know. All I do know is that it was awkward. One minute I'm lost in bees and books and the next I'm standing in Awkward Town with a stranger from Old Country. An Old Country escapee? Refugee? Little Town never fails to surprise.

Did I mention his eyes were really blue? If my eyes were as blue as Pavel's maybe Erin F would have been all over me like a tramp on a sandwich.

MENTAL MEMO: DO NOT INTRODUCE PAVEL TO ERIN F IN CASE SHE WANTS TO DIVE RIGHT INTO THOSE BABY BLUE BLINDERS HERSELF.

'How long have you been in Little Town?' I asked.

Pavel counted on his fingers.

'Two hours we arrive since.'

'Why come here?' I said. This was a genuine question because I was deadly interested why Old Country people wanted to decamp here. HERE! Maybe they wanted to stand shoulder to shoulder with us against rotten Regimes? Maybe they felt they could somehow be freer here, have an opinion that was safe to voice? If only they knew the half of it. It wasn't as if we had a load of cool amenities or tourist hotspots. We did have a couple of bookshops, a not-so-inviting park and a shopping street where you could get your hands on last year's fashions, if you had the funds. By the look of Pavel I didn't think he was into fashion. Or books.

'Why Little Town?' I asked again.

'Parents make come choice.'

'Parents, eh?'

'Old Country no good for parents any longer more.'

'Why?'

'Too much of shit.'

'Was it, like, dangerous?'

'For parents dangerous. Every night scared.'

'So you couldn't, like, go to the flicks or anything?'

'What flicks?'

'Sorry, it means cinema.'

'No. No cinema go for us.'

'So that's the reason why you came to Little Town? Because Old Country was too dangerous.'

'This is reason, yes.'

'That's terrible, Pavel. I'm sorry to hear that.'

'Please call to me Pav. Pavel I no like. Pav much better.'

'Pav's good for me.'

'And your name one more?'

'Charlie,' I said. 'Charlie Law.'

'I hear not this name before.'

'It's old.'

'Is typical Little Town name, yes?'

'It was my grandfather's name,' I said.

'He dead?'

'A long time ago.'

'Shot?'

'No.'

'Prison?'

'No.'

'Torture?'

'No,' I said with a tiny sneer.

From what Pav was asking it seemed as if Old Country was utter Bandit Country. *We're heading the same way as that place,* Dad would mutter from time to time, but I never considered that Little Town would ever get that bad.

'Grandfather live in no gun time?' Pav asked.

'A long time ago, yes,' I said.

'The luck man. Maybe we make the big fook-you time machine and go back,' Pav said, laughing massively from his gaunt belly.

I laughed too.

Our first.

'Who taught you to swear in the lingo?' I didn't correct his mispronunciation.

'First words we learn.'

I showed Pav around the backyard and told him the best times of the day to see bees, which cats enjoyed it when you chi chi chied them. He let me hear all the swear words he'd learnt in the lingo. Impressive enough. If only he'd put the same learning effort into grammar foundations and sentence construction, then he'd have been on to a winner.

Pav liked bees and cats. He liked the flowers as well. Insects. Animals. Plants. Three things in common, not a bad start. I didn't want to push my luck and talk about books; my gut feeling was that he wasn't much of a reader.

'So how old are you, Pav?'

'I have fourteen years.'

'Same as me.'

'I will fifteen years after summer.'

'Same as me again.'

'Ah, yes?'

'So that means you will be attending my school then?'

'School near station?'

'That's the one.'

'I no like school.'

'Don't worry, Pav, I'll look after you. Anyway, we still have loads of the summer to go before we think about school.'

The idea of getting in some decent work experience and helping Pav with the lingo popped into my head. He would need a helping hand in case he made a complete arse of himself at school. And for reasons that baffled Mum and Dad, I wanted to be a teacher when I left school.

We saw four different species of bee that afternoon. My record was three. Was Pav my four-leaf clover? Sadly we didn't discuss books, but Pav told me some of the reasons why he and his family came to Little Town.

5
Shed

There was a rickety old shed at the bottom of our shared backyard. Nobody ever used it, so me and Pav decided that it would be perfect as our sanctuary place. Our boom-boom room. Our lad pad. Pav wanted it to be called THE DEN, that special place where fellas can chat about the ladies, football and Governments.

'Did you have a girlfriend in Old Country, Pav?'

'Don't like girl.'

'Really?'

'I no like.'

'Look, it's OK with me if you eat your soup with a fork. I'm down with that.' Pav looked confused. 'I mean, if you prefer boy hugs it's OK. I couldn't give two hoots, but you have to know that I'm a self-confessed ladies' man,' I said.

'No. No. No. No,' Pav said, waving his arms around. 'I like the girl and the lady and the woman. I NOT kiss the boy.'

'OK, Pav,' I said. 'But it's totally fine if you –'

'I like the girl, Charlie!' he said.

'OK,' I said.

I wanted the shed to become a type of classroom, a backyard school kind of place. Somewhere I could practise my teaching skills and get Pav's lingo up to scratch before school started.

A small table and two chairs would definitely fit inside the shed, at a push a third chair. There weren't any other kids my age on our block, and my friends from school weren't in the habit of dropping by because of the patrols and the curfew, but who knows, maybe if Erin F could get away from looking after her poor mum for a few hours, she'd want to come shedside for some chat and chill of an occasion? I think Erin F needs some quality R & R. Some time just for her. So, a guest chair was an absolute must.

Problem Number One: I didn't have a clue where to get my mitts on a table and chairs. It's not like they were just lying around in the streets any longer beside bags of old manky clothes and stinking mattresses. When I was a little kid in Little Town you could easily go around and ask your neighbours or family friends if they were lobbing out any old rubbish or unwanted furniture. People don't open their door any more to random knocks.

'Do you have any extra chairs in your house, Pav?' I asked … You never know.

'One chair have we. And one big chair.'

'Big chair?'

'Long.' Pav extended his hands to show me what he meant.

'A sofa, you mean?'

'Sofa, yes. One chair and sofa.'

'It's important that we get our hands on some chairs if we want our shed to be comfortable.'

'We need to be the thief?' Pav said.

He clearly hadn't learnt the rules of Little Town yet. 'No. No stealing,' I said.

'No?'

'No, we'll just have to keep a close eye on the street in case anyone is throwing away old chairs. Ask people in the know.'

'I peel my eyes,' Pav said.

'It's keep your eyes peeled, Pav. But good effort.'

For someone so scraggy, Pav was strong. An Old Country ox. When we cleared the shed to make our den, Pav lugged these weighty metal poles and heavy pieces of wood out on his own. He didn't want any help either; he dived right into the work, chopping through the task like a machete through honey, heaping stuff on to his bony shoulder before piling it all up directly behind the new den. I was no lugger, but my supervisory role was vital just the same. I was more than happy to be the brains and logistics guy of the operation.

Once the place was fully cleared we stood at the doorway gazing at the empty shell we'd created. What Pav had created. A blank canvas of possibilities. I high-fived Pav, who reached up to meet my hand. Slap! His pits were sweaty and pungent. Humming in fact. I tried not to breathe through my nose too much, as the mix of Pav's body ming and stale shed was eye-watering stuff.

'We need lock,' Pav said.

'First thing we need to do, Pav, is keep this door open and let some air circulate.'

'Best idea for to get smell out. I agree, Charlie.'

'It's a shame there's no electricity.'

'No worry. We use fire and battery.'

'You mean candles?'

'Yes, fire candles.'

'I can probably get my hands on some candles,' I said.

Every house had stashes of candles for when the electricity was clicked off. I always thought that owning a small candle shop in Little Town would bring me untold riches, but standing in a candle shop day after day would've melted my mind.

'Must first get lock to thief stop,' Pav said.

'We don't have anything worth stealing yet.'

'When stuff come thief will too.'

'Not necessarily, Pav.'

'In Old Country you know what they do to thief?' Pav said, all serious and tense.

'I've heard rumours, but I'm not sure if they're true or not.'

'It true, Charlie. It true.'

'So they actually do … do … that … then?' I turned my right hand into an axe or a butcher's knife and made a chopping motion on my left wrist. Bringing the hack down twice.

'It true. I see happen.'

'Really?'

'They come to school, bring teacher outside and do this.' Pav did the same chopping motion as I had.

My mouth was wide and circular.

'What did the teacher do?' I asked.

'They say he money thief.'

'Bugger me,' I said, which made Pav laugh. I'm not big into the swearing game, but whenever I swore Pav found it hilarious. This conversation badly needed a swear word. 'And was he guilty?'

Pav shrugged his shoulders.

I was going to say another swear, but I said it inside instead, only much harder this time. A real bad one. A belter of a swear word. One that Mum and Dad would have skelped me for if I ever said it out loud.

'And his hand? Did they just leave it lying there on the ground?'

'They bag hand.'

'Was there lots of blood?'

'Like splashing pool.'

'And your teacher, Pav, what happened to him?'

He shrugged his shoulders again.

'God, and I thought *here* was bad.'

'What happen to Little Town thief?' Pav asked.

'Depends who catches you. If it's the Regime you'll go to prison or get a huge fine. But if any of the Rascal gang members nab you, well, you might lose a kneecap or they'll force you to work for them. Not sure what's worse.'

'Fook saking,' Pav said.

'So, best not to steal anything.'

'I think yes I agree.'

'Not even as much as a grain of sand,' I said, sounding as if I was warning Pav, educating him on Little Town rules. Someone had to.

'Why thief want sand, Charlie?'

'No, Pav, it's an expression ...'

'Ah, I yank your chain. I yank good.'

Pav's thin belly and skeleton shoulders bobbed up and down with all his giggling.

It was time to explain to Pav the rules of Little Town. We sat at the doorway and I carefully went through Charlie Law's Ten Laws of Little Town for him.

*

'Norman, this is Pav,' I said.

'All right, Pav,' Norman said.

'Pav, this is Norman.'

'Please to meet,' said Pav.

Pav came closer and extended his hand. Norman took it.

'You the friend good of Charlie?' Pav said.

Norman looked at me.

'Pav and his family just moved here from Old Country,' I said.

'Old Country?' Norman said. His eyes opened further, forcing his eyebrows to shift skywards.

'So they don't speak the lingo too well,' I said.

'Oh, OK,' Norman said. 'I dig that.'

'Not yet anyway,' I said. 'I'm going to teach the life out of him before we go back to school.'

'Oh, brilliant! Can I come? Can I? Can I? Please?' Norman's mocking tone made me want to rip out his tongue. He didn't mean it of course; he liked playing the joker, as he did all the time in school, in the street, at home, everywhere. Norman liked to call himself *a man about town*, which meant he knew stuff that we didn't. *Stuff in the subterranean, my friend, stuff in the subterranean.* He knew some of Little Town's Rascals, who could get their hands on things ordinary people couldn't; these men did the dirty work, got down to the nitty-gritty, took the flack but were given the slack. Norman wasn't as stupid as many people thought, oh no; a proper clever devil, in fact. He just couldn't be bothered with school. He always knew things that most of us struggled with, stuff like history and religion and philosophy, just didn't go on about it much. Norman got all his information from books, which meant that he couldn't have been the scallywag Dad thought he was. But the fact that Norman happened to know some proper bona-fide scallywags who lived in Little Town was exactly the reason I wanted to speak to him. That's why I'd invited him to our pre-shed meeting.

But if I'd known what this would all lead to, I'd have never have got involved with Norman.

'So, Old Country, eh? Is it as mental as everyone says it is?' Norman asked Pav.

'It very bad place.'

'Did those bastards chase you out?' Norman probed.

'We come Little Town for bester life,' Pav said. I didn't want to tell Norman too much about why Pav and his family were in Little Town; it wasn't my place to open my trap about the family secrets. Anyway, Pav had told me as a trusted friend and, as a trusted friend, I will take whatever secrets are told to me to the grave. I knew Pav wouldn't have said anything to Norman.

'What? You came *here* for a better life?' Norman said.

'Yes.'

'Jesus! Was this the only place you could have come to?' Norman asked.

'Only place we get papers for. Only place Dad get job.'

'What does the old fella do?'

Pav looked at me.

'Norman wants to know what your father does here for work, Pav?' I said.

'He work at hospital,' Pav said to Norman.

'Is he a doctor?' Norman said, as if impressed.

'He floor and wall clean,' Pav said.

'Shit. All the way to this shit town to do some shit job in a shit hospital. Cleaning people's shit all day. No thanks.'

'He no floor clean in Old Country.'

'Pav's dad had a good job there,' I said to Norman.

'Let me guess, Pav. Your old man worked in a shirt and tie job in Old Country?' Norman was practically in his face. Kissing distance.

'He was scientist,' Pav proudly said. 'He working for big company, but we must to come Little Town when Government –'

'Gave them permission to go,' I said, stopping Pav in his tracks.

'So, Charlie, you wanted to show me something?' Norman said without taking his eyes off Pav.

'I did; it's down at the end of the garden.'

Pav went first and I led Norman to the bottom of the backyard. I opened the door and we all looked inside the empty shed. Norman entered; standing bang in the middle, he did a three-sixty. I sort of knew what he'd say.

'What's this ming heap, Charlie?'

I should have been a betting man.

'It is *now*, Norman, but it won't always be; that's why I wanted to talk to you,' I said.

'Talk. I'm listening.'

'Well, as you can see, it's bare. Barren.'

'You mean it's got sweet FA in it?'

'Exactly.'

'So where do I fit in?'

'We need three chairs.'

'Three chairs?'

'And a lock.'

'Three chairs and a lock?'

'And maybe a table.'

Norman stopped craning his neck around; he fixed on me.

'Do I look like a furniture shop to you, Charlie?'

'Oh, come on, Norman, you know some people who can get this stuff no bother.'

'Oh, do I now?'

'We both know you do.'

'And what people would that be then?'

'Well, there's those … those … erm … subterranean people.' I felt that it wasn't the time to mention The Big Man at this stage. I didn't want to scare Norman away.

He paused.

'Do you have any dosh?'

'No one has any dosh, Norman. You know that.' That wasn't quite true; some of those Rascals had plenty of dosh. They were rolling in it. 'It's just a tiny problem.'

'I wouldn't say that. I'd say it's a massive problem,' Norman said.

'I was thinking of negotiating some manual labour or an I-scratch-your-back-you-scratch-mine type of arrangement.'

'Not really how things are done these days, Charlie.'

'Come on, Norman, is there nothing you can do? Not even with your contacts?'

'Please, Norman,' Pav said.

Norman looked at Pav. I could see his face soften. At least I think it did.

'What's in it for me?' Norman said.

'Well, for starters you can come around here anytime you want; it can be a three-way den instead of just for me and Pav.'

'But I don't live near this block, Charlie.'

'We won't say anything.'

'But if the Regime catch me in another block when it's dark, I'm buggered. You know that.'

'They won't.'

'Want a bet?'

And he was right: he *would have* been buggered and I couldn't say for sure that he'd be OK and that they wouldn't catch him. They haven't been here for ages, but that's not to say the night beat aren't due a mooch around here soon.

An idea came to me.

'I'll do all your homework for a month?'

This was like my sucker punch. My up-the-sleeve ace. Norman's brain was spinning in his head.

'Until Christmas,' Norman said.

'For two months,' I said.

'Until Christmas, or nothing,' he said.

'OK, until Christmas.' My head was twisting at my rubbish negotiating skills.

'Right, I'll see what I can do,' Norman said.

'Fantastic time,' Pav said.

'I can't promise anything,' Norman said.

'Three chairs, a big lock, a table and some candles,' I said.

'You didn't say anything about candles.'

'Ah, just throw them in as a goodwill gesture, Norman.'

'You're a chancer, Charlie, do you know that?' Norman said.

'Where will you get the stuff?' I asked.

'There are a few possibilities. Leave it with me.'

I sucked some air in and puffed out my chest.

'Are you going to try The Big Man?' I said nervously.

Just by uttering the words I knew I'd crossed the line.

Norman's eyes tightened, as did his whole body.

'Ssssshhhhh, for Christ's sake,' Norman said, indicating to Pav.

'Sorry.' I looked around for any eavesdroppers. 'Pav's OK. He knows zilcho.'

Obviously I didn't know The Big Man personally, I'd only heard about him; everyone in Little Town had heard of The Big Man. He was like the king of the Rascals. The Grand Mafioso. The one whom everyone feared. The rumour was that The Big Man had some of Little Town's Regime firmly by the gonads. Norman's parents used to live in the same block as The Big Man before he became THE BIG MAN so that's why he knew him. I think his dad and The Big Man were pals back in the day. Or he used to do some pick-up work for him. Whatever. They knew each other.

'Don't ask me about The Big Man, Charlie. OK?'

'Got it.'

'No, I'm serious about this. Don't mention him. The Big Man talks about us, not the other way round, OK?'

'OK.'

'Right, let's leave it at that then.'

'When will we hear from you?' I said.

'I'll let you know as soon as,' Norman said, before saying his goodbyes. He left us without shaking hands. We all had to do hand punches instead. He must have seen people doing it on television.

'Charlie?' Pav said.

'Yes.'

'What is Big Man?'

'You don't want to know, Pav. You don't want to know.'

6
Reflections

Every now and then, Mum and Dad get all sentimental about how life used to be, and I begin to understand how much it's changed in Little Town and why Dad gets so angry and Mum gets so frustrated. Of course I don't remember any of it, but back in olden times, before the Regime took over, a footloose and fancy-free young couple enjoyed life.

- They went out to the pub, cinema, dancing, bingo, etc without worrying about a wrist-slapping for disobeying the dark curfew. *(Little Town introduced the dark curfew only after the old Government of the People was lobbed out and replaced by the Regime, our new Government. Since then it's been all them and us and us and them. Dad says the people don't have the resources or power or money to get them out. He also says that all the new Government wants is to have full control over everything and that there'll never be a free vote in Little Town. Not in his lifetime anyway.)*

- They used to have all these passionate political chats and debates with friends and colleagues over a few glasses of vino. *(The Regime and Rascals don't like it if you complain about stuff, especially in public, so everyone stopped chatting. If you are seen to be a complainer they'll make your life a living hell. And there are far too many ears and eyes in Little Town so it's best to keep your mouth shut. Dad says that the Rascals are nothing more than the Regime's henchmen and enforcers. Nothing more than a secret illegal police.)*
- They used to have pals who supported the Regime. *(Now we all live separately side by side. Dad says that the Regime supporters don't like books or music or poetry or art. How can that be? And that their supporters are the ones with the best jobs and most money.)*
- They didn't feel the need to look over their shoulder every time they popped out of an evening. *(Mum says that now Little Town living is tension-filled and not good for her blood pressure. The security can stop you at any time, ask some daft questions, pull stuff out of your bag, all because they want to hassle you up for the fun of it. Because they can.)*

- Mum used to make her money teaching at the local primary school. *(After I was born they replaced Mum's job with a man. The security feels that women should not do too much money-chasing work. I think that's why she goes ballistic with me at times. Maybe she blames me for her being stuck inside the block day after day; that would drive anyone round the twist.)*
- Dad used to write all these cutting-edge and important articles. *(Now everything he writes has to go through his 'editor', who then sends it to the security people before it gets published in the paper. He says what he now writes now is soulless censorship rubbish and not proper journalism.)*

When the Regime came into force, before I was born, their security people asked Dad if he wanted to become a 'special driver'. For *security people* read: Rascals. He told them where to stick their special driver offer. Mum said it was just another illustration of how they wanted to control everything.

Dad turned them down because he said he believed in *democracy, not criminality,* as well as *staying alive*. Now Dad's stuck in his boring desk job, never to get promoted because he's not friends with the Regime or the Rascals. Like many people in Little Town, they are punished because they don't voice their support. Mum stays home with her inhaler to keep her company. But, silver lining, I, Charlie Law, am their pride and joy. And I know the rules and obey the rules and play with the rules of Little Town.

7
Riot Van

We couldn't sit on our hands and wait for Norman to appear with the gear, so we kept our eyes open whenever we were out and about. But almost three weeks had passed since I'd asked him and still nada. Our shed was empty.

On the street, people were milling around, some walking alone; others were in small groups, which was OK because it wasn't dark yet. Me and Pav were looking out in case anyone in our area had been shunted from their home – all you had to do was get behind with your rent or annoy the wrong people and you got booted out, kids and all. If they had, we'd be there like a couple of rabid dogs to snaffle what they discarded. It didn't usually happen down our way though, not because it was full of toffs with decent jobs, but because it was full of true-blood Little Towners: people who lived in silence and didn't criticise. I'm sure if we went up behind the station we'd have maybe got our mitts on something cool, but that wasn't my territory.

Pav had been keeping a low profile for a few days. We were now at the stage in our brief friendship where I could tell when he wasn't being himself. Some telltale signs told me he was on another planet:

- He didn't laugh as much when he swore.
- He didn't eat like it was the first time he'd seen food after ten years of living on a desert island munching on leaves and bugs.
- He didn't change his clothes.
- He didn't follow my lead.

'We'd better get back before it gets dark, Pav,' I said.

I hadn't heard the wagons yet, but the patrols always started just before sunset. Some said that The Big Man ran the wagon fleet, but nobody knew this for sure; I'd say he definitely did.

'Come on, Pav, we're losing light.'

'I no care.'

'Don't be stupid. You know about the curfew. We can't be out after dark.'

'Little Town *stupid*.'

'Have you any idea what will happen if we're caught?

They might throw us in a cell for the night or, worse, give us a real sore skelping.'

'I no scare of them, Charlie.'

'Is everything OK?' I said.

'I here, in this place,' he said, throwing his arms up into the air. 'So no OK.' He stopped walking and looked at the ground. For a moment I thought he was going to have a psycho breakdown before my eyes; at the very least I thought he was going to start sobbing in the street. My mind was going haywire thinking of different scenarios: will I have to give him a cuddle? Stroke his cropped hair and bony back? I hoped not. Imagine what a disaster it would've been if the wagon had spied these shenanigans going on, on their turf? How do you go about explaining that one?

'Pav, what's the matter?' I asked.

'I angry man, Charlie,' Pav said.

His eyes looked sad.

'Why?'

'Mum cry for three day.'

'Is she ill?'

'She cry because …'

'Because you're missing Old Country?'

'No, Charlie. Because bad men give Dad big hassle.'

'What bad men?'

'Little Town bad men. They come to him all time.'

I'd heard a bit about what happened sometimes to Old

Country refugees if they got on the wrong side of the Little Town Regime. The Rascals would be dispatched for a small word in their shell. But who knew for sure? It was only hearsay. Still, if I were Pav's dad I'd have been keeping a low profile.

'All the time? When?' I asked.

'They always to hospital for to see Dad. They make the bad crap for Dad when he try to work.'

'Why?'

'Because we from Old Country, Charlie, and they no like this. They make Dad size of this.' Pav made the gap between his thumb and forefinger about two centimetres wide.

'Bloody toerags.' I felt the anger rise up inside me. 'What do they say?'

'Always same.'

'What?'

'Papers, papers, papers. They want see papers.'

'But haven't you got papers?'

'I not sure, but Dad scare he lose job.'

'Best just to keep the head down,' I said. 'I'm sure it will pass, Pav. These things normally do.'

'I hate Little Town. Mum hate Little Town. Dad hate Little Town.'

'Oh, don't say that, Pav. Things will get better.'

'I doubt.'

'They will. Promise.'

'But why you let these prick Rascal men run this town, Charlie? Why?' Pav said. I knew he didn't mean *me* personally.

'What can we do about it?'

'I have idea.'

Pav made his finger into the shape of a gun, or a pistol, and fired a shot. Followed by another.

'Have you any idea how dangerous these men are, Pav?'

Pav nodded his head in agreement.

'Too much dangerous, Charlie.'

'But they give protection to Little Towners.'

'I don't believe.'

'They do.'

'No. They *no give*. They take.'

'It's called protection, Pav.'

'From who protection?' Pav's baby blue blinders looked hard at me. Some blood webs were in the whites of them now. A stare-off. 'From who protection?' he said again. I think he wanted me to say protection from Old Country's Government, but I wouldn't say it. I couldn't.

'Protection from those people who want to do bad stuff to Little Town, that's who,' I said.

'Dad no want to do Little Town bad stuff.'

'I know he doesn't, Pav. I know he doesn't.'

'He good man, just want to work, eat, sleep, live.'

This was probably not a good time to tell Pav about my special TO BE and TO HAVE verb charts. He'd have blown the idea out of the water, telling me to shove my Little Town lingo straight up my funnel. Best to wait until the heat inside him had cooled.

The light was fading fast. Most of the streets were deserted; those still outside were either trying to get home or dicing with the devil. There had been rumours that a storm was coming to Little Town, and I'm not talking about the weather. Dad was always saying, *They're going to send in the big boys to sort out these problems. Then they'll have another bloody problem on their hands, a bigger one.* I listened but didn't ask.

Heaven knows what we were still doing outside. The sound of the wagon patrols could be heard in the distance, like they were all waiting for some big race to begin. And as soon as that sun went down it was a green light for them. All systems go. Red for us.

'Come on, Pav, we'd better get home.'

'I no go.'

'Pav, don't be mental. We have to go.'

'I look for chair.'

'It's getting dark. Can you not hear the wagons?' I said.

Pav put his ear to the sky.

'I no hear.'

'Pav, if they find you wandering the streets, things will be worse for your mum and dad, don't you see that?'

'Worse how?'

'For a start they'll know you're not from here ...'

'I not.'

'They'll soon discover that you're from Old Country ...'

'I *from* Old Country.'

'I know that. But they might lob you in a cell, skelp you around a bit or take you directly home. Then they might give your mum and dad a massive fine for not being able to *control a minor*.'

'What is minor?'

'A young person. You. And me. We are minors, Pav.'

'I a minor?'

'Yes.'

'Cool.'

'This is no time for cool, Pav. We have to get out of here.'

The sound was getting closer. We could hear their engine splurt along some parallel road. Pav's eyes flashed towards the sound.

'How massive fine?' he said.

'I don't know, a week's salary?'

'Christ mighty!'

'Maybe even two weeks,' I said.

His eyes widened.

'Could be more, Pav. I don't really know. I've never been caught.'

The switch had been flicked.

'OK, we get fook out.'

'Right, let's go.'

We didn't run. Didn't want to attract attention. We walked at a steady pace. We were like those Olympic walkers when it seems as if their bums are chewing caramel.

Four blocks to go: my heart was going as fast as my feet. Pav's too. I could hear his breathing.

Three blocks to go: my muscles were beginning to get sore with this new walking technique. Pav was lagging behind. I needed to slow down.

Two blocks to go: it was pitch-black. All I could hear was the vehicles closing in. I could smell their guns and petrol.

One block to go: I could see the lights of our block. My heart calmed. My feet were fierce sore.

Our block came into sight.

Our block:

Damn!

Blast!

If only we had been able to reach it.

8
Into the Darklands

The pain of not reaching our block stuck in my head like a poisoned arrow. I didn't want to be annoyed at Pav, but I was a tiny bit. I'd spent my whole life avoiding trouble. Now we got huckled for disobeying the dark rule. How stupid is that?

The wagon had pulled us up just before we got home.

'Leave the speaking to me, Pav,' I said as a man rolled down the window.

'OK, I say nothing,' Pav whispered.

The window man leaned out, rested his elbow on the door and gave us the big cheesy. Teeth galore. His smile took me off guard, as everything I'd heard regarding the night wagons before that was all about them being pure nasty. Like, how they strip you down to make sure you aren't carrying any weapons under your clothes, in your bum or between your legs. The images flashed through my head. I saw myself standing in some corner of a cell, shaking with terror while they laughed at me and told me to put my clothes back on. Horrible images that made my body shudder with fear.

'Good evening, lads,' the window man said.

'We're just going home, sir,' I said.

'That's what they all say,' he said.

'Sorry for being late; it was an accident. My fault entirely.'

'Names?' The man didn't pull out a pen or pad. His smile had drifted off somewhere else too.

'I'm Charlie Law and this is Pavel Duda.' I nodded my head towards Pav; he was still sloping behind my back. The window man clicked his radio on and said our names into it. A loud crackling sound shot out, followed by the words '*Affirmative, over.*'

'Duda, eh?' the window man said to Pav. He drew his eyes from Pav's toes to the top of his head. 'You're not from around here, are you, son?'

'I live there,' Pav said, pointing towards our block.

'Don't get cheeky, Duda. You know what I mean.'

'He moved here recently, sir,' I said. The window man stared at me, a teacher's stare at insolent boys. 'From Old Country.'

'Am I asking you, Law?'

'No, sir.'

'So shut your trap then, OK?'

'OK.'

He took his teacher stare away from me and passed it on to Pav.

'Old Country not good enough for you lot, Duda?'

Pav said nothing, not because he didn't understand the window man's question, but because it was a dim-witted one.

'Old Country chuck you and your family out, did they? Speak up against someone important, did you?' the window man said.

'They left because of –' I felt Pav squeeze my love handle area. It's not like I was going to tell the window man anything, was I? I'm not that stupid.

'Am-I-talking-to-you-Law?'

'No, sir.'

'So button it then. Mouth.'

'Sorry, sir.'

'So, what's your story, Duda?'

'No story,' Pav said.

The window man sniffed about a litre of snot up through his nose and gobbed it straight at our feet.

A green, slimy splat.

He gave Pav the once-over again.

'Who cut that hair of yours, Duda? The blind barber?' The window man's smile returned, then he sniggered, laughed, howled.

'No,' Pav said. 'Mum cut.'

The window man's howl stopped.

'I don't like cheeky oafs, Duda. Got it?' He pointed aggressively at Pav. 'And I especially don't like cheeky oafs from Old Country.' The pointing made Pav's body tense. Mine too. 'Got it?'

'Got it,' Pav said.

'So, can we go home now?' I asked.

'Now he's asking if he can go home,' the window man said to the night air.

'Would that be OK?' I said.

'Now he's asking if that would be OK.' He was being strange, or *extracting the urine*, as Dad would say. 'Sorry to break it to you, but you two clowns are going nowhere.'

'But ...'

'There's someone who wants to meet you two numpties. So, sorry to say, you won't be setting off together into the night.'

'Who wants to meet us?' I said.

'Get in.' The window man pointed to the back of his truck.

Pav stepped behind me, gripping on to my back. I heard a tiny whimper from his mouth. I reached and held his wrist. Just to let him know that I was there for him, that I was his buddy, that I wouldn't abandon him.

'Where we go?' Pav said, stepping back into view.

'Rap it, Duda,' the window man said. 'In!'

'But who wants to see us?' I asked again.

'Don't make me get out of this vehicle, Law.' He clicked open his door a little. 'Do not make me do that.'

'OK, we're coming. We're coming,' I said, and pulled the heavy back door open. I jumped in first, then gestured for Pav to follow. He reached for me. I took his hand and pulled him into the wagon. The sweat almost made him slip away. The inside reeked of chemical bombs, or it could just have been sweat and farts.

'Right, the pair of you, sit there. One word and you'll get a severe clout.'

We said nothing.

'Got it?' he roared.

I didn't want a severe clout. A severe clout would make me cry. God, imagine Erin F seeing me bubble. Doesn't bear thinking about.

We said nothing.

Travelled to the sound of our hearts pounding.

9
Money

The place they took us was minging.

Manky dripping water fell from the roof. It wasn't even raining. It reeked of salt, damp towels and dog shit. The stink was so bad that if you opened your mouth it was as if you were actually munching on some dog shit; it got stuck into the back of my throat. Weird: no pets were allowed in Little Town. Weirder still: I couldn't hear any barking sounds.

'Right, that's you. Out.'

The window man didn't turn off his engine. He didn't get out himself. He didn't tell us where we were or what we were supposed to do. We were standing outside a big barn, factory or farm. I wasn't sure. His only instruction was:

'See that door over there?'

'Yes.'

'Move your arses through it.'

We watched him driving off into the night again, searching for stragglers.

We were alone. The door faced us. I looked at Pav, directly into his eyes. I could tell he was thinking the same thing as me: if we went through that door, we might not get back out. If we didn't open it, something worse would happen to us.

When I opened the door, Pav gripped tightly on to my elbow, as though he wanted me to be his eyes. His leader. His protector.

'I no like this, Charlie,' Pav said.

'Tell me about it.'

'I tell you. I tell you.'

'No … I mean … oh, never mind. Just keep close.'

'This never happen in Old Country.'

'Pav, do me a favour?'

'What favour?'

'Don't mention Old Country in here, OK?'

'No Old Country. My mouth zip.'

'Try not to show that you're scared.'

'But I terror scared, Charlie.'

Pav gripped harder, moved closer towards me; we were almost hugging. After about twenty yards we stopped walking. It was pitch-black; you couldn't even see your hand in front of your face.

My mind was spinning:

What's that smell?

Who wants to meet us?

Why do they want to meet us?

Are we going to be hurt?

Can they damage Pav instead of me?

Am I in trouble because Pav's my newest pal?

Is this a set-up by Pav and his Old Country mob?

Do Mum and Dad know I'm here?

'I smell the shit,' Pav said.

'Me too.'

It felt as if the smell had dragged us to the ground and kicked the living daylights out of us.

From the other end of where we were standing a light shone. Someone had opened a door, allowing the light to shoot out and make a run for it. I was thinking of doing the same when a voice shouted, 'Can you hear me?' twice. The first time normal. The second time like he was peed off.

'We can hear you, yes,' I shouted back. My voice echoed.

I really tried to sound calm, but calmness had been sucked out of my body and replaced by panic and fear. My echoed tones vibrated with worry.

'Can you see the light?' the voice shouted.

'Yes,' I returned.

'Walk towards the light then,' the voice said.

Our steps were baby ones.

The light was on us, bright and sharp. We could see now.

'Come through here,' the voice said, indicating with his hand for us to go through. 'Come. Don't be afraid.' Terror must have been painted all over our faces.

Inside the door was a desk. A computer sat on it, along with a lamp and a phone. Behind the desk was a chair. A comfy, swingy leather number. On the chair swung a man. Longish hair. Lush beard. All in black. His head was gigantic, his belly colossal. Too many burgers and beer. Swinging on that chair was the man they all spoke about. In every way he was the man they spoke about. I knew who he was as soon as I set eyes on him.

The Big Man was exactly how I'd pictured him to be.

'Law and Duda, correct?' he said.

'Yes.'

'Which is which?'

'Well, I'm –'

'Wait! Let me guess,' he said, swivelling on his chair from left to right and back again, eyeballing us. 'You, skinny drawers, you must be Duda.' He pointed at Pav. 'And you, mega mouth, you must be Law, right?'

'You're right. That's right. Very right. Yes,' I said.

'Thought so,' he said, placing his two hands on the table in front of him and leaning forward like a wildcat getting ready to pounce. I shivered. Pav clutched me. 'Do you know who I am?'

'Erm … I think so,' I said.

'And who might that be then?' he asked.

I gulped.

'Come on, mega mouth, who do you think I am then?' He raised his voice.

I gulped again.

'I think ... that ... erm ... you might be ... erm ... The Big Man,' I said.

The Big Man did a three-sixty in his chair, laughing all the way around.

'That's right. Here, before you, sits The Big Man.' He did a crucifix with his arms while saying this.

'Pleased to meet you, Big Man.' I didn't know what else to say. My thoughts were frozen. The last person any teenage boy in Little Town wanted to meet was The Big Man. I'd take the reality of the Regime any day as opposed to the myth of The Big Man.

'And what about you, skinny drawers?' he said to Pav.

'He doesn't know who you are,' I said.

'Let him speak for himself,' he said, looking directly at Pav. 'Do you know who I am, Skinny Malinky?'

I gave Pav a wee nudge.

'I not know,' Pav said.

The Big Man stood up – and boy, was he a big man – came round from the table and stared hard at Pav.

'You're not from Little Town, Duda, are you?'

'He's –' I tried to say.

'Shut it!' The Big Man shot at me. He pointed a stiff finger towards my chest. Like he was holding a gun. My whole body rattled.

'Well?' he said to Pav. 'Where are you from?'

'I from Old Country,' Pav said.

The Big Man nodded his head.

'How long have you been in Little Town?'

'The few week,' Pav said.

I cringed.

'I'd say so, given how shit you are with our tongue.'

'I sorry, I soon to learn with Charlie,' Pav said.

'Not to worry, you'll get there.' The Big Man moved closer to Pav. 'Know who else is from Old Country?' he asked.

'I no,' Pav said.

'My grandmother.' I'm sure The Big Man winked.

'Really?' I said.

'She came here when she was a few years younger than Skinny here.'

'Ah, yes?' Pav said. Eyes widening, grip loosening on my elbow.

'Those Old Country bastards forced her family out.'

'We leave also because Old Country bastards,' Pav said.

'I hear you, Skinny, I hear you,' The Big Man said.

'That's mad,' I said.

The Big Man put his hand on Pav's shoulder, like a father would do to a son who'd done reasonably well at school sports day. In that moment I was glad Pav was here to take the heat out of the situation.

'You need to be careful of those Old Country bastards, Duda. They don't like it when their people come to live in Little Town. There's talk that they're going to take Little Town down.'

'Old Country people?' I asked.

'They don't like how we live, Law. They want to destroy it,' The Big Man said.

'Destroy it with what?' I said.

'Anything and everything they have,' The Big Man said.

'But that's a lot,' I said. 'Then what happens after they destroy it?'

The Big Man sniggered.

'Don't worry, Law, that won't happen.'

'How can you be so sure? Old Country is strong. It has lots of money.'

'Oh, there's people in place to make sure that it doesn't happen.'

'People like you?' I said.

'You better believe it,' he said. 'There are many who want to protect Little Town. Every day, people come and ask to help.'

'I want help,' Pav said.

'Hold on, tiger,' The Big Man said. 'There will be time for that soon. First things first.'

'Are we in trouble?' I asked. Something told me that we hadn't been brought here to chew the fat about Little Town versus Old Country.

'Trouble?' The Big Man said.

'Yes.'

'Not that I'm aware of, unless you've been out stealing any of my stuff and playing silly buggers.'

'We broke the dark curfew.' I kind of bowed my head. 'Sorry, Big Man.'

'Ah, we all do that from time to time. I wouldn't worry about that, Law.'

'So … we're here because … ?' I asked.

'Yes, why here?' Pav asked.

'Well, lads, you're here because it's come to my attention that you want to get your hands on a few chairs and other bits and bobs. True?'

Chairs? Bits and bobs? I let out a comfort sigh. The Big Man had popped my fear balloon. I could've hugged him … well, not really.

'Have you spoken to Norman?' I asked.

'Indeed,' The Big Man said.

'You get chair?' Pav asked.

'I can get whatever I want,' The Big Man said.

We looked at each other and smiled.

'A big lock?' I said.

'Anything,' The Big Man said.

'Cool,' Pav said.

'Norman tells me you're after three chairs, one table and one lock? Am I right?'

'Yes,' I said.

'Yes,' Pav said.

'And all this is stuff for a shed?' The Big Man said.

'You know about our shed?' I asked.

'There isn't anything I don't know about, Law,' The Big Man said.

'Oh, OK,' I muttered.

'Norman good friend,' Pav said.

'Give me a few days and I'll get it sorted.' The Big Man said.

'For the stuff?' I said.

'For the stuff,' The Big Man said.

'Very brilliant,' Pav said.

'Great,' I said. This was a great moment in my life, as nobody – apart from my parents – had ever done anything nice for me before, without wanting something in return, that is.

Click: light switch moment.

'We have no money to pay.'

The Big Man waved his hands. 'Ah, don't worry about money,' he said.

'How pay we?' Pav said.

'I told you, don't worry about the dosh.'

'Are you sure?' I said.

'I'm sure. What's a few chairs and a lock between friends, eh?'

We looked at each other and shrugged our shoulders. Dad always told me never to look a gift horse in the mouth. So, right there and then, I decided not to look inside The Big Man's gub.

'Thanks,' I said.

'Thanks,' Pav said.

The Big Man organised a car to drop us off back at our block. 'I'd take you myself, but I can't be arsed,' he said.

As the car was leaving the smelly factory The Big Man waved us down. We stopped. The windows were electric. I felt rich. He leaned his head inside the car, smiled.

'Remember, lads, don't worry about any dosh.'

'Thanks …' I said.

'We'll sort something out later, eh?' The Big Man winked before slapping the roof of the car two times.

Our shed would soon be an ultra cool place to hang out in, doing quality things like reading, teaching, chatting and generally having some sanctuary from life in Little Town. But it wasn't the coolness of the shed, nor the comfy chairs, nor the smooth table, nor the safe locks that I was thinking about on the journey home. I wish it had been. I was thinking about what The Big Man said before his car slap.

We'll sort something out later, eh?

Sort out what?

10
My Book

On return from The Big Man's place, cave, den, factory or warehouse – I wasn't too sure what to call it – my face was the colour of snow. In the mirror I saw beads of sweat on my brow. My pupils were dilated. My tongue bone dry. I stared intently at the figure in that mirror, wondering who was staring back. Thinking to myself: *What have you done, Charlie? You've allowed The Big Man into your life, what have you done?* I knew then and there that life would be different, that there would be a Charlie Law pre The Big Man and a Charlie Law NOW.

But maybe I was wrong. Maybe it was all about a few chairs and a lock. Maybe it was a favour and nothing more. A decent gesture by a decent man. Maybe I'd got it all wrong about The Big Man being some crazed tyrant. He seemed

OK after all. He didn't do any of the things that were part of Little Town's urban tales: headbutting, kneecapping, blow-torching, nail-yanking. He treated us well. He liked us. Sure, what type of malfunctioned brain would you have to have if you decided to blowtorch a couple of fourteen-year-olds? No, The Big Man had his wired up properly. I was a good judge of character and could tell his brain was functioning well.

So why did he say it? Why did he say those words? Why did he tell us that *we'll sort something out later, eh?* I couldn't figure it out. All I wanted to do was lie in bed, get excited about the shed and think about how I could improve Pav's lingo skills, which books would help me achieve this, which approach was best suited to Pav's needs. Yet my mind wouldn't let go of The Big Man's words. I didn't want to sort anything out later.

I really didn't.

Mum and Dad used to speak fondly about the library that Little Town once had. Apparently they used to cart me along to it when I was a toddler. The Regime closed it down when I was six so I don't have much of a memory for it. They did say that a brand spanking new one would be built instead. Still waiting.

However, Little Town did still have a bookshop. Called The Bookshop, it sold books, obviously, pens and paper. All colours. Except white pens. My mission was to get my hands on a lingo book with loads of exercises and diagrams in it, a book that was simple to follow for the basic speaker (Pav), a book teeming with so many new words that it would seem as if they were being fired at you like a hundred-rounds-a-second Uzi.

Boat BOOM!

Dish towel BOOM!

Lampshade BOOM!

Shoelace BOOM!

Tank BOOM!

Grenade BOOM!

My job would be to tie them all together with my own diagrams, verbs and innovative teaching style. Easy. When my eyes opened from a troubled dream, that was my day's mission.

Our table, when it came, would look so much better with some books and a few pens strewn over it. I wanted the shed to be a beautiful functioning thing. A home from home for me and Pav. It should never be empty. After all, a chair without a bum on it is just a chair. The good guy in me thought it would be nice to put a smile on Pav's chops as well; the poor fella had been dragging his chin off the floor lately.

Pav said the worst thing was how everybody made vile comments about refugee folk from Old Country. His mum felt that Little Town was one giant women's prison. Like Pav's dad, she'd had a big job in Old Country, writing for papers and stuff (like my dad). But here she was chained to a bread maker and manky dishes. And his dad was still getting hassled by thugs at the hospital. No one ever had anything good to say about these poor Old Country people.

As if they knew any proper Old Country refugees.

As if they knew what it was like to live in Old Country where their top brass pestered you every day.

As if they knew what it was like for refugees to live in Little Town without properly knowing the lingo.

As if they knew that living in Little Town with rubbish lingo skills was akin to being a deaf mute.

As if they knew all that.

Talk about being slow. These people were slower than coastal erosion. That's why I kept telling people at school to read books.

I thought that if I could just help Pav to speak the lingo a little bit better, he'd be able to help his folks, and the world of Little Town would get a bit easier for all of them. The bookshop mission turned out to be a disaster.

Reason One:

I hung about the *Teenage Reading Section: Boys* far too long, scanning through all these books I couldn't afford to buy. Who could? Regime workers and their supporters, that's who. I had to make do with second-hand ones at school and home, sometimes third, fourth and fifth hand-me-downs. Here I loved nothing better than to feel their spines and get a good whiff of new book covers. I worshipped the tang of new books. It's not like I needed to be on some deviants' register or anything, I just thought the reek of a new book screamed out information and knowledge. If something took my fancy, which it always did, I'd try like a desperate man to speed-read a first chapter so I could then speed-read the following chapters on my next visit. That was the only way I could get my hands on a proper new book. Far too much time wasted in the *Teenage Reading Section: Boys.*

Reason Two:

I almost died. Properly died. Heart attack material! A heart attack so massive that it could've resulted in a triple or quadruple bypass, maybe even a transplant. A heart attack so titanic that the moment it started pounding away I thought it was going to explode from my body and splat on to the wall behind the shop assistant, leaving a red mess dripping behind her head. I'd never felt that way before.

Reason for this Major Organ Malfunction:

Guess who I spied flicking through the books at the *Teenage Reading Section: Girls*?

Eh?

None other than the amazingly stunning and utterly gorgeous Erin F.

YES, *THAT* ERIN F.

I moseyed into the *Learning Section* and plucked a book from the shelf, a book big enough to cover my face. A4 size.

I didn't care what it was just as long as it kept me incognito. *Elevator Engineering throughout the Years: The Ups and Downs* made it possible to sidle up and get a good glimpse of Erin F. It was nice to see her out and about, away from her infirmed mum for some quality *her* time. I couldn't see what she was reading. It didn't matter. It didn't matter because I was sharing her air space, seeing how her tummy went up and down to the rhythm of her breathing, which I then copied. Seeing how she stood with one foot crossed over the other, which I then copied. How her hair hung over her face, which she would occasionally place behind one of her ears. The right one. Why do boys have to have such short hair in Little Town? I was close enough to see how her jeans were turned up, revealing sockless ankles. Skin. To see how her flowery blouse was cut at the shoulders, revealing her long, slender arms. No hair. Smooth skin. More skin. Lovely skin. Erin F's skin. My body shuddered because I was in the vicinity of Erin F's skin, being able to stare at it without being told off or being laughed at by her friends. She looked so alive and radiant.

With one foot in the *Learning Section* and the other in the *Teenage Reading Section: Girls*, the nerves were going ninety because of the possible danger this one foot could bring. It wasn't that boys weren't allowed in the *Teenage Reading Section: Girls* area, it was just really bizarre to see them in there among all that girl stuff. Why are you in there? What are you looking for? Who are you looking to supply? So it was best to tread with super caution.

Erin F put the book she was reading back on the shelf and made her way to the *Learning Section*. Big relief. Neutral territory. She picked up a learning book – *How to Speak a Foreign Language in Two Weeks* – and began flicking through it. I wondered what lingo Erin F wanted to learn. Maybe I could teach her too?

> **MENTAL MEMO:** WHEN ERIN F REPLACES *HOW TO SPEAK A FOREIGN LANGUAGE IN TWO WEEKS*, TAKE IT OFF THE SHELF, HAVE A GOOD GANDER AND WHIFF OF IT. MAYBE EVEN BUY IT, IF IT'S IN MY AGE RANGE.

I followed her movements. With her back to me she ran her hand across the spines of books like a piano player would do for their final crescendo. She stood on her tippy toes and tried to look at some top-shelfers, stretching her Achilles tendon to do so, which was sensational to see; it made the butterflies dance away inside my stomach. I heard her cough once, a tiny cute-as-a-button cough. Poor soul. A piece of dust maybe. Or the dry air we were breathing. Our shared air. I did a tiny cough as well, in solidarity. Perhaps she had a slight cold and that's why she couldn't be around her mum that day? Makes sense. I did another little cough.

'Charlie, I know it's you.' Erin F's voice floated over my head.

Elevator Engineering throughout the Years: The Ups and Downs had failed me.

'Charlie, stop hiding behind that awful book.'

I froze as if I'd been left in a freezer for twelve days. Everything froze, even *that*. A frozen twig.

'I know it's you so there's no use denying it,' she said. Her voice was closer. I lowered the book.

'Oh, hi, Erin F, I didn't see you there.'

I could hear the crack in my voice.

'Don't talk garbage, Charlie.' She shook her head. 'You've been totally gawping at me for the last ten minutes.' She wasn't angry. Praise be for that. Result!

'Have I? I wasn't aware that –'

'Yes, you have.'

'Sorry, I didn't mean to gawp. But you know when you think you know someone and you do a double take and it *is* that person you think you know and then you don't know what to say to them after that but you've already moved closer to them and the only reason you've moved closer to them is because you thought you recognised them in the first place. Know what I mean?'

Erin F looked confused.

'I haven't the foggiest idea what you're going on about, Charlie.'

'I just wanted to say hello, Erin F, but I didn't know how to go about it, that's all.'

'Just say hello then. It's no big deal, is it?'

Now wasn't the time to tell Erin F that she was the last thing in my head when the lights flick off at night. Now wasn't the time to mention to Erin F that together in my dreams we have snuggled up in a chilly igloo, snowboarded in our swimming togs through a giant mudslide and heave-hoed, heave-hoed during a mighty one-on-one tug-of-war session. Or that every time I laid eyes on her my heart suddenly became the fastest, highest and longest triple jumper in all of Little Town.

Hopping.

Skipping.

Jumping.

Bouncing.

'No, you're right, it's no big deal,' I said. 'I should've just come over and said hello without all the cloak and dagger stuff.'

Erin F looked confused again. I knew the look by now. It was her usual expression whenever we had our brief chats. This, in fact, was the longest chat we'd had since her mum became unwell.

'You should have,' she said. 'I don't bite, Charlie.'

'How's your mum doing, Erin F?' I wanted to punch myself for jumping right in with two giant feet, especially when she was probably trying to forget about all that stuff for a few hours.

'Fine. Yours?' she said.

'Erm ... yes ... fine too ... So are you buying a book then?'

'Just browsing. You?'

'I was after a good lingo book for my mate Pav,' I said.

'Pav?'

'Pavel Duda, to be exact.'

'Weird name,' Erin F said.

'He prefers to be called Pav.'

'Does he speak the lingo?'

'Not too well. That's why I thought I'd help him out a little.'

'Where is he from, this Pav guy who doesn't speak the lingo?'

'He's from Old Country.'

'Oh,' Erin F said; then she looked to her right and left.

'Pav's a top bloke, Erin F.'

'I'm sure he is, Charlie.'

'He is.'

'No doubt.'

'You should meet him. You could come round to my place and meet him.'

Erin F hesitated, as this sounded like an overenthusiastic invitation. We paused. Big-time awkward. I've never invited

Erin F to anything before. Not even to read my recommended books.

'Only if you want, that is,' I said.

My mind was screaming at my tongue to put a sock in it. Not only did this sound like an overenthusiastic invitation, but it also sounded as if I was trying to play Little Town/Old Country Cupid. Hands across the barricades and all that jazz.

'Erm … is he our age?' Erin F said.

'He'll be fifteen soon, same as us.'

'So he'll be coming to our school then?'

'Yes, after the summer.'

'Jeepers, Charlie. I hope you're going to keep an eye on him at school. You know what some people can be like.'

'I'll have his back, Erin F. Don't worry about that.' I sounded like a hip dude, someone who had his eye on the ball and knew the score. The ear-to-the-ground guy.

'And you know what the teachers think of non-lingo speakers, don't you?'

'I do. That's why I'm going to teach him the lingo.'

I think she was impressed at my heroic nature.

Erin F's eyes left mine and shifted sideways towards the assistant's desk. The assistant was scowling at us. She lifted the phone receiver and put it to her ear. Her eyes never left ours. A warning? You never knew who was watching you in Little Town. Her fingers slowly pressed the buttons on the phone. Regime eyes everywhere.

'I think we better make like a banana, Erin F,' I said.

'Eh?'

'Split!'

Erin F looked at me. Her face suggested that if I wanted further chat I'd need to improve the patter.

'Yes, I think we should go, Charlie.'

'Me too.'

DID SHE JUST SAY *WE*?

Erin F's block was in the opposite direction, over the big hill, whereas mine was past the shops and through the park. I didn't want our confab to be over. I didn't want to watch her naked Achilles tendons saunter away from me on their own. I wanted to stand outside The Bookshop and chew some serious fat with Erin F. Make her giggle. Make her flick her hair over her ear. Make her touch my arm cos she'd been laughing so much and needed to steady herself. Make her say, *We should do something together sometime, Charlie* because she couldn't face the thought of us being separated. What I didn't want was for her to give me a lazy little wave followed by a *See you around, Charlie* before bolting.

'Well, see you around, Charlie,' Erin F said. 'Got to get back. Mum, you know?'

'Oh, yes, of course, I know. I know.'

She threw me a lazy little wave and made her way to the big hill. I watched each step she took.

Step one.

Gutted.

Step two.

Absolutely gutted.

Step three.

Swift-kick-to-the-balls gutted.

Step four.

A monstrous voice arrived on my shoulder: *Do something, Charlie.*

Step five.

Same voice: *Say something, Charlie.*

Step six.

Charlie, say something. Do something. Anything. Charlie.

Step seven.

CHARLIE!

Eight …

'We have a shed,' I said.

LOUDER, CHARLIE.

'We have a shed,' I shouted.

Erin F's arm-swinging stopped. Her hair fell to a flop. Her ankles halted. She turned.

'What?'

'I just thought you'd like our shed, Erin F,' I said as soon as she was back within chatting distance.

'Speak the lingo, Charlie. What are you going on about?'

'Me and Pav have ourselves a wee shed.'

'Where?'

'At the bottom of the garden behind our block.'

'How?'

'We just found it and then we cleared it out – well, Pav did. You should see him in action, Erin F, he's, like, dead strong and stuff.'

MENTAL MEMO: STOP TALKING ABOUT PAV BEING SO GREAT.

'And what's in this shed now?'

'Nothing yet, but we're getting chairs and a table and a lock. We're going to make it into a pad. A place to hang out. Just us and our mates.'

'Yeah, right!'

'We are, swear to it.'

'Where are you getting the stuff from?'

'Contacts, Erin F. Contacts,' I said, trying to sound like one of those dudes who knew all the comings and goings of a place.

'I'll believe it when I see it, Charlie.'

'If you want you can come round and see the shed?' She looked at me. Silence. 'Only if you want, like,' I said. I think my heart was sweating as well as my pits. Time slowed. Everything slowed.

'OK, I will, Charlie. Thanks.'

'You will?'

'I'll take you up on the offer of seeing your shed.'

'Brilliant,' I said, before remembering to play it cool. 'So, will I just text you or something when the chairs and stuff arrive?'

'Yes, that's probably best.'

Erin F pulled out her phone and gave me her number. I took Erin F's number and put it in my phone. Imagine, Erin F's actual phone number sitting pretty in my phone. When the info shot over to the main phone-receiving depot they'd see that it was only Erin F's number I'd put in my phone. Nothing sinister. They'd see that Erin F was no infidel or social problem or rogue trader. Erin F just happened to be the diamond in the rough of Little Town, and her number was snuggled up tight in my phone. In fact, this number would be going straight into my brain. Cemented. This number would be my tattoo.

'I'll text you then, Erin F,' I said.

'Cool,' she said.

'Cool,' I said.

'Cool,' she said. 'See you then, Charlie.'

'See you then, Erin F,' I said, to the back of her head. Erin F walked off to the right and out of sight. I watched her every step of the way.

Every step.

11
Politics

My mum was one of the few people who didn't look forward to the summer holidays. She hated me getting under her feet at home. If we had the money I bet she'd have sent me off to a snobby boarding school somewhere to fester my teenage years away. But who else would take the journey to get her inhalers?

Our summer holidays were almost over and Pav's lingo had not shown significant improvement in spite of my best efforts. Also, The Big Man hadn't come up with the goods yet. There was no sign of our chairs, table or lock. No sign of The Big Man himself. No sign of Norman. I was totally relieved with not seeing The Big Man. However, the dream shed we had in our minds was just an empty box of nothingness at the bottom of the garden. I decided to cut The Big

Man some slack, understanding that he was probably knee deep in organising manoeuvres, patrols, checkpoints and some other serious stuff.

And there was serious stuff brewing in Little Town. You could cut the atmosphere with your finger. Tense didn't even cover it. TV reports speculated day after day about some military build-up by Old Country. No wonder people were tense! I didn't really like watching the news – but Mum and Dad were completely addicted. Dad huffed and tutted and argued noisily with the guys in ties on a daily basis. The Old Country threat was nothing new, but it fuelled the lack of friendliness towards Pav's family and the other Old Country refugees who'd accidentally – or unfortunately – found themselves stuck in Little Town for the rest of their days.

It wasn't surprising the last thing on The Big Man's mind was our shed furniture.

But bombs or no bombs, a promise is a promise. Just saying.

After my brief encounter with Erin F, I had revisited The Bookshop and bought a lingo-learning book and a grown-up novel with dosh I'd borrowed (I'll pay it back with interest) from the secret stash (in the soap powder box) Mum kept in the kitchen for emergencies. I hadn't had the courage to call Erin F, especially without a suitably welcoming shed in which to entertain her loveliness. I wanted to be able to play a word game with her on the table, sip specially made (by yours truly) smoothies with her and have some deep chat. But the shed was not yet ready for seduction or wordplay.

I finally plucked up the courage to send her a message:

Hope you are well Erin F. See you next week at school. Hopefully. Charlie

Erin F's reply was brief:

Yes

I didn't know whether to take the YES as a positive or negative. I shilly-shallied about making my next big courageous move after receiving her YES text. Yes *is* positive, isn't it?

The shed is coming on, looking forward to having you in it.

As soon as I sent the text I instantly regretted what I'd done and frantically pressed all the buttons on my mobile, attempting to UN-send it. No chance. These mobile phones aren't programmed to give you a few seconds' grace period for regret texts. Mobile phones don't do emotion. Thankfully Erin F was a clever cookie so she'd have known that when I wrote *looking forward to having you in it* I didn't mean that I was looking forward to actually *having her* in it. Erin F's reply was longer this time:

Me too.

Like I said, clever cookie.

A week before we were due back to school the guy in the tie who reads the news interrupted our programmes with *an extraordinary special announcement*. By the look in his eyes I knew that the special announcement wasn't going to be a joyous one. The news guy looked as if he'd been howling floods of tears just a few seconds before the cameras rolled. He managed to hold it together for the *extraordinary special announcement*:

Good evening, residents of Little Town. It is with great sadness that I inform you of tonight's imminent events. Our intelligence reports indicate that Little Town will come under a sustained attack sometime before midnight … We expect this criminal act to be catastrophic for some of our residents …

The news guy continued speaking but what came out of his mouth, or rather what entered my lugs, was *nanananananananananananananananananananananananan* instead of words and sentences. People talk about having a numb feeling when something drastic happens. I thought they meant a numb feeling like when it's F-word cold outside and you're freezing your rocks off. How wrong was I? Me, Mum and Dad sat in our triangle of numbness, staring at the television news guy as if it was his fault that Little Town was about to come under attack. While he advised us of what we should do, everything he said sounded like an inaudible slur.

- If you have them, assemble in the basements or bunkers of your homes.
- Turn off all lights in your homes.

- Under no circumstances go outside.
- Do not drive.
- Good luck and stay safe.

When the numbness wore off I sat shaking my head. Dad sat with his hands on his thighs, stiff. Mum sat on the edge of her chair with her knees pressed together, like people in wheelchairs do. She took two puffs on her inhaler before shaking it to check how much she had left.

'Attack us for what reason?' I asked.

'Because they can,' Mum said.

'It's easy,' Dad said. 'They want our Government out and they want to come in instead. To control from within.'

Mum and Dad still said Government – they still believed in the sense of Government – but really they should've said Regime.

'But they don't live here, they're not from here,' I said.

'Try telling them that,' Mum said.

'They think some parts of Little Town should be theirs, and to get it they think they should overthrow our Government,' Dad said.

'But that's a good thing, no?' I asked.

'No, it's not a good thing, Charlie,' Dad said.

'But I thought you hated our Reg– … Government, Dad?' I said.

'That may be true, if you can call them a Government –

more like a cabal of hoodlums! I want them overthrown through democracy and diplomacy, Charlie. Not with bombs and bullets.' Dad pointed to his head and mouth. 'I want to do it with this and this.'

'So why do they want our land?' I asked.

'They say they have a right to it,' Dad said.

'It's written somewhere apparently, Charlie,' Mum said, taking yet another puff.

'Your mum's right,' Dad said.

'So? Some guy writes it somewhere and everyone believes him?' I said.

'That's about the size of it,' Dad said.

'That's hardly a law,' I said.

'It's illegal, that's what it is,' Mum said.

'That's what they believe,' Dad said. 'That's what they live by.'

'And so that means you have to start bombing people out of their homes just because you believe in some tripe that was written, like, a million years ago?'

'It's a world gone wrong, morally mad,' Mum said.

'That's just crazy stuff,' I said.

'I couldn't agree more, son,' Mum said.

I bowed my head and tried to gather my thoughts. Mum stood up and looked out of the window. The news guy was now off our telly screen. Our screen was blank. Obviously all the television-making people had done a runner. No chance would I have stayed peering through a camera; I'd have been offski too. Stuff that, waiting to film bombs being fired straight at you.

Mum whispered from the window, 'So this is it then?' and just before she sat down she said, 'The place is deserted.'

In all the books I'd read about bombs and coups and death there is always this big moment of panic before everything hits the fan. But that was fiction. Here in the reality of Little Town my family sat in silence. A strange sort of calm washed over us. Usually at this time of night Mum would be busting my chops to do the dishes, tidy my room or to stop ripping *her* knitting. Instead we sat in the silence of our own thoughts.

'Can't they just live here with us ... in harmony ... or whatever?' I said. 'It's not as if they're perfect.'

'It's not as easy as that, Charlie,' Dad said.

'It's not, Charlie,' Mum said.

'Why?' I said.

'The fact is, they don't like us and we don't care much for them. We're not compatible. End of. And anyway, replacing one controlling Regime with another is hardly a progressive move, is it?' Dad said.

'Our ways are different, Charlie,' Mum said.

'But how can I not *like* them when I don't even know any of them?' I said.

'But you do know them,' Mum said.

'No I don't,' I said.

'What about your wee buddy across there?' Dad said, pointing at our front door.

'Who?'

'The Duda fella,' Dad said.

'Pav?'

'Yes.'

'He's not one of them,' I said.

'He is, Charlie,' Mum said.

'He's only from there,' I said. 'That doesn't make him one of them.'

'I'm not so sure,' Dad said.

'But Pav and his family don't want our land; they only came here for protection, like refugees. Pav's dad earns an honest crust. It's not like they pure love our Regime or anything.'

'We know this, Charlie, son,' Mum said.

'And he was a major player in some brainy job back in Old Country.'

'I know this,' Dad said.

'How do you know?' I asked.

'This is Little Town, Charlie. We do know a thing or two about who comes in and who goes out. People talk … well, whisper. People listen,' Dad said.

'So if you know what he did why can't he get a similar job here then?'

'It's not as simple as that, Charlie,' Dad said.

'But he has the skills,' I said.

'And so do many Little Towners,' Dad said. There was anger in his voice. Maybe it was fear. 'Our Government don't want skills, they want control, or men who'll exercise that control.'

Dad was meaning people like The Big Man.

'So you're telling me that people in Old Country don't like Pav's family, and people in Little Town don't like them either?'

'It's not a question of *like*, Charlie,' Dad said.

'But they came here in order to feel safe,' I said.

'They are safe here,' Mum said.

'Try telling them that,' I said.

'Well, they're probably safer here than they were in Old Country, aren't they?' Dad said.

'Not after tonight they won't be,' I murmured.

'You don't know that, Charlie,' Mum said. 'We don't know what will happen tonight.'

'They'll probably launch a few warning shots,' Dad said. 'Without much damage, just to remind us that they're right there over the border, watching. It's all about control and paranoia.'

'But what happens if Old Country soldiers find Old Country refugees living in Little Town?' I said. 'They'll definitely know the names of those people who left.'

Mum and Dad shifted their eyes to the floor. Then my mind flashed towards poor Anne Frank and her family. I'd read the book about their hiding exploits at school once.

Surely Pav's family wouldn't have to go into hiding from Old Country soldiers? Surely they wouldn't have to go into hiding from folk here who think they've just arrived from Old Country to pinch their land, nick their jobs and dilute their culture? I looked at Dad. I looked at Mum. Surely no Law family member would grass them up. I looked at Mum. I looked at Dad. Surely not.

'They hate Old Country more than you do,' I said. In truth I didn't know this as a fact, but why else would they come *here* if they didn't? They had to hate Old Country.

'Well, I'm not too sure about that,' Mum said, and sat back in her chair, taking in a big puff.

Dad sat back in his chair as well. Both let out a massive sigh. Me too.

Dad broke the stalemate.

'Well. I suppose we best do something about these bloody bombs then.'

And it arrived. My chest felt compressed; the reality of it all jolted my emotions into action. I looked at my mum and dad and cried.

We didn't have a basement or a bunker. We didn't have a lock-up. The shed was too rickety, and it was mine and Pav's anyway. We didn't have a cellar. We didn't have a shelter. We had nothing big and bomb-resistant. The only thing we had was bed covers. Huge duvets. When the bombs came, just before midnight like the news guy said, I was underneath mine in the foetal position, snug as a bug. Mum and Dad were in it with me.

Then it happened.

They sounded far away, as if they were on the other side of Little Town, somewhere near the station. The bombs didn't thud the way I'd expected them to thud.

There was no BOOM.

There was no BANG.

There was no ROAR.

They echoed like fireworks going off in the sky; the echo was so fireworky in fact that it teased and tempted me to get up from the foetal position and look out of my window, mouth open in awe at the beauty of Little Town's sky of many colours. *Stay under* was the call from Dad so I stayed under. At other times the bombs seemed just like cracks of thunder. Definitely not like bombs in the films I'd seen or in the books I'd read. The sustained attack lasted for six minutes. Under the duvet I counted. Six whole minutes of fireworks and thunder.

After the six minutes of sustained attack a hush came over Little Town. That lasted for seventeen minutes. Under the duvet I counted. Seventeen minutes of Little Town being dead as a dodo. A place fireworked to buggery. I was now going to be living in a desert of rubble and ruin. My new home. Under that duvet I imagined the amount of buildings destroyed, the amount of people missing, the amount of money the clear-up operation would cost and the amount of stress parents would have on their plates. I lost count.

Little Town was then shunted back into life. A life with a severe limp, that is: the sirens started up; even from under my duvet I could see their blue, red and orange lights illuminating the walls.

Blue.

Red.

Orange.

Dark.

Blue.

Red.

Orange.

Dark.

Blue.

Red.

Orange.

Dark.

The combination of the police, ambulance and fire brigades' sirens made a shocking crescendo of sound. Then the screams kicked in again and every sound went up a notch, from shocking to terrifying level. I squashed my face into the pillow, pulled up the sides so it fully covered my ears. Blocking it all out. The noise still managed to find its way through the duvet though, through the pillow and right into my lugs. It was clear that loads of people were out of their blocks. Folk shouting, questioning and just being nosy. People were yelling for their family members who'd been out and about. Screaming for them. I don't think anyone gave a monkey's about the dark curfew.

'Charlie? Charlie?' Mum said.

'Yes?' I muttered. My face still deep in the pillow.

'Are you OK, son?'

'I'm good now,' I said, taking my face off the pillow. My mouth and pillow were sodden with saliva. We pulled the duvet from over our heads and breathed normally again. 'Is it over for the night, do you think?'

'I think so,' Mum said. 'Do you want to sleep with Dad and me tonight?'

'No, I'm OK here.'

So it was all fine and dandy cuddling up to Mum and Dad when I thought we were about to be blown to bits, but now that wasn't the case, not a chance was I sleeping with them. I was almost fifteen, for God's sake; time to unshackle the MAN.

'OK, then,' she said.

'I don't think the bombs reached us, Mum.'

'They mostly bombed up near the station, I think,' Mum said.

'Does that mean there won't be any trains coming and going from Little Town any more?'

'It's probably too early to tell, Charlie.'

Mum sat on the edge of my bed and stroked my hair. No doubt she was worried sick for her son's mental safety. I was fine apart from the wet mouth, clammy hands and bumpy heart rate.

'You should try getting some sleep, darling,' Mum said, lifting the duvet away from the bed so I could lie down properly. This was going back to the old days of stories and kisses and songs and hugs and alphabets. Mum seemed to enjoy it. I thought it was weird but I put my head down and allowed her to tuck me in, peck me on the head and tell me how much she loved me before she left my room. Classic old-school mummying.

It was way too noisy to sleep. I was way too adrenalin-pumped. The real reason I didn't want to sleep was that I was afraid I wouldn't wake up again. I was scared the bombs would come back and bounce off my head. That they'd return to our part of Little Town and I wouldn't see the light of day again because of them. Or worse, I would be stuck under an avalanche of debris and dust and left for days on end before finally perishing from dehydration and lack of vital-organ oxygen. But the amazing thing was that I did see the light of day again and I did manage to get some sleep. One minute I'm lying watching the blue, red, orange, dark spin around my room, listening to the muffled street sounds and thinking about Pav and how he and his mum and dad were coping with all this, how they were processing the fact that it was *their* people who'd done it, *their* mob's mental politics who lobbed bombs at us, and the next minute I'm creaking my eyes open at sunlight sneaking through my window. It wasn't as if I'd slept like a baby, but I'd slept.

The next morning was spent glued to the telly screen until something or someone came on. The news guy eventually returned with his eyes even more mangled than they had been the previous night. It was clear this man definitely hadn't slept like a baby. He said that he was broadcasting from a *secret and secure location* because of *circumstances outwith our control* and went on to tell us about the *criminal devastation* Old Country had caused. You could hear a smidgen of a pin being dropped in our house when he was reading out the list of destruction.

DEVASTATION OLD COUNTRY HAD CAUSED

- Shopping Area: bombed to smithereens.
- Train Station: bombed to smithereens.
- Metal Factory near Station: bombed to smithereens.
- Sports Stadium: bombed to smithereens.
- Little Town's Town Hall: bombed to smithereens.
- Three Hundred and Twenty-Seven Souls (and Rising): bombed to smithereens.

In his secret location the news guy shuffled in his seat. He then paused. The pause gave the viewers time to swallow what he'd told us. Once again we sat in open-mouthed silence. Mum puffed her inhaler and then put her hand over her mouth and shook her head. Dad's eyes had a look of revenge about them. As always Dad broke the silence, but when he said, 'Rotten murdering bastards,' it wasn't meant as a conversation starter.

The news guy perked up once more and told us about the many things that weren't bombed to smithereens but merely seriously damaged or semi-destroyed:

- Some Schools: just damaged.
- The Bicycle Tricks Park: just damaged.
- The Big Supermarket: just damaged.
- Mobile Phone Transmitters: disabled.
- Six Hundred and Forty-Two Souls (and Rising): just damaged.

All this info left me with some serious questions of my own to mull over:

- With the transmitters down, how was I going to find out if people were OK? Mainly Erin F.
- How were we going to be educated?
- Where were we going to do bike tricks now?

- How in the hell's fire were we going to get scran in our bellies?
- Who was going to help the relatives of the hundreds of poor souls with all their tears and pain?

And the biggie:

- Was The Big Man dead?

12
Monsters

After the bombs came I didn't get out of bed for two days except to watch news on the telly. Mum and Dad were glued to the sporadic news broadcasts, trying to find out as much information as possible. Apparently, Old Country soldiers were spreading through Little Town, but we hadn't seen any yet. I read, slept, thought, shook and one time cried when I heard people wailing outside. It was probably all in my mind but the smell of everything crept into my room: a pungent mixture of burning, blood, dust and death. It dried my throat and latched on to my skin. I worried about Pav and his family, wondering if they were huddled behind a wardrobe, too scared to show their faces. Hungry. Exhausted. Terrified.

I thought about Erin F and wondered if I'd ever get to see

her again. Tears filled my eyes. In fact, who would I get to see again? More tears.

On the third night there was a thud. I thought I was still dreaming. The non-dream part was Mum telling me to stay in my bed, Dad saying through gritted teeth not to make a sound or else we'd be next. He didn't say *next* though, he used another word.

The first THUD made sure I wouldn't be finishing my dream. The second THUD woke me up proper. And the third THUD shuddered my innards. I got up and went to see what it was. Mum and Dad were hunched together at our main door, listening to what was happening at the other end of our shared block. Directly outside Pav's place.

'Charlie, get back to bed at once,' Mum whispered with her angry voice. It didn't have the same impact as the bellowing voice she normally uses so I chose not to return to bed.

'Keep that shut,' Dad whispered, and drew a zip across his mouth. 'If they know we're in here listening, we're done for.'

That's when I knew it was serious. So did my heart. I ran an imaginary zip across my own mouth and lobbed an imaginary key over my real shoulder. We were all huddled beside the door. Listening. It reminded me of Anne Frank again. Even our eyes didn't move as we listened.

'You. Stand there,' said the voice from behind our door.

'You. Stand there,' the same voice said.

'You. Stand there.' Same voice again. But there was more than one person because we could hear them shuffling about. Maybe three. Maybe more. Speaking the lingo. The voice sounded agitated and annoyed.

I just knew that Pav, his mum and his dad were lined up outside their front door totally shitting themselves. I was too scared to look through the letter box. I'd heard all about these night visits. We all had. I didn't know if they were true or not. Nobody had actually experienced seeing one in action; it was just some eejits at school full of bravado who said that these raids happened. They'd probably upped the ante since the bombs. Someone must have grassed on Pav and his family, that's all I can say. Told these thugs about Old Country folk living here.

'Who else is inside?' a second voice said.

'We are just three,' Pav's dad said.

'You better not be lying to us,' Voice Two said.

'No, go see inside; we are just three,' his dad said again.

'What do you think they want?' I whispered to Dad.

Mum put a finger to her lips. Dad's lips said *shut up* to me. His eyes became zombieish, as if to say *I'm going to kill you Charlie if you don't rap it, son.*

'All clear,' a third voice said.

'Papers,' Voice One said.

You could hear the man rustling through Pav's family papers: ID papers, entry and exit papers, birth papers, marriage papers, religion papers, employment papers, education papers. All the essentials needed for Little Town Rascals.

'Are you Jan Duda?' Voice One asked.

'I am,' Pav's dad said.

'Are you Danica Duda?' he asked Pav's mum.

The silence seemed to last for ages.

'Speak!' Voice Two said.

'What's the matter with your tongue, woman? Don't you speak the lingo here or something?' Voice Three came in, which brought a bit of sniggering from the other two voices.

'I not so good,' Pav's mum said quietly. They probably thought that she was scared stiff of them, but what they didn't know was that Pav's mum was a smashing woman who always spoke softly.

'Are you or are you not Danica Duda?' Voice One asked again.

'My name is Danica Duda, yes,' Pav's mum said.

'And you, you must be Pavel Duda?' Voice One said.

'My name is Pavel Duda.' Pav's voice suggested that he was a tough little nut.

'How old are you?' Voice Three said, as if he was trying to trip Pav up.

'I have fourteen years,' Pav said.

The thug Rascals howled.

'*I have fourteen years*, that's brilliant!' Voice Three said, mimicking Pav.

'I fifteen years after summer,' Pav said. I wanted to open our letter box and scream: *Don't say another word, Pav; please schtum it. Don't give them the ammo to shoot you with.*

'They've tried to butcher our town and now they want to butcher our lingo as well,' Voice Two said.

'Disgusting,' Voice One said.

'Funny though,' Voice Three said.

'It is funny,' Voice Two said.

'Very funny,' Voice One said.

More howling and giggling.

I suspected that all the neighbours in our block were terrified to even breathe heavily; I was glad Mum didn't need a puff to keep her going. She was on puff rationing.

Then all three Rascals hit Pav's dad with a quick-fire torrent.

'Why did you come here?'

'Why did you leave Old Country?'

'Did they boot you out?'

'What did you do?'

'Tell us.'

'Who were you against, Duda?'

'Spit it out.'

'We can find out, you know.'

'Scum too much to handle in Old Country for you then?'

'Yeah, full of scum, was it?'

'Riddled with them, was it?'

'Stinking the place up, were they?'

'Mingers.'

'Filth.'

'Tramps.'

'Beggars.'

'Vagrants.'

'Infidels.'

BACK OFF A LITTLE AND GIVE THE MAN SOME SPACE TO SPEAK, WOULD YOU?

They started up their laughter routine again.

'Why you want us?' Jan Duda asked.

As quick as a light being switched off, the sniggering stopped. Routine over. Mum and Dad changed their facial expressions. Dad shook his head. Mum put a hand to her mouth. I did an inside swear word.

'What was that?' Voice One said.

'What the hell did you say?' Voice Three said.

'You don't ever ask why we want you, got it?' Voice Two said.

Silence.

'Got it, Duda?' Voice Three said.

'Got it, yes,' Jan Duda said.

'See, you Old Country people, you're all the same,' Voice One said. 'Think you're better than everyone else, think you've got a right to everything here. Well, I've got news for you, Duda.'

'You lot come to Little Town and think you own the place,' Voice Two said.

'What your mob have to remember, Duda, is that Little Town is ours,' Voice Three said.

'A few bombs isn't going to change that,' Voice One said.

'So, we'll be keeping an eye on you,' Voice Two said.

'See, we know where you work, Duda. We know where you live. We know everything in Little Town,' Voice One said.

'You wouldn't want that information to be passed into the wrong hands now, would you?' Voice Three said.

'People who might come and take that pretty little wife of yours away while you're out scrubbing floors,' Voice Two said.

'Old Country psychos perhaps,' Voice One said.

'Oh, I can imagine what they'd do to a cute thing like her, can't you, Duda?' Voice Three said. 'Everything has a price. Information is costly.'

'Especially information with benefits,' Voice Two said.

'Consider yourselves watched,' Voice Three said. 'Any shit against our Regime and we'll come for you.'

'Unless Old Country beat us to it,' Voice One said.

'And you might not see that lovely wife of yours again,' Voice Two said.

'Or that skinny kid,' Voice Three said.

'Got it?' Voice One said.

'Got it, yes,' Jan Duda said. 'Can we go sleeping now?'

The voices did more hyena sniggering.

Then a long pause.

'Go,' Voice One said. 'Get out of our sight.'

We could hear the sound of Pav and his parents shuffling back into their house.

'Remember,' Voice Two said. 'Be good.'

These were definitely the Regime's Rascals. Thugs with legitimacy. You'd never see any of the actual Regime enforcing their brand of law and order like this. When all that stuff about Pav's mum was going on, Dad squeezed my mum tight into his chest.

When the Duda door slammed shut Mum's shoulders drooped; once again Dad drew an imaginary zip across his mouth, just in case the voices were still hovering about. I didn't sleep too well that night. I certainly didn't do any more dreaming. All thoughts of Erin F had to be put on the back burner for the time being.

I couldn't even read; the words weren't going in the way they should have. I lay awake thinking about poor Pav and his folks. They were well and truly on the Rascals' radar now.

When I thought about the raid on Pav and his family I was embarrassed to be a Little Town person, knowing that *my* people could do shocking things to *those* people. These were my initial feelings, but when logic hit the brain I thought: *Come on, Charlie, cop yourself on, son. Who else is going to look after us here? Who else is going to make sure Little Towners don't have bombs lobbed at them again and again? Who else is going to keep buses, cafes, markets and parks panic-free and safe? Get a grip.* That didn't mean what happened to Pav's family benefited any of us.

The morning after the raid on Pav's, Mum and Dad slurped their tea, crunched at their jammy toast, nosed a local paper – the first since the bombs – and listened to some guy on the radio prattle on about how everything in Little Town would be back to normal in no time. Regime propaganda, no doubt. Not a ditty about any late-night raids by their Rascal thugs, not even from Mum or Dad. Nothing.

It was as if nothing had happened.

Say nothing, do nothing, pretend it didn't happen. Was this how things were going to roll in the Law household?

'Do you have a pen, Mum?' I asked.

They both looked up from their reading material.

'What are you planning, Charlie?' Dad said.

'I'm not planning anything. I just want a pen. That's not a crime now, is it?' I said.

'Watch it!' Dad said.

'There.' Mum handed me an old biro. Blue. My favourite.

'Any free paper floating about?' I asked.

'Charlie!' Dad said.

'What?'

'Here.' Mum gave me an A4 sheet whipped straight out of Dad's bag.

I needed to stick my oar in and help Pav's family. But how? The only thing I had to help the Dudas was Charlie Law's power of language. It was time to make a start with getting the lingo on to Pav's tongue. I didn't want to think about bombs and raids and refugees and death any longer. It was time to start living again.

To get us started I drew two little charts, carefully covering my A4 from Mum and Dad's eyes. The charts consisted of the verb TO BE and the verb TO HAVE. The most important ones. First, I intended to go through them with Pav and explain the basics before having him fill in the blanks in column three.

I am Pav.

I am happy.

I am sad.

I am from Old Country.

Surely they had verbs and stuff in Old Country lingo?

To cement things in his head I'd get him to do more blank-filling homework tasks. I was sure he would flip his lid with excitement when he saw them; I hoped at least it would take his mind off the Rascal thugs who carried out the raid.

VERB: TO BE

SUBJECT	VERB	COMPLEMENT
I	AM	
YOU WE THEY	ARE	
HE SHE IT	IS	

VERB: TO HAVE

SUBJECT	VERB	COMPLEMENT
I	HAVE	
YOU WE THEY	HAVE	
HE SHE IT	HAS	

What we needed to pull it all together was that table and those chairs. Doing it standing up would do bugger all for Pav's concentration.

'What's that you're scribbling?' Dad asked.

I flipped the A4 over.

'Nothing,' I said.

'Nothing?'

'Nothing,' I said again.

'Nothing's nothing,' Dad said, which didn't make much sense to me.

'Oh, Bert, leave him alone. You know what he's like,' Mum said.

'I don't want any trouble, Charlie,' Dad said.

'Like I do?' I said.

'Just be careful,' Dad said, grabbing his bag and jacket. 'Right, I'm off.'

'Where are you going, Dad?' I said.

'What do you mean, *where am I going*? I'm going to work.'

'But –'

'It's OK, Charlie. Things will be fine. I got a call last night. The office has reopened.'

'But what if –'

'Don't worry. Right, I'm off.'

'Bye, love,' Mum said.

'Bye, Maggie.' Dad gave Mum a peck on the cheek, which she held out for him. He kissed her longer than usual. Not the best thing to witness first thing in the morning, but cute as well.

'Bye,' I said.

'Remember, no trouble, Charlie. Got it?' Dad said, sounding like the Rascal thugs.

I stared at him for a moment. He knew what I was thinking. He was many things, my dad, but Mr Thick wasn't one of them.

'Got it,' I said, sounding like Pav's dad.

13
Concrete Streets

THINGS I DID BEFORE THE BOMBS CAME

- Got really bored because Little Town had a lack of teenage things to do. *(If there's a word below LACK that's what we have now, which means we also need a word below BORED)*
- Went to school for an education that would allow me to get a decent job. *(Then I would escape Little Town, maybe find my fortune some place else)*
- Dreamt that one day I'd become a doctor, lawyer or teacher. *(Without education I'd be lucky to get a job cleaning the schools)*
- Browsed bookshops. *(Browsing days have been destroyed)*
- Dreamt about Erin F and the possibility of … you

know what. *(I still do actually. The bombs have had no bearing on that. Still, I've no idea if she survived)*

- Didn't feel that I had to protect my mate Pav from his people *and* mine. *(Who'd be an Old Country refugee these days, eh?)*
- Ate whatever I wanted to. Well, what Mum made me to eat. *(I can't believe how fussy I was pre-bomb days; now I'd munch on a scabby dog if it filled me up)*
- Walked miles to get Mum her inhaler. *(She's had to decide how much breathing to do throughout the day. Something good to come out of this: her shouting at me has reduced)*
- Never cried myself to sleep because I was starving. *(In old-time lingo, Dad calls it being Hank Marvin, after some song-and-dance guy from way back when)*

After four days I left the house.

No one knew how many Old Country troops were on the ground. How do you go about counting? But it seemed as if they were everywhere, like a plague of sewer rats infesting Little Town. Each one carried a gun, or had one slung over their shoulder. Some of them were so young it looked as if they'd just completed their schooling. No wonder Pav and his family wanted out quick style. The guns were huge, long metal contraptions. Any false move, sprint in a different direction or suspicious behaviour could mean a bullet in the neck or a butt on the nose. That's why we all walked towards the checkpoint areas with special care. In a weird way I was happy to see the Old Country troops; it meant that there'd be no more bombs. I mean, what country would lob bombs on top of their own army? Not even Old Country's Government is that daft. Are they?

School was closed, and all my friends were shut up in their houses – I didn't even know if they were all still alive. I didn't really want to go out but someone had to get Mum's inhaler. The reek attacked me as soon as daylight hit; this burning smell hovered thick in the air, as if it was the day after a bonfire. Not the comforting smell of smouldering embers though; this smelt like human flesh and fear. The sky was a grieving grey colour too; it seemed to be in mourning with us. The outside was eerie. The people walking didn't speak. Food hunters? Relative hunters? Whatever, no one spoke. I didn't feel like speaking either. As I walked further along, towards the park, another rank smell battered my senses. Rubbish. Garbage. Trash. The rubbish hadn't been collected; it was strewn along the streets, definitely more than a week's mess. I had to dodge the bags, paper and rotten food as I shifted along the pavement. I tried not to think too much about the food. This was Ratland. Give it a few days and we'd have an actual rat infestation.

At the park's entrance the burning smell grew stronger. Four figures huddled in chat. Smoke drifted my way. Two of them had fags dripping from their mouths. Khaki combats tucked into bovver boy boots. No helmets. They saw me coming. The smokers chucked their stubs away. Their conversation ended. Smiles disappeared. Eyes my direction. Sussing me out. I tried not to make eye contact with them. It was no use though. The sight of them was magnetic. One of them was female, dark hair pulled back into a ponytail. She was an odd sight in her boots and swagger. Maybe she was their leader? It was the closest I'd been to Old Country troops. My neighbours. Oppressors. My stomach rumbled, again. My heart plundered my chest. *Put the head down and keep walking, Charlie,* my monster said. *You've done nothing wrong, son. You've done nothing wrong.* I could feel their eyes and sniggers burrowing into me. I clocked their hanging guns. I was scared senseless. They knew it. They revelled in it. My brothers and sister across the border. How did it come to this? They gave me my very own guard of honour. One gobbed at my feet, khaki coloured like their combats. *Walk with a purpose.* If one of them had stamped their boot on the ground I'd have soared like a firework. A male voice guffawed. The female voice chuckled. I advanced. *That's it, nothing to worry about.*

'Stay on path,' one of them shouted when I was beyond them.

The see-saw that I used to go up and down on when I was at primary school had been snapped in two. The see was missing from the saw or the other way around. The roundabout was lying upside down with no chance of spinning again. Of the six swings that swung before the Old Country days only one remained, and that was buckled and wrapped around the top metal bar. Broken glass, like little diamonds, glistened off the ground. Booze bottles mainly. The grass surrounding the playground was a cow's dreamland. Long and tired. This park was no more, only a tiny memory for people my age. Sad, that. In a few weeks it would become a dumping ground.

The smell of burning got more intense. There were little pockets of smouldering fires dotted around the park with soldiers clustered around them. So many of them. Various heads turned to examine this lone figure walking on through. One jittery move and I knew it was curtains. All it would take was a reach into the inside pocket of my jacket, an aggressive yank on my belt. That's all the excuse they'd need. The soldiers were burning the rubbish and rubble. Where were the people of Little Town? The Regime? Our Rascals? The men who hassled Pav's mum and dad? Had we given in so easily already? Near the exit of the park a pile of shoes and boots of all sizes were waiting their turn to be cremated. That's when I thought that maybe it wasn't just the rubbish they were burning. My stomach turned. Not for the first time.

When the shops came into view my body relaxed a bit. I refocused and went to get Mum her inhaler.

I knew before it came into view that it wasn't there any more, that it hadn't made it through the bombing. My nerves jangled more at this than at the sight of the Old Country troops. Its sign remained, but only the letters CHEM were visible. The IST part had been blackened. Burned out. Gone.

Gazing into the dark shell of the chemist shop it dawned on me that Mum would have to cut down on her daily breathing. At least until we could find her a place that sold inhalers. A hidden chemist, perhaps.

Talk about trouble and worry.

14
Fighting the Law

If anyone was going to break CHARLIE LAW'S TEN LAWS OF LITTLE TOWN it was Pav. If someone had a gun to your head and asked you who'd disobeyed CHARLIE LAW'S TEN LAWS OF LITTLE TOWN you'd have blurted out Pav well before trigger time. But guess who did violate CHARLIE LAW'S TEN LAWS OF LITTLE TOWN? Charlie Law, that's who. The worst law of them all. Law number nine: NO STEALING. Only the eejits and brainless dare break law number nine.

The eejits.

The brainless.

And me.

Charlie Law.

The night before the NO STEALING law was butchered

I spent an hour listening to my belly make sounds that the percussion section of an international orchestra would have been proud of. You'd have thought a quality baker was mixing cakes inside my stomach. Cakes. If only.

Since the bombs, and the arrival of Old Country's (hungry) troops, food was seriously scarce. Well, everything was scarce. I'd visited every known and unknown chemist trying to get an inhaler for Mum. No luck. It wasn't panic stations just yet, but it was getting dangerously close. Mum couldn't go out – the air was still debris-dusty from the bombing, and the sight of Old Country troops on the streets made her chest tight. Great tidal waves of hunger pangs engulfed us all, but it was much worse for poor Mum because she had to cope with breathing issues on top of those waves. The main shopping centre had been destroyed. The borders were closed, and the farmers didn't seem in a hurry to get food to Little Town. It was clear that supplies just weren't reaching us. Maybe due to drivers' fear of entering Little Town. Maybe out of Old Country's refusal to allow them entry. Either way, food was running low in everyone's gaff.

For the past week we had had soup for dinner. Two potatoes, two carrots, an onion, a bit of turnip (I found some turnip and carrots in the street, result!). Add some water, mush together with a little salt and pepper and hey presto! Soup. Soup for three. Soup that would have to last a week.

Delicious, tasteless soup. No dipping bread. Just soup. Bland Little Town Veggie Soup.

That night I didn't lie in bed thinking about Erin F's hair in my hands or Pav's family's safety or Mum and Dad smiling again or The Big Man handing over some plush chairs. God, The Big Man. I wasn't even sure The Big Man was still alive. I watched my dream shed flutter away. It was food which consumed my every thought now. Nothing else.

Food.

And food.

And more food.

It was as if my head was a supermarket's conveyor belt with all this wonderful, scrumptious scran passing through, with me pouncing like a rabid dog to get my chops on it. My head and stomach rumbled constantly. I was beginning to think that the first major casualty of these bombs – this war – was food itself. Or lack of it.

That night I couldn't read a book as my concentration was below gutter level. I decided to cry instead. For an hour. At first a drip. Then a flow. Followed by a flood. I couldn't stop it.

The only shop that was still doing any business was FruitLoop; I'm not sure why, as surely there was only a tiny amount of produce left to sell. Shame because FruitLoop used to have every fruit and veg type under the sun. When Little Town was in calmer times, Mum occasionally sent me there to pick up her messages when she couldn't be bothered herself. The shop only survived because it sat in a little parade which the bombs hadn't obliterated; even so FruitLoop was now a sorry sight. The main colour from the display outside was fire-damaged brown. But each time I walked past FruitLoop the temptation killed me. The monster's voice appeared on my shoulder, whispering into my lug:

Go on, Charlie, who's going to notice? Go on, Charlie. You'll never in a month of Sundays get caught. Go on, Charlie, I've got your back on this. You're a shoo-in.

Now, I'm fully aware that shoplifting is high on my list of Little Town DON'Ts, but I let my fingers run wild and free. I ran them gently over the fruit and veg, caressed an apple, placed all five digits over its waxy skin. Its bruising didn't matter to me. I only saw this juicy, delicious apple sitting pretty, waiting to be picked up, examined, breathed on, rubbed on a thigh and plunged into my mouth. I held it. Smelt it. I hadn't eaten fruit in weeks. The little monster mumbled:

Go on, Charlie. Stick it in your bag. No one has clocked you. Remember, I've got your back.

I looked left and right, unzipped my bag and plonked it in.

Good on you, Charlie. Walk away. Slowly does it. Don't want to attract any attention.

But I didn't walk away. I reached out and nabbed another. One for Mum.

Enough, Charlie. Leave it now.

Then blagged another. For Dad.

Oh, sweet Jesus, Charlie, what are you doing, son?

RUN! RUN LIKE THE WIND, CHARLIE. RUN LIKE THE BLOODY WIND.

I didn't hear exactly what the FruitLoop man said, but it was something like, *There's no use in running, Charlie Law. I know it's you. Just wait till they hear about this. Just wait till I tell them what you've done.* I couldn't hear anything after that; my heavy breathing and thunderous heart drowned out his ranting.

When I got to our block I went directly into the shed and waited for my body to calm down. I dug deep into my bag, fished out the three apples: vile, repulsive excuses of apples, further bruised with the bashing they took during my scampering. I lofted them up like trophies. Turned each one in my hands. Held them. Smelt them. My belly didn't rumble with much excitement. My tongue didn't lick my lips. My eyes didn't bulge. The hunger had jumped ship and left my tummy, hadn't it?

Mum and Dad should never find out that their son was nothing more than a common thief. I couldn't tell them. It would have to be a waiting game. Waiting for *them* to come and get me. Waiting for the FruitLoop man to knock on my door, flanked by some burly Rascal bruisers ready to dish out what had been coming to me. I could face anything, or so I thought. But a life of parental fear? No thanks.

Bombs? Pure doddle.
Bullets? No problem.
The Big Man's Tough Guys? Easy.
Searches? Effortless.
Nicking three putrid apples? Terror alert.

15
Elbow

Pav stared at the piece of paper for ages. I gave him some space and didn't peer over his shoulder during his thinking time. He was muttering stuff in his own lingo. Thinking words. I was standing at one end of the shed. Pav was at the other, struggling with the contents of the paper.

'Do you want me to go over it one more time, Pav?' I said.

'No, I have answer.' He came towards me, showed me the paper and pointed to where the apostrophes should go. 'You put here and here.'

'This one's right, Pav. This one's wrong,' I said. I gave him a tick. I didn't give him a red pen 'X' in case it psychologically damaged his confidence. 'That's not bad, Pav. Fifty per cent, that's good.'

The lessons would need to be of high intensity before

school started. If we only knew when that would be. I'd heard that part of the building had been hit, but we didn't know what to believe. We didn't venture that far to find out – there was still no phone signal. Although I did bump into Norman in the street and he gave me the utterly fantastic news: Erin F was alive and kicking; apparently Norman had been given the task of taking vital medicine to her mother's house. Who gave him the medicine? I didn't ask. But I had my ideas. I didn't care. Erin F was ALIVE.

Food shortages and troops clamouring about our streets I could just about swallow, but having my school closed was a total head-wrecker.

It was hard to get any quality work done standing up. Still no sign of The Big Man. Something told me that Pav's mind wasn't up to studying anyway. The whole bombing and thug thing had hurt him, dented his mind. A sadness had returned to his baby blue blinders again.

'Sure you don't want to go over it just one more time, Pav?'

'My brain is fook melt, Charlie,' Pav said.

'Are you OK? Is everything OK?'

'Little Town hating us so no OK.'

'They don't, Pav.'

'We not bomb Little Town. Bastard from Old Country did bomb. Not us Duda.'

'I know that, Pav.'

'We run from Old Country bomb many times. Old Country hating us too.'

'I know that. I understand.'

'Yes, but not every others,' Pav said, indicating with his head the blocks that surrounded us.

'They do, Pav. They know you're refugees. They know that you ran from the Government in Old Country. They know that you hate them more than we do. Everyone knows this.' I tried to reassure him.

'Yes, but look they still with the dagger eye at us.'

'It's not you. They're just scared of the Old Country troops now.'

'I not patrol troop, Charlie.'

'I know you're not, Pav.'

'I fook hate Old Country troop.'

'Me too.'

'More me.'

Pav folded the paper and put it in his shirt pocket. His shirt flapped around his tiny body like a sail in the wind.

'And how are your mum and dad?'

'All time in house. Shitless scared.'

I knew Pav's dad was still working at the hospital, which thankfully had escaped bomb night. An Old Country tactic? But Pav's dad could no longer ride the bus. It was too dangerous in case Old Country patrol did a quick-fire stop check. There had been news of some Old Country refugees being hunted down, discovered, taken away, questioned and never seen again. Game over. Pav told me that his dad had to be smuggled to work in the boot of a compassionate co-worker's car. I wasn't sure if I wanted to know this info or not. Imagine that I myself was dragged in for interview by Old Country troops one day and asked to provide them with any relevant info about traitors, plotters or schemers I knew of. I don't think I could hold my tongue if they brought out the water buckets. Maybe it was better to know nothing. Head down. Nose clean. Say, do, see and know nada.

'I'm sure it will ease off, Pav. I actually think that the Old Country troops will leave.'

Pav sniggered. 'Don't be eejit, Charlie. They want own Little Town. Make like Old Country. Soon they bring Old Country people to live here. So troops be here to protect these people. They no go anywhere. Trust in me.'

'You think?'

'I hundred per cent sure.'

'My dad says this will happen as well,' I said.

'Then all Old Country people be the most hated in Little Town.'

'Yeah … I think you may be right there, Pav.'

It was hard to disagree with Pav. No one really wanted mega numbers of Old Country folk arriving thinking they owned the place. Popping up their shops everywhere and speaking a lingo nobody understood. I wouldn't have a clue what was going on. Imagine the confusion and all the kerfuffles. Maybe having their own shops was the reason for flattening the shopping area on bomb night. A part of me was thinking that perhaps life would be better with new shops: different places to go, a selection. Choices. We'll see.

'I no want to be person everyone hate, Charlie,' Pav said.

'You won't be. Not while you're in my company anyway.' I pointed to the folded paper in his pocket. 'You want to continue with the apostrophes?'

'Let have break, Charlie.'

'Sure thing, Pav. We can do some vocab instead.' Pav groaned. I was unsure if it was his hunger pangs or his passion level. 'I'll tell you what I'll do, I'll just point out random things and you can tell me what they are. OK?'

'OK,' Pav said, with all the enthusiasm of a dead pig.

'Come on, Pav, the brain still needs to be active. Keep it ticking over. A healthy mind and all that.'

Pav looked at me as if he was chatting to someone from another planet.

'You know what I mean, Pav?' I said.

He shook his head.

'It doesn't matter. Anyway, let's start, OK?' I said.

'OK.'

'Right.' I looked around the empty shed. I pointed to my shoe. 'What's this?'

'Feet.'

'No, *this*?'

'This is shoe.'

'And this?'

'This is floor.'

'Or you could say ground.'

'Floor ground.'

'It's one or the other, Pav. You choose.'

'I choose floor.'

'Good man. And this?'

'This is arm.'

'Yes, but what specific part of the arm?'

'Middle arm.'

'Good guess, Pav, but not right.'

I moved my arm up and down like I was pumping iron.

'Muscle,' Pav said.

'No, this part.'

I pointed at the specific part.

'I not know.'

'It's I *don't* know, Pav. I *don't* know. Not, I *not* know.'

'I don't know.'

'I'll give you a clue; it begins with the letter E.'

Pav's eyes shot through me. Clueless.

'I don't know. My head empty.'

'What I'm pointing to is my elbow, Pav.' Pav touched his own elbow, all jaggy boned. 'Say elbow.'

'Elebow.'

'No, not elebow … el-bow. Say it slower; it's like two little words.'

'El-bow.'

'Brilliant.'

'Why I need know this, Charlie?' Pav said.

He had a point.

'Well, in case you hurt it and you need to go to the doctor,' I said, trying to think of good uses for elbows. 'Or if you want to rest it on your knee when you're knackered after a hard day's graft. Or if some beautiful hot stuff does a romantic stroke on it or, even better, she wants you to hold on to hers because she needs protection.' Pav was blank. Then the major significance of this word came to me. 'But, most importantly, Pav, you're not allowed to put these on your desk at school.'

'Why?'

'OK, I think we can move on,' I said.

More groans. Not the hunger pangs.

'What is this?' I said, pointing to my bum. I thought it was time to inject some fun into the day. See if Pav's eyes could glow. 'Come on, you know this, Pav.'

Pav's body tensed with the hard thinking.

'Arsehole!' said a voice from the shed's door. 'What are you two fudge-packers up to then?' Norman's head popped around.

'Blooming hell, Norman,' I said, putting my hand on my heart. 'I pure shat it there.'

Pav didn't budge.

'Not to worry, it's only me,' Norman said. 'You didn't think it was one of those Old Country dickheads, did you?' Norman's eyes flicked towards Pav. 'No offence.'

'It no offend,' Pav said.

'How did you know where to find us?' I said.

'Where else would you two weirdos be?' Norman stepped into the empty shed. With Erin F in mind I noted that there was no overcrowding problem. Result!

'We're just …' I started, Norman put his hand up like a stop sign.

'No need to explain anything to me, Charlie me old China, I'm a man of the world. Each to their own and all that,' Norman said. 'How are you, little man?' he said to Pav.

'I good, Norman. You?'

'Getting by, getting by,' Norman said. 'I see the lingo is coming on.' Norman winked at me.

'It's getting there, isn't it, Pav?' I said.

Pav shrugged his bony shoulders.

'You lost a bit of weight, Norman,' I said.

'Tell me who hasn't, Charlie?' He stretched out his arms to show me his body.

'Where have you been? We haven't seen you in yonks,' I said. Norman's face changed position, as if I'd just offended his mother or something. 'Just thinking of our chairs and table and lock. That's all.'

'Are you blind, Charlie?'

'No. Why?'

'So look around you.'

I looked out of the tiny window in the shed. I looked at Pav. He looked at me. I looked at the ceiling. I looked at Norman. I looked at Pav again, who stuck out his bottom lip.

'I didn't mean for you to actually look around you, did I?' Norman said. Sometimes it was easy to extract the urine from Norman.

'So have you come with news of our stuff?' I said.

'Jesus, Charlie! Little Town is a disaster area; it's hard to do a slash now without thinking you're being watched or followed.'

'What is slash?' Pav said.

'I'm telling you, it's easier trying to find a diamond in a haystack than getting your hands on a loaf of bread these days, and all you're worried about is a crap chair and a lock?'

I didn't want to tell him it was *needles*.

'Three chairs actually, Norman. It was three chairs.' It was my turn to put my hand up like a stop sign.

'We met with The Big Man, Norman,' I said.

'Yes. We meet,' Pav said.

'I know, he told me,' Norman said.

'Is he OK? I mean, he's not ... erm ... he's not ... like ... erm ...'

'No. He's fine, just up to his eyeballs in stress and stuff because of these Old Country pricks getting in the way of business.' Norman pointed outside towards the Old Country pricks. Then he looked at Pav. 'No offence.'

'I no offend,' Pav said.

'Well, at least he's not ... you know,' I said.

'He's sound. That's partly why I'm here.'

'Why?'

'The Big Man wants a word with you two,' Norman said.

'What word?' Pav said.

I wasn't sure if this was Pav's lingo deficiency or he was making a real joke. If it was a joke it was a chuckler. But I was part delighted and part nervous. Delighted because maybe The Big Man could get his hands on an inhaler for Mum as well as our stuff. Delighted because we'd finally be able to kit out our shed. Delighted because Erin F's company in it was becoming real. However, I was nervous because it was The Big Man we were talking about after all. Nervous because he might still want to *sort something out, eh?*

'He wants to see the both of you,' Norman said.

'What do you mean?' I said.

'What do you mean, *what do I mean*?'

'Well, does he *want a word* or does he *want to see us*, Norman? Which one is it?'

'Does it matter, Charlie?'

'Yes, it does matter, Norman. *Wants a word with you two* is very different from *he wants to see you both*. Very different indeed.'

'How?' Norman said.

'Well, for a start one's a threat and one's a request, that's how,' I said.

'What do you think, little man?' Norman said to Pav.

'I not know.'

'Thought so.' Norman took a deep breath. 'The Big Man wishes to speak with you pair of fannies. Is that better?'

'Does he have our stuff?' I said.

'Did he tell you that he'd get you the stuff?'

'Big Man say he get,' Pav said.

'OK, so if he said he'd get you the stuff he'll get you the stuff. The Big Man's word is good.'

'So when does he want to see us?' I said.

'He'll send someone over to pick you up,' Norman said. 'It's dodge central out there on your own so it's better that way.'

'You go out there,' I said.

'Yes, but I know the score, Charlie. I know the ropes.'

'Sure you do, Norman,' I said.

'Right, I can't stay round here shooting the breeze with you two head-bangers all day. I've got to go see a man about a canine.'

We all shook hands like we'd done a business transaction or just put down a mysterious Mafia deal.

'Well, cheers for the heads up, Norman.'

'No worries,' he said. 'I'll see you two cats later.'

We watched as Norman slammed the door shut behind him.

'What is canine, Charlie?' Pav asked.

'A dog, Pav,' I said, staring at the slammed door. 'A dirty dog.'

16
Critical Mass

As soon as the car skidded its brakes beside us my brain went into overdrive: I feared Pav would be taken away for a full-on question-and-answer session. In an instant he might've been snatched and I'd never set eyes on him again. Pav would equal past tense.

I wasn't sure if the dark curfew was still in force or not. All sense of Little Town rules had been muddied after the bombs came. It wasn't dark yet, but it was getting there. Creeping in. It felt eerie being outside, knowing Old Country troops were lurking with their guns. Knowing the Regime's Rascals could pounce from the shadows at any time. Even though the Old Country troops and the Regime appeared to be coexisting in some bizarre peaceful hostility you could feel the pressure on the streets; it hugged your body and kissed your face. The tiniest act of aggression from any Rascal thug could result in a blaze of bullets. Occasionally we'd heard them whizzing far in the distance.

This wasn't an Old Country car, oh no; this was a manky Little Town Rascal vehicle. It rattled and crunched along, trying to blend in with the rest of the motors, which were just as shabby and tired. The few cars that were on the road drove with extra caution, each one attempting to draw zero attention from Old Country patrols. The last thing any driver wanted was to be smithereened.

The car that stopped next to us was a shambles. A metal tramp on wheels. A tinker with electric windows. The window slid down.

'How are you homos?' the man said, leaning out. It was the same window man who took us to see The Big Man that first time, just before the bombs rained down on us. A crappier vehicle, but the same dude.

Pav twisted his head away.

'It's OK, Pav. It's not Old Country,' I said. 'Really, it's OK.'

Pav twirled to face the window man.

'Duda, right?' the window man said.

'Pavel Duda, yes.'

'Old Country boy, eh?'

'He hates Old Country,' I said.

'Was I asking you, Law?' I said nothing. 'Was I?' I shook my head.

'I hate man from Old Country,' Pav said, nodding his head up in the air. The window man laughed. 'I hate. Is true, Charlie?' Pav looked for support.

'It's true, he does hate them,' I said.

The window man continued with his smiley face.

'Don't we all, Duda. Don't we all.'

'They pure bad,' Pav said.

'It's true, that's what he thinks of them,' I said.

'Old Country bastard.' Pav gobbed a massive spit on the pavement. This wasn't anger for show. This was legit. The window man looked at me.

'Old Country bastards.' I gobbed a spit of my own that didn't get past my chin. Rubbish! I wasn't much of a spitter.

'I no like. Go back,' Pav said, again nodding his head to the sky.

The window man looked confused.

'He means that he thinks Old Country troops should go home, not you,' I explained.

'Sure that's what he thinks?' the window man said to me.

'It is. Hundred per cent true,' I said.

'Is that what you think, Duda?' the window man asked.

'Yes. I think,' Pav said.

'Well, you can think what you want, Duda, but you can't escape from where you're from, or who you are, can you now?' the window man said.

That sounds familiar.

His smiley face was no more.

'He's not living in Old Country any more,' I said.

'That doesn't matter, Law. He's still one of them.'

'He doesn't feel like one of them,' I said.

'As I said, you can't escape where you're from.' He pointed his gloved finger at me.

'But he's from here now. He lives in Little Town. Therefore he's from Little Town,' I said, wiping gob away from my chin and mouth.

'I from Little Town,' Pav said.

'It's true. He is,' I said.

The window man leaned out a little further; it was his turn to sniff up and gob on to the pavement. Missed our shoes by inches. Your typical Little Town Rascal. It was clear that the presence of Old Country troops had burst these thugs' bubble, which probably sent them into a wind tunnel of rage. They had no one left to bully. No one left to flex their muscles at. No one left to bug. Apart from easy targets like Pav and me.

'Very big true,' Pav said.

'Here's the thing, Duda. I don't think it is true,' the window man said. 'I think you could be a dirty little spy.'

'Never spy man,' Pav said. 'I no dirty little spy.'

'You watch your tongue when you speak to me, Duda,' the window man said, glove pointed at Pav.

'We haven't done anything,' I said.

'That's what you think, Law. That's what you think.' Then it struck me: he must have been talking about the apples. Of course, he was talking about the apples, what else could he have been talking about? We (I) hadn't done anything else to stray from the system. Before the bombs you might get a slap around the chops, but now you could get a bazooka up your arse.

'What we have done?' Pav asked.

'We haven't done a thing, and it's not dark,' I said, glaring at the window man.

'In the back.' He thumbed towards the back seat.

'Why?' Pav said.

'He wants to know why,' the window man said to nobody.

'Yes, why?' I said.

'Now *he* wants to know why. Get a load of these two cheeky little …'

'Where we go? You tell where we go?' Pav was standing with his arms folded, face scowling.

A grin cut across my mouth. I was thinking, *On you go, buddy. Get in there, pal. Stand your ground. Be all defiant and brilliant*. I could have thrown my arms around his skinny neck and hugged him tight.

The window guy was hopping with rage. One second his eyes were glued on us, then they flicked to the rear-view mirror. His eyes see-sawed like that. He was clearly scared shitless in case Old Country patrol clocked him talking to us. Terrified in case Old Country patrol exposed him as nothing more than a Little Town Rascal, doing The Regime's dirty work for them. Petrified in case it was his time to be q and a'ed in a dark and disused warehouse somewhere. His flicking eyes uncovered his fears.

'Look, just get in, lads. There's someone who wants to see the two of you.'

'Is it The Big Man again?' I asked.

'He has chair?' Pav said.

'Of course he has chairs. What are you on about, Duda?'

'No, he doesn't mean that. He means, does he have our stuff?' I asked.

'Look, he wants to see you, that's all I know. Now don't make me get out of this vehicle, Law.'

'I've heard that one before,' I said.

Eyes still jammed to the rear-view, a bead of sweat on his brow. 'You've got three seconds, then I'm out of here. And if that happens The Big Man will come and get you himself, which will make him severely pissed off. Is that what you want?'

We didn't answer. I looked at Pav and raised my eyebrow. Pav shrugged his two twiggy shoulders.

'He's not a man to be messed with, lads.' Rear-view eyes properly bricking it. 'It's up to you.'

'We'd better get in, Pav,' I said.

Pav went first.

*

This location was different from where we'd first met The Big Man. I suppose that factory, or wherever, didn't make it past the bombs. Instead we pulled up outside a normal block not too far from ours. Nothing suspicious about it. Ingenious. The window man told us to go up two flights of stairs. Once there, someone would be waiting to take us to The Big Man. We hopped out of the vehicle and watched as it huffed away. We were alone. My bones started rattling.

I led Pav into the block. Fire and waste still polluted the air. It hurt your tongue. Slowly we went up the first flight of stairs. Then the second. On to the landing. An empty landing. We stood still. Rooted in fear. I held my breath. Tensed my stomach. Pav edged closer. I felt his scrawniness on me. Our scrawniness together. A door clinked down a corridor. Then another, closer, heavier. Boots sounded, closer, heavier. Something appeared: The Big Man?

No.

No, standing before us was a mega-muscled colossus of a man. He eyeballed us from top to bottom, snorting loudly through his nose. The crack of his bones echoed around the landing as he stretched out his back.

'What are you pair of bawbags doing here?'

Quite possibly this was the biggest man I'd ever seen in my life. A human mountain. Pav let out a tiny whimper. I put my arm on his and squeezed.

'Eh?' Muscles said.

I gulped.

'Erm ... the guy who ... erm, dropped us off said that ... erm, The Big Man wanted to see us.'

'That he does,' Muscles said. 'That he does.'

'Where is he?' I asked.

'Through that door.' Muscles pointed to a door down the landing.

When he stepped out of the way and opened his arm like a matador would to a couple of crazed bulls, his jacket flapped open. I spied a gun in an underarm holster. A flash of steel.

My face ticked.

'Do we just go in?' I said.

'Be my guest,' Muscles said.

If they were giving out nappies for fourteen-year-olds then I'd have been at the front of the queue. I opened the door and baby-stepped inside the flat. Pav behind me, the leader. A long hallway awaited. Carpet on the floor. Everything dark.

'Charlie?' Pav whispered.

'What?' I whispered back.

'What is bawbag?'

'Eejit. Or idiot,' I said. 'Keep close, Pav. Keep close.' Bit by bit we made our way to the door at the end of the hall. Behind which The Big Man would be, wouldn't he? Sat in a gold throne or something.

'You have many word for stupid people in Little Town, Charlie.'

'That's because Little Town is full of them, Pav.'

A crash course in synonyms could be just what the doctor ordered.

I knocked twice on the door.

Two dinky knocks.

'Come in!' a voice boomed.

17
Big Man's Bitches

On the first *come in* we hesitated. Pav looked at me for guidance. The second *come in* sounded as if whoever said it was totally peed off about something. Probably with us. The tone pricked my ears. This voice didn't help with the fear. Pav nodded for me to advance. Chalk-white face, sweat-soaked body and googly eyes, I opened the door and entered the room. If I was to ever smuggle suitcases of Class-A drugs from one country to another I'd be caught before reaching the check-in desk. Mum called me an open book of a boy. I just didn't have the face for a life of crime.

The room was rank and bare. The carpet was so knackered that it was all leather in parts after years of feet beating. I kept my eyes on the floor.

'Here they are, my two favourite numpties,' The Big Man

greeted us. He was sunk into a figure-hugging leather chair, flanked by two bruisers like columns in a Greek temple. Ugly Greek columns. This time round there was no phone, no big swing chair, no desk and no computer that my eyes could see.

'The driver and the guy on the landing said you wanted to see us, Big Man,' I said.

'You have our stuff?' Pav butted in.

'Wow, wow, wow. Hold them horses, Duda,' The Big Man said. He was neither smiling nor snarling. Then he snarled, 'I don't know if you're aware or not, but we're in a war zone right now and all you're interested in is a couple of bloody chairs.'

'No … he … didn't mean …' I tried to say.

'Don't you be his mouthpiece, Law. That's not cool.' The Big Man pointed up at me from his seat. 'This little skinny arse here knows exactly what he's all about.' The Big Man fixed Pav with a hard glare. 'Don't you?'

Pav didn't answer.

'We just thought that when you wanted to see us it was to do with the stuff we asked for, Big Man, that's all,' I said.

The Big Man's full lips and mouth softened.

'Look at the state of you two.' Me and Pav looked at each other. We were clean and I'd shampooed two days previously. It's not as if we'd been cutting around like Huckleberry Finn and the Artful Dodger. I didn't know what to say. 'You're like a couple of butcher's pencils standing there. When was the last time you had a proper feed?'

'Ages I no eat,' Pav said.

'I can see that, Duda. I can see that,' The Big Man said. 'What about you?' he said to me.

'I eat what I can, which isn't much.'

'You're like a flick knife, Law. How the hell are you going to carry these chairs I've got for you into your block, eh? I've seen more beef on a dog's cock.'

'So you have stuff?' Pav said. The Big Man glared at him.

'When The Big Man says he'll get you something, he means he'll get you something,' he said.

'Thanks,' I said.

'No need for thanks, Law. The world is full of thanks; what I'm looking for is action.' I didn't know what he meant by this. Pav was totally lost. 'But first things first.' The Big Man rose. He stood bigger than the two columns. 'I think it's time you lads had some decent scran inside your bellies. What do you think?' We nodded. Of course we nodded.

He went over to one of the columns, very close. So close we couldn't hear what he was saying.

'You eat meat, Duda?' he said.

'I eat.'

'What about you, Law?'

Weeks ago I was seriously considering life as a veggie, but with all this carnage in Little Town I'd have happily munched on a scabby dog or my own arm if there was any chance of meat being on it. It's amazing how quickly principles get chucked out of the window when needs must.

'Yes, I eat meat.'

The Big Man pointed to Pav.

'Burger?'

'Burger, yes.' Pav's eyes were like two plates.

'With cheese?'

'With cheese, yes.' Two dinner plates.

Then he pointed to me.

'Burger?'

'I will, thanks.'

'Same?'

'OK.'

He flicked his head to one of the columns, who did what any thick bruiser would do: he followed orders without uttering a word.

It wasn't any of my business how The Big Man managed to get his mitts on a pair of burgers; I was just salivating at the prospect of attacking it. I was too scared to ask that question. Not Pav though. He was in like Flynn.

'How you get burger?'

'You mean, how do I get my hands on a couple of burgers when no one else can?' The Big Man said.

'Yes, how you get hands on this burgers,' Pav asked.

I was willing him to rap it, but at times Pav liked nothing

more than diving in at the deep end, with concrete slippers on.

'Christ, Duda, you need to brush up on the lingo if we're going to be seeing more of each other.

'There is nothing I can't get in Little Town, Duda. Even with those dirty, rotten Old Country bastards thinking that they now run the place. I can still get my paws on anything I want.'

'Well, that's good news for our stomachs,' I said with a chuckle. Nobody else chuckled. The Big Man certainly didn't chuckle; he shot me a look which sent shivers up my spine. He took two steps closer. I smelt stale fags, booze and fried food.

'I have a bone to pick with you, Law.' My nose hardly reached his chest. My heart sped up.

'What … have I … erm … done?'

'I'll tell you what you've done, fannyman. Shall I?'

'Erm … please.'

'It's come to my attention that you have been pilfering stuff that belongs to me.'

Pav looked at me as if I'd let him down. How did he know what pilfering meant?

'Pilfering? You … erm, mean …'

'Apples, Law. You've been blagging bloody apples. *My* apples.'

'Your apples?'

'If you nick anything from Little Town shops you're nicking stuff from me, clear?'

'I didn't ... erm ... know that the apples were yours.'

'Well, you know now.'

'Sorry.'

'Everything you see, Law, belongs to The Big Man. Everything. This Old Country invasion changes nothing.'

'It won't happen again, Big Man, promise it won't,' I said.

The Big Man stepped back, scanning us both.

'So, you're a thief, Law,' he said to me. 'And you, Duda, you're from Old Country, which makes you all sorts of things.' He then grinned from ear to ear. 'You know what I call that, chaps?'

'No, what?' I said.

'It's an asset, that's what it is,' The Big Man said.

'What is asset?' Pav asked.

'Something that will benefit The Big Man, Pav,' I told him.

'Like talent?' he asked.

'Exactly, Duda. You and Law here are a uniquely talented pair of eejits who can help me. No. You can help the people of Little Town.'

'Help how?' Pav asked.

'A few odds and ends now and again. Think of it as doing a civic duty.'

'That's all?' I asked.

'Oh, I'll need to think about that, but the way I see it, you owe me for the kind gesture of providing the furniture for your doll's house and for being good-hearted enough not to break Law's sticky little fingers for tea-leafing *my* stuff in *my* town.' That's when my sphincter opened and closed again and again like a camera shutter. 'I'd say you two owe me big time, but to show that I'm actually a humanitarian deep down, the burgers are on the house.'

I wanted to swear out loud. Shout obscenities at Norman. Skelp myself in the chops. Burn down the shed. Get the flock out of Little Town.

We stood there, feet nailed to the bogging carpet. Two numb numpties. The Big Man flopped back down on his chair. Folded his arms.

Soon after the door flew open and one of the columns thrust greasy big burgers into our hands. Piping hot, they smelt like a trip to paradise. The Big Man gestured for us to sit and enjoy. The burgers eased the fear.

The thought came to me as I chewed my burger in silence. If The Big Man was right, if there was nothing he couldn't get in Little Town, then maybe, just maybe, he could help Mum get her hands on some inhaler medicine. I was about to jump up and ask him there and then if he could. Lay it on thick. Tell him that Mum's life depended on it, that her fight for breath was a constant battle. That me and Dad were at our wits' end with worry. But I didn't want Pav to hear. He shouldn't be involved in this request. This was purely a private matter.

A beep beep sound came from one of the column's pockets. He took out his mobile phone, looked at the message before showing it to The Big Man.

'Right, there's a van waiting downstairs for you.'

Pav, still ploughing through his burger, stopped munching and raised his eyes towards me. It was his you'd-better-say-something-fast look.

'To take us where?' I said. The fear kicked in again.

'Home, Law. Home.' The Big Man noticed my chest heaving with relief. The penny dropped. 'Where else would you be going. Eh?' Then the penny dropped again. Much harder this time. 'What do you think I am, Law? What do you take me for, some Old Country barbarian?' He looked at Pav. Pav poked the remaining bit of his burger into his mouth. 'Do you think I'd ever lay a finger on two nothings like you?'

'No, I just thought –'

'Never mind what you thought. Just get your arses down-stairs to that van or else you'll be walking home.'

'OK, Big Man,' I said. 'Come on, Pav. We'd better go.'

'We leave?' Pav said.

'Go! Get the hell out of my sight,' The Big Man said.

'Thank for burger,' Pav said.

'Get your arses out of here.' With a nod The Big Man asked one of the columns to escort us down the stairs to the van. I pretended to be getting my jacket on and sorting myself out; I waited until Pav was through the door.

'Are you deaf, Law?' The Big Man said.

'I just wanted to ask you a favour, Big Man.'

'What? Another one?'

'I'll be quick.'

'Make it.'

'Well, you know the chemist has been bombed.'

'Right. So?'

'So, the thing is …'

'Get to the damn point, Law.'

'My mum used to get her inhaler medicine from there and now she … erm … It's serious, Big Man. She's really struggling. She needs it.' The Big Man's palm stopped me.

'You want me to get her medicine, Law. Is that it?'

'Erm … I suppose so … yes.'

The Big Man glared. Stared. Flared his nostrils. 'OK, give me the details. I'll see what I can do.'

'You will?' I said, wanting to hug him.

I wrote down the details on a piece of paper, which he looked hard at.

'*Inhaler medicine for Mrs Maggie Law*?'

'Right,' I said.

'OK, now get the hell out of here.'

Mum would go off her nut if she knew The Big Man had her vitals. Maybe I should have said the inhaler was for me. Kept Mum out of this mess.

*

We didn't speak too much on the quick trip back from The Big Man's place. The taste of succulent burger still coated my mouth. Most importantly, my belly was full, as was my mind. A part of me wanted to run into my house and tell Mum that I'd soon get her medicine, that she'd be OK from now on, that I'd look after her. But hearing The Big Man's voice saying my mum's name made my stomach clench. As the van trundled towards our block we looked out at the deserted streets. I could tell that Pav was going over what had happened; his face had that scrunched-up appearance. Confusion. Intrigue. Fear. Excitement.

As the van hit a particularly dark spot I saw my own reflection in the glass; my face looked the same as Pav's. One part of the brain was delighted that The Big Man had come up trumps with our goodies, meaning Erin F would definitely be getting invited to our luxury shed. The other part of the brain was wondering what we'd agreed to do for The Big Man. What we'd agreed to become. Had we agreed to be his lackeys? His errand boys? His new young bucks? Vital cogs in his inner circle? I just didn't have a clue. All I knew was that The Big Man had gone out of his way to scratch our backs and now he was feeling the itch himself.

When the driver got out of the van, he was acting as if he was an international spy; this was a man who clearly didn't want to be seen outside his zone, especially with two boys handling some second-hand furniture. He gave us a hand carrying the stuff to the shed, before bolting. Me and Pav flopped on a chair each and released the air that was trapped in our lungs.

'God, I'm glad that's over,' I said.

Pav shook his head, despairing of me.

'It no over, Charlie. This is the begin.'

'Yes, the beginning of our independence in here,' I said, gesturing around the shed, changing the subject. 'Think about it: we could create a library and other cool things in here.'

'No, Charlie, this the begin of you and me being danger men.'

'In danger, you mean?' I said.

'Exact.'

I knew he was right, of course; I knew he was. I was trying to block everything out but that bloody cheeseburger kept repeating on me, transporting me back to The Big Man's. Back to his clutches. To his new-found control over us. I wished I'd refused that bloody cheeseburger. I wished I'd left those bloody apples alone.

'It'll be OK, Pav. You'll see,' I said, but I think I was trying to convince myself more than Pav.

'What we do, Charlie, eh? What we do?'

'We enjoy our new shed, that's what we do. We invite some people around and maybe have a shed opening. Erin F can be our first visitor.' Pav sat shaking his head. 'We do nothing, Pav. Just keep our heads down and do nothing. There's too much going on in Little Town for him to worry about us two.'

But what would happen to Mum if The Big Man did forget about us? Sitting there in my comfy chair, I imagined her in the house, wheezing, famished, trying to ration her inhaler puffs, limiting herself to short bursts of breaths. If I'd sold our souls to The Big Man for the sake of a couple of chairs, I might as well make sure something good came out of it. My family badly needed inhalers. The Big Man had Mum's last breath in his hands.

'The Big Man will probably forget all about us anyway,' I said.

'He not forget, Charlie. He like huge elephant.' Pav pointed to his temple.

'Look, if the worst comes to the worst, the most he'll want us to do is run a few errands for him. Go to the shops. Keep an ear to the ground. Stuff like that. Nothing we can't handle.'

'I not believe,' he said.

'Don't believe what?'

'That Big Man only want small thing from us.'

'Of course he does, Pav. What else would he want us for? I mean, we have nothing to offer.'

'That what I worry. Why he give stuff, eh? You OK, Charlie. Me? I refugee. No one want here. Big Man very powerful. He do big damage to Dad work. They do the bad thing to Mum. Me? I no get choose; I must do what Big Man say.'

'I'm not OK either, Pav. You see, I asked him to get medication for my mum. If she doesn't get it,' I said, feeling my throat vibrate. 'If she doesn't get it, who knows what'll happen to her. She might … she could …' I rubbed my eyes. 'I guess what I'm saying, Pav, is that The Big Man's got us both by the short and curlies.'

Pav's chin was practically on the floor. Not the grand comfy shed opening I'd imagined. 'Look, I'm sure everything will be OK,' I added.

'I no want to be bitch of Big Man, Charlie.'

'I no want to be bitch of Big Man either, Pav.'

'I no want to be bitch like Norman, Charlie.'

'I no want to be bitch like Norman either, Pav.'

It seemed that Pav's lingo ability was improving a tad, while mine was being ripped to shreds. His influence was strong.

'Little Town no good for me if I caught with stealing. They send me back to Old Country or put me in jail with men who want to do the sexy with me.'

'Listen, I'll go back and speak to The Big Man and ask him what exactly he wants from us. OK?'

'When you go?'

'I'll leave it for a week or so, to see what happens, and then I'll go see him. Deal?'

The very thought of going to see The Big Man alone sent shivers up my legs. I was afraid that he'd eat me alive for going to him without an appointment. Or one of his muscle men would. That image of The Big Man sitting on his huge leather chair in that dingy room was still very much alive in my mind. If I was going to get through this with my sanity intact, I'd need to buck up my ideas.

'OK,' Pav said. 'You speak to Big Man.'

We used the sturdy lock to secure our shed from thieves. But not bombs though.

'Charlie?' Pav said.

'Yes?'

'What short and curlies mean?'

'Hair around your willy area, Pav.'

18
Good Tidings

It was Sunday afternoon. Three weeks since the bombs came, ten weeks since Pavel Duda arrived in Little Town, a few days after I traded my freedom for some chairs and a cheeseburger. We were due to start school the following week. The Old Country invaders seemed keen to get things back to normal. Fortunately for me our school *had* survived the bombing. Pav wasn't exactly cock-a-hoop about the notion of educating himself. His face was thunder at the very thought of going to a new school. A fresh group of jokers ready to welcome him with open mouths; a brand new set of Old Country refugee haters waiting to pounce.

I had a feeling that Pav wasn't your typical A-grade learner. No, Pav would be your up-the-back-of-the-class-head-on-desk sprawler type of guy peeking up at the clock every two minutes because he believed all this learning guff was the most excruciatingly painful experience of his entire life.

Mum had managed to get her hands on some spanking trousers for my first day back. Cheap and nasty. Electric shock numbers. But new. She'd bleached some of my shirts from last year so that the yellow sweat marks and bogging collar stains were only a memory. My three shirts were pressed, hanging up and raring to go. I'd been busy swotting up. A complete nerd? A weedy geek freak? Whatever people wanted to call it. I'd read three books for our English course, two plays for Classics and two biographies for history. I tried to go through some of it with Pav as well, but he was having none of it. Pav told me that he'd be wearing the same school clothes he wore last year in Old Country. Neither of us would have new bags.

Since the transmitters were thankfully back up and running I'd sent Erin F a text inviting her to our newly furnished shed. No reply. Perhaps the network was still scrappy.

That Sunday I was busy rearranging and rejigging the shed furniture. I did it so many times that I couldn't tell what the best position for things was. I read a book once about this mad oriental technique of furniture organising that was supposed to help soothe the soul and make your life all harmonising and groovy, but when I tried it out in the shed it didn't work for me; instead it seemed to have the opposite effect: muddling my head and sending me into a wind tunnel of confusion. I asked Pav if it would be better to have one chair near the door, one below the window and one in the corner? What didn't help was that Pav's answers to my questions seemed to take the shape of:

'It bloody chair. I no mind.'

or

'Put there. I no shitting care.'

A career in interior design was definitely not Pav's future bag.

'Forget chair, Charlie. When you go to see Big Man?'

'I …'

'You promise, Charlie.'

'I know I did, Pav, but I've had stuff on my mind and I just haven't got round to it yet.'

'You make huge promise to me.'

'And I'll keep it, Pav. I will.'

'If you no speak to Big Man, Charlie, it mean he has our short and curlies. You know this.'

'I know, Pav.'

'I no want my short and curlies in Big Man's hands.'

I sat down, not knowing what to say. The truth was I was scared to death of going to see The Big Man again. The very thought of it knotted my tummy. We sat in silence for a moment. Then something weird happened: a tear fell from Pav's eye and landed on his cheek. I watched it trickle down, until his hand came up to wipe it away. I looked closer in case it was a tear mirage. It wasn't. I saw the trickle from my own tearless eyes.

'Are you OK, Pav?' I asked.

He said nothing.

Sniffed up the snot that fell on to his top lip.

'Pav?'

I began to worry.

He ran his sleeve across his mouth, cleaning that hard-to-shift snot.

'Pav, speak to me.'

He looked up; another tear dropped on to his cheek. Smaller this time.

'What's up, Pav?'

More sleeve-wiping.

'Pav, what's wrong? Is there anything I can do?'

'No.'

'Has something happened?'

No answer, which told me that *something* had happened.

'Hey.' I reached out and touched his elbow. He didn't flinch. I gripped harder. 'Speak to me, buddy.' I gave his arm a soft pal rub. 'I'll go see The Big Man, promise.'

'That not problem, Charlie,' Pav said.

I released my grip on his elbow.

'Is it the thought of going to school? Are you scared?'

'I handle school.'

'Look, if you'd rather not talk about it that's OK with me.'

'No, I want.'

'Listen, take your time. My ears are yours.'

'I no want take ears from you, Charlie.'

'No, it's just an express– … oh, it doesn't matter. If there's anything I can do, just say.'

'It is Mum,' he said, wiping more tears. 'My poor mum.' I wanted to hug him. I thought about Erin F's mum and wondered if Pav was going to have to care for his in the same way she cared for hers. A sentence for both of them.

'She's not ill, is she?'

'No, but she cry all time.'

'Your mum? Why?'

'She thinking too much about my sister.'

'Your sister back in Old Country?'

'Yes.'

'That's understandable, Pav. Natural.'

'There is mass problem.'

'What problem?'

'My sister not in Old Country no more, Charlie.'

'She's not?'

'No.'

'Where is she?'

'She here.'

'Here?'

'Yes, here.'

'Here? Like in Little Town here?'

'Yes.'

'But I thought …'

'Mum see my sister three day ago.'

'In Little Town?'

'In patrol.'

'An Old Country patrol?'

'Yes, she working for Old Country patrol. Mum see her.'

'Did your mum speak to her?'

'No.'

'Why?'

'My sister no see Mum.'

'But she's sure that she saw your sister in an Old Country patrol truck though?'

'Sure one hundred of per cent.'

We spent a minute or so thinking. I tried to imagine what Pav's sister looked like; was she as gaunt, pale and hungry as her younger brother? I tried to imagine her dressed in a uniform with a killing machine slung over her shoulder. All mean-faced in search of any scallywag Little Towners. Wow! Pav's sister an Old Country troop? It was hard to believe. The shame and dismay his parents must have felt.

'Maybe they grabbed her off the street, Pav. You can't be sure she wasn't.'

Pav shook his head, almost sniggering at my naivety.

'She not taken by them, Charlie. This is thousand of per cent definitely.'

'Really?'

'Really yes. My sister wear the Old Country uniform, Charlie.'

'The military one?'

'Yes.'

'So your sister works for Old Country?'

'Yes, she works.'

'But … how?'

I scrunched my eyes, confused. I didn't understand how Pav and his family could loathe the Old Country Government and Military so much, yet his sister decided to hobble off and get herself a position with them. Surely that was a major betrayal of her family?

'Why does your sister work for the Old Country Military, Pav? I just don't get it,' I said.

'She work for a while, they wash her brain when at university. Say to her many lies. Then one day she leave me, Mum and Dad to work for Government Military.'

'No explanation?' I said.

'Nothing.'

'She just got up and left like that?'

'Yes.'

'And you never saw her again?'

'She leave home.'

'And never returned?'

'Only one time for tell Mum and Dad they must become Government supporter.'

'Your sister *told* your mum and dad that?'

'She say we support or we have much troubles.'

'When you say *troubles* what you really mean is … ?'

'Troubles. I mean troubles, Charlie.'

'Like she was going to kill you if you didn't support the Government or something?'

'No! I no mean that.'

'To me *troubles* means bad stuff, Pav.'

'Bad stuff, yes. But not die. My sister not psycho maniac.'

I don't know so much. Let's look at the evidence: she's part of an Old Country Military who gained entry here by bombing us to bits. She's now part of those ground troops who tell us how we should be living our lives. And if we don't live our lives according to the way they want us to, they'll make that life a tough one … or worse. So I'd say *psycho maniac* just about covers it.

'I'm not saying she is, Pav. I just thought –'

'She tell to us, without supporting Government it best leave Old Country.'

'Wait,' I said, putting my hands up to my chest so Pav could hold them wild horses back for a second. 'So you're telling me that it was your sister who told you to leave Old Country?'

'Yes, she say.'

'Say or told?'

'Told.'

'Like a threat?'

'No, like told.' Pav was firm.

I couldn't see the difference, but I think Pav had convinced himself there was one.

'Better to leave than to be like chicken on toast, no?'

Sorry … what?

Excuse me?

Come again?

This must've been a direct Old Country lingo translation; I didn't get the chicken on toast thing. Pav's hands were wide open; he was expecting a response. I gave him one, of sorts. Nodding my head in agreement.

'No, you definitely don't want to be the chicken on the toast, Pav. That doesn't sound like a good place to be.'

'Exact … so that why we come here.'

Collating it all in my head, it became clear that the reasons the Dudas came to Little Town wasn't because their daughter had joined up with their Government's Military; it wasn't because she had tried, and failed, to have them follow in her footsteps; it wasn't because she had threatened them with experiencing some *troubles* (yeah, right!) if they didn't show their support. No, it was all because the Dudas were scared shitless that someone from the Military – maybe their own daughter – was going to force them to lie under a giant metaphorical toaster like a family of chickens. I don't think so somehow.

'Is your mum afraid?' I said.

'Afraid. Sad. Angry. Every things.'

'Does she think that your sister and her Old Country buddies will come for you?'

'Yes and no and maybe. Her head is the spaghetti plate at moment, Charlie.'

I got this meaning.

'So what you're telling me is that your sister works for Old Country Military?'

'Yes, she work.'

'And that she's now on the ground here in Little Town?'

'She in Little Town, yes.'

'And that she and her cronies might be on the lookout for you and other Old Country refugees?'

'True it could be.'

If ever there was a swear moment this was it. I was having so many of them since I'd met Pav. I said it into my head. A whole sentence full of them.

'A bit of advice, Pav.'

'What advice?'

'Whatever happens, do not mention any of this to anyone. Not to Norman and definitely not to The Big Man.'

'You also no say Erin F too,' he instructed me.

'Erin F doesn't even answer my texts, Pav, so don't worry about me; my lips are zipped.' I pulled an imaginary zip across my mouth. Pav did the same, then we pretended to lock them with an invisible key. We even swapped lock keys and put them into our pockets. That's the sort of silly thing mates do, isn't it? I'd have buried my key for Pav. It made us laugh. We needed a laugh.

'What are you planning on doing? Your mum and dad, that is?' I said.

'We keep head down, like always.'

'Well, nobody knows about the shed, so maybe this would be a good place to keep the head down. It's safe anyway.'

The words had barely left my mouth …

Bang!

Bang!

Bang!

Went the shed door.

After the initial fright we froze.

The adrenalin arrived tsunami style.

Everything jingled-jangled inside our bodies.

Bang!

Bang!

Bang!

The wooden door almost flew off its hinges. But The Big Man's lock held firm. Just.

'Open up,' the voice said.

'Who is it?' I said.

'Open up or I'll break the thing down.'

'What you want?' Pav said.

'You've got three seconds,' the voice cried.

I was afraid that Mum, Dad or the Dudas would hear the commotion and investigate.

'One!'

'We do nothing,' Pav shouted.

'Two!'

'Open door,' Pav whispered.

'You open it,' I whispered back.

'Three!' the voice howled. At least the voice spoke the lingo, which meant that, whoever it was, it wasn't an Old Country patrol hunting down dissidents and refugees. 'I'm warning you two, I'll boot this thing down.'

'NO! DON'T!' I said. 'Don't break down the door, mister. I'll open it.'

'Move it then,' he said.

As soon as the door opened I recognised him straight away. It was none other than our *good friend* Muscles, standing upright with his biceps flexed, head to toe in black clothes – bouncer clobber.

'I don't have time for this crap, especially from you two clowns. You'd better start toeing the line here.'

'Sorry,' I said. 'We were just shifting some furniture around and then the knocks gave us a fright, that's all.'

'I'll give you more than a fright,' Muscles said.

'Want to come in?' I stepped aside so he could enter.

When he came into our shed it didn't feel as big and spacious any longer. Pav sat in one of the chairs, almost hugging it for special protection.

'So this is the hole you two are busy rearranging?' He looked around our shed, shaking his head. 'What's happened to the youth these days?' he said under his breath.

'Do you want to sit down?' I asked him.

He didn't give me a reply. 'It beggars belief to think what you two lesbians get up to in here day and night.'

I could see Pav shifting in his chair, ready to pounce and correct Muscles. Fortunately, without Muscles noticing, I managed to give him a little shake of the head, telling him to stay calm.

'Nothing much,' I said.

'Nothing much, eh?' Muscles said.

'We do no things,' Pav said.

Muscles stood hovering over him.

'You'd be lucky to get a bird in an aviary, Old Country, so if I were you, I'd take what I can get, son.'

Pav gave him his death stare.

Muscles looked away first.

Victory to Pav.

After losing the contest, Muscles laughed, then flopped himself down on one of the other chairs. He pulled a small rucksack from behind his shoulder and placed it between his feet.

'This isn't a social call,' he said.

'Aw, that's a pity,' I said.

'Watch it, Law,' he said, pointing to his mouth. 'This is going to get you into some deep shit one of these days if you're not careful.'

I didn't reply. Pav snorted.

'That goes for you as well, Old Country,' he said to Pav.

'So why are you here?' I asked.

'Yes, why here?' Pav said.

'The Big Man wanted to give you a little something.'

'The Big Man?' I said.

'What Big Man wanting?' Pav said.

'What he *wants*, Old Country. What he *wants*. Jesus, you'll have to learn our lingo properly, son, if you want to get by in this town.'

'What does he want to give us?' I asked.

'A few presents.' He looked around the shed. 'Let's call it a house-warming gift.'

He dug deep into the bag, pulled out two Moleskine notepads and handed them to us along with a pen each – one of those pens that had a choice of four different colours. Each colour huddled together in the same pen. Genius. I'd always wanted a Moleskine notepad. I tried to hide my smile. Pav didn't need to try.

'He knows you're going back to school tomorrow. He just wanted to give you a little starter pack.'

He rummaged again. Deeper. When his hand came out it was clutching a small brown paper bag.

'This one is for you, Law.'

'What is it?' I said.

'Open it and see.'

I made to unwrap the paper.

'NO! DON'T OPEN,' Pav shouted. He was on his feet with his hands out towards me.

Everyone stopped.

'Could be boob prize, Charlie,' Pav said.

'A what?' I said.

'A what?' Muscles said.

'Like bomb of nail,' Pav said.

'Don't be so ridiculous, Old Country. Do you think I'd bring a nail bomb in here and sit watching while he opens it in my presence?'

Muscles had a point.

Pav saw his point.

'What sort of tripe goes through that Old Country brain of yours?' Muscles pointed at Pav's head. There was a tense moment as he waited for his answer. 'Do you think I'm a numpty, son? Eh?'

'Erm … No … I no think this,' Pav said before sitting back down again.

'Open it.' Muscles said. 'Go on.'

I raised the bag up to my eyes in order to peek inside.

'BOOM!' Muscles shouted, then laughed as if he'd just heard the funniest joke ever. Or seen someone walk into a glass door. 'Only kidding. Go,' he said to me.

I opened the brown bag.

APPLES.

THREE APPLES.

THREE BIG APPLES.

THREE BIG, JUICY APPLES.

Apples like the ones I'd blagged, except more edible. An apple for each of us. My hand rummaged further. Hidden underneath the apples were two, TWO, inhaler medicines for Mum. Packaged up with the fruit, subtle.

'Want one?' I said, holding out an apple towards Muscles.

'Don't mind if I do, Law. Don't mind if I do.'

I tossed it to him.

'Pav?'

Pav almost took my arm off he was so quick to grab the apple off me.

We all bit into our apples together. Munched and crunched in silence. I could feel the apple drop into my empty stomach. Joy of joys. Muscles' mouth was so mammoth that he ate his apple in about three bites. Core and everything.

'You'll be hearing from The Big Man soon,' Muscles said as he stood up to leave.

Pav threw me the eyes.

'Can I see him tomorrow?' I said.

'You can't just come round, Law. It doesn't work like that.'

'I just want to thank him,' I said.

'I'll thank him for you,' Muscles said.

'No, I'd rather thank him myself. Tomorrow's good because I can come to his block after school.'

'He might not be available, Law.'

'I'll take my chances,' I said.

'He take chance,' Pav said.

'Right, I'll tell him, but he might not be happy and, like I said, he might not be available.'

'That's fine with me.'

Muscles stared at us in silence. He spat out a couple of apple pips as if he were firing bullets at us.

Notepads, eh?

Pens, eh?

Apples, eh?

Each *gift* cocked and loaded.

19
Take Down

It was utterly terrifying. I didn't wait until after school – I went that same night, without Pav. I wasn't able to knock on the front door; I didn't even get that far. Some guy whom I'd never laid eyes on was standing at the top of the landing – waiting for me? I don't know – and frogmarched me right back down the stairs. My feet barely touched the steps. Outside he put a firm hand on the back of my dome and bundled me into the rear of a car, just as they do with criminals leaving court after being accused of some horrendous crime. Inside the car sat another man whom I hadn't seen before either. He grinned. I smiled back.

'All right, kiddo?' he said.

But before I had time to say, *Eh, not really, mister,* he'd chucked some sort of blanket or hood over my head and forced me down on the seat. I struggled to breathe. I didn't want to die. *This* wasn't my time. I wasn't ready yet. I wasn't prepared. I'd too much to do before all that death palaver hit me.

I survived that car journey by taking tiny short breaths: in through the nose and out slowly through the mouth.

I didn't speak.

I didn't ask my usual questions.

I didn't annoy anyone.

I concentrated on breathing.

The driver and blanket man didn't speak either.

The car didn't speed or swerve or roar its engine.

A tear ran from my left eye over the bridge of my nose and down on to my right cheek. I realised I had no idea who these people were or where they were taking me. I had no Pavel Duda by my side to make me feel brave.

When the car came to a halt I didn't try to get up. The hand on my head prevented this anyway. Not a word was muttered. *Stay calm, Charlie, stay calm, son.* The driver got out. I heard his feet crunching through the gravel as he walked around to my side. The blanket man lifted his hand from my head.

'Time to go, kiddo,' he said.

The driver opened the door and the blanket man shoved me out. The air rushing up through the blanket/hood was like having the kiss of life. How good is air? I thought he was going to whip the thing off my head but he didn't. I took in huge man-size gulps of air.

The ground wasn't smooth. Because the driver had his hand on my head I was staring at my feet, which kicked away little stones as they walked. My shoes were getting dirty. Mum would go spare. If dirt got on my trousers it would be enough for a quick skelp on the kisser.

Mum and Dad would be deranged with worry if I didn't come home. Since the Old Country troops stormed into Little Town they wanted to know my every move. I knew Mum was suspicious about the sudden appearance of the inhalers I'd given her that evening – she knew no shop in Little Town could supply these. She didn't ask where I'd got them, a sure sign that she knew she wouldn't like the answer. I suppose her ability to breathe properly was more important. I could say I'd been out doing some pre-school studying because I wanted to hit the ground running, or something. But out all night? No chance could I blag that one.

One of the heavies opened a heavy metal door. It made that chinking noise when pulled, dragging metal along the ground. Inside, the place smelt of decay and unemployment, the pong that suggested hard work used to happen a while back. We walked about twenty steps. Stopped. Another door opened; this time it sounded like a shopping trolley being yanked along the concrete. I was pushed in. Another room? The shopping trolley door rattled closed.

'Right, time to breathe,' the driver said, and pulled the blanket/hood from my head. Everything was black. Talk about relief! Talk about uncontrollable terror! Everything was pitch-black. We were standing in a rickety old lift. Going down. Super fast. Going down below the ground. To the depths of Hell? My eyes had difficulties adjusting. Strangely, I was calm.

'Where are we?' I asked.

'No questions, son,' the driver said.

'But …'

The man put his finger to his mouth.

The lift hit the ground with a thud. My knees felt the impact. The man pulled the trolley door open.

'Right you are, kiddo,' he said.

'Do I get out?' I said.

'This is your stop.' He gave me a coaxing shove out. 'Cheerio, for now,' he said, pulling the lift door shut. I watched him rising to the daylight. My head followed him ascending. No wave.

Alone now. All calmness gone. My eyes were beginning to penetrate through the dark. I stood still. Not moving forward. Not shifting left or right. Glued rigid with dread and apprehension. When I saw movement in the distance I swear my stomach could have made cheese. The movement came into view. More than one figure.

'Aw, if it's none other than Charlie Law.' The voice echoed through the space.

I screwed up my eyes.

'Big Man?' I said. 'Is that you?'

The Big Man was standing with his hands behind his back, flanked by Muscles and some other dude I didn't recognise. At least it wasn't the Old Country troops. Who'd have thought I'd be relieved to lay eyes on The Big Man?

'You wanted to see me, Law?' The Big Man said.

'Erm … yes. But … how did … ?' I said.

'I've told you before, Law. This is my town; everything that goes on in my town The Big Man knows about. You only have to *think* something and I know.' He twiddled his left hand's fingers in front of his face as if he were a magician. 'Where is that Old Country friend of yours?'

'Home, I think.'

'We'll get to him soon enough.'

WHAT DID THAT MEAN?

Don't ask.

'Erm, right,' I said.

'I'm glad you came, Law.'

'Thanks for the inhaler medicine,' I offered.

'No problem; there's more where that came from if you play your cards right.'

That's what I intended to do.

'Thanks.'

'You know what this place used to be, Law?'

'Not really, no.' If this had been a school expedition or a

history lesson I'd have been interested as hell, but now wasn't the time for interest. My breathing was heavy.

'This used to be an old coal mine.'

'Is that right?' I said, trying to inject enthusiasm into my voice in case this was The Big Man's special place. I didn't want to offend him.

'My dad worked here.'

'Really?'

'And his dad before him.'

'Your grandad?' I said.

'Nothing gets past you, Law. Eh?' The Big Man said this to the heavies next to him. They chuckled, only because they were afraid to do anything other than chuckle.

'You know why I didn't work down here, Law?'

How the bejesus would I know that?

Because they shut the thing down?

Because you got more dosh from street hustling?

Because it seemed too much like hard work for you?

Because it was a shitty job?

Because Rascal work pays better?

'No idea,' I said.

'Because I need to have air in my lungs every day, know what I mean?'

'I think so.'

'I need to see daylight.'

I KNOW WHAT YOU MEAN, BIG MAN.

'I can understand that,' I said.

'But the thing is, Law, there is no daylight any more.' The Big Man walked towards me. 'Little Town has been cast into permanent darkness. Know what I mean?'

'Erm ...' It was hard to think. Hard to answer his questions. Hard to breathe.

'And do you know who's responsible for this darkness, Law?'

'The bombs?' I said.

The Big Man's voice changed. It became more sinister, husky. His eyes opened up. His shoulders arched. He walked slower, but closer. Sweat seeped through my clothes.

'Those Old Country bastards put Little Town into darkness, Law. That's who's responsible.'

My mouth was as dry as Gandhi's slipper.

'It's not right, is it?' The Big Man said to his lackeys, who, right on cue, shook their heads. 'And now their troops are everywhere, trying to make us into an Old Country clone. Changing the rules. Taking away our freedom. It's not right, Law, is it?'

'No, it's not right,' I said.

He leaned into my face, his pronounced nose almost touching mine.

'What are you going to do about it?' he whispered.

'I don't really have any solutions, Big Man,' I said, which was true.

'Do you know what we have to do, Charlie?' We were eyeball to eyeball by this stage. His eyes wide. I was unsure if the *we* he was referring to was me and him. Or was The Big Man using the royal *we*? I think he said *Charlie* to butter me up, thinking I'd believe we were pals.

'No, I don't know what we have to do.'

He smiled a massive toothy one.

What happened next made the huge coal mine narrow into one tiny dot in my eye. The Big Man reached behind his back, pulled a gun from his jeans and pointed it right in my face. I couldn't speak, as if some hand had entered my mouth and blagged my breath. I didn't cry. The sound I made was worse than crying; I think it was the sound of a trapped rabbit.

'I'll ask you again, Charlie Law. Do you know what we have to do?'

I WISH I DID KNOW WHAT TO DO. I WISH I HAD ALL THE ANSWERS.

Just say something, Charlie. Anything.

I had no words for him; my mind went blank. My eyes stared directly inside the hole of the gun. Or is it the barrel? I didn't know. Trapped rabbit. If ever there was a time for words, and I loved words too, this was it. Here I was, like a fool, with none.

'Let me tell you what we have to do, shall I?' The Big Man said. I can't be sure but I think I nodded. 'We have to take this fucking town back, that's what we have to do.'

The gun was still staring at me.

'People like you and me have to resist those bastards.'

The Big Man refused to lower the gun from my forehead.

'You've got a brain in there, Charlie.' He tapped the gun off my head. The metal was cold against my skin. 'A good brain. We could use that brain.' He rested the barrel on my head.

'P … P … Please don't sh … sh … shoot, Big Man.'

Tapped three times.

'P … P … Please, Big Man. I haven't done anything,' I pleaded.

'You stole those apples.' His tone had changed.

'I was hungry.'

'*My* apples.'

'I didn't know they were yours.'

'You do now.'

'I'm sorry. I'm so sorry, Big Man.'

The Big Man's thumb pulled back the little lever on the top part of the gun; I didn't even know the name of this part, that's how un-guns I was.

The gun clicked.

Click!

Real tears fell down my cheeks.

'Close your eyes.'

'Please, Big Man. Please.'

'Close them.'

'Don't.'

'Close.'

I closed my eyes as tightly as possible. Snot streamed out of my nose.

'I loved those apples, Law.'

'I'm so sor–'

'One thing I hate is thieves.'

'I'm not a thief, Big Man, I was hun–'

'Keep 'em closed.'

No more pleading. I accepted my fate. I accepted that this was it. I squeezed my eyes hard until little white dots appeared under my lids. Waited.

Waited.

Waited.

'You can open them now.'

Right one first, followed by the left.

The Big Man and his brain-dead heavies laughed. Their bellies laughed. Their hair laughed.

'I'm just screwing with you, Charlie. Come on, get up.'

JUST SCREWING WITH ME?

'Up.' The Big Man directed me with his gun.

I got up.

'I thought you were going to shoot,' I said, wiping snot from my chin and tears from my eyes.

'Obviously I wasn't going to shoot you, was I?'

'I thought for a minute–'

'What do you take me for, Charlie? An Old Country scumbag?' The Big Man put his face near to mine. He saw how watery mine was. 'You OK?'

'I think so.'

'Sure?'

'Yes, I'm fine.' Snotters still streamed out of my nose. I had to use my shirtsleeve as a hanky.

'That the first time you've had a gun pointed at you?'

'No, the patrol have done it.'

'Apart from that.'

'I think Old Country have them pointed at us in the street, but we don't see them.'

'Here.' The Big Man held the gun out for me to take it. 'Have you ever held one of these, Law?'

'No, never.'

'Take it.' He thrust it towards me. I flinched. 'Come on. Don't be shy. Take it, go ahead. It's OK.' I stared at it. It wasn't the gun's fault for making the tears flow.

'It's only a gun, Charlie. It won't bite.' I wanted to hold it. I lifted up my writing hand. The Big Man placed the gun into my palm. The metal was heavy, much heavier than I'd have imagined it to be. Two, maybe three kilos. Heavier than a bag of sugar. The handle was warm from The Big Man's hand. Sweaty.

'It's heavy,' I said.

'You need a strong arm.'

I lifted the gun upwards and looked through the small V-shaped aimer. It wasn't intentional but I pointed at them.

'Careful now,' The Big Man said.

'I am being,' I said.

I straightened my arm to a locked position.

'I bet you'd love to,' The Big Man said. The gun wasn't pointed directly at him, but it was close enough.

The little monster on my shoulder arrived:

I bet you'd love to, Charlie. I just bet you would. Go on, squeeze. Come on, Charlie, just give it a little squeeze. In fact, three wee squeezes. One for each of them. You'll be OK, not one of them is faster than a flying bullet. Not one of them. Aim. Fire. One down. Fire. Two down. Fire. Three down. Easy-peasy. No one would ever know because no one will hear. Jump in that lift and you're free. Go on, you heard the man: I bet you'd love to. Put that little finger of yours on the trigger and DO IT! He deserves it. He's scum of the earth. One little squeeze. Boom!

I put my finger on the trigger, rubbed it up and down, inside it and out. I aimed to my left, to where The Big Man was standing. *Big Man first. Floored. One metre to the right. Muscles. Floored. Two metres to my left. Square chops. Floored. Lift. Up. Daylight. Air. Happy days. Easy.*

'It would feel good, eh?' The Big Man said.

'Maybe.'

'I'm afraid you can't, Law.'

'I think I could,' I said.

'That's not what I mean; it's not a question of you having the bottle or not.'

'I do.' I did.

'The thing isn't loaded.'

Another blow. Another dagger to the heart. I dropped the gun and swung my arm by my side. It hurt a little with the strain.

'Do you want to fire it?' The Big Man asked.

I didn't need to think for a minute.

'Yes.'

The Big Man nodded to Muscles, who went off into the darkness.

'You have to listen and do as I say, do as I tell you, got it?'

'OK, got it.'

Muscles emerged from the darkness with a case. The Big Man took the gun from me and handed it to Muscles. He put bullets in the gun, loaded it up. Handed it back to The Big Man, who then handed it to me.

'Do not even think about squeezing that trigger, Law.'

'OK.' The gun felt even heavier.

Muscles put his hand inside the case and pulled another gun from it. It looked identical to mine. He handed it to The Big Man. We had our guns. A duel? To the death? The guy with the square jaw walked out of the darkness – I hadn't seen him go – wheeling a clothes-shop mannequin. The target.

'There it is, Charlie. Just pretend it's an Old Country whore you're firing at.'

I didn't want to shoot any Old Country whores.

'Before we shoot, Big Man, I wanted to ask you something.'

'Shoot,' he said. Everyone laughed like it was the best joke they'd ever heard in their lives. I sniggered out of fear.

'Am I meant to be working for you now?'

'You're far too young to be working for anyone.'

'Pav just thought, you know, you might want us to run errands and stuff.'

'Does he now?'

'And Norman said something about scratching our backs and then we have to scratch his, or yours.'

'You leave Norman to me.'

'I suppose Pav wants to know what plans you have for us,' I said.

The Big Man looked to the heavens and gave one huge howling laugh.

'What plans I have for you? That's good, I like that, Law.'

After that he pointed the gun at me again. The gun with the shiny little bullets loaded inside it.

'Are you Old Country's bitch, Law?' The Big Man asked.

Twice in one day that female dog word had been chucked in my direction.

'No, I'm not.'

The gun got closer.

'Why didn't he come and ask me himself?'

'He's scared.'

'Of what, me?'

'Everything in Little Town.'

'Including me?'

I could smell the closeness of the gun once again. Loaded this time. Mine hung down at my side, but my mind was ready in case I needed to be a quick draw.

'Including you, yes.'

'Me? I'm a pussycat, Law.'

'He's just worried in case he gets into trouble, that's all.'

'How would *I* get him into trouble?'

'Don't know.'

'Are you saying The Big Man's a troublemaker, Law?'

'No. He is scared that he'd get into trouble with Old Country troops, his mum and dad or at school. Just trouble in general.'

'He's an Old Country refugee, your mate? An abandoner.'

'Yes, I suppose he is.'

'So getting into trouble with the troops wouldn't be good for him, now, would it?'

'It'd be terrible.'

'He wouldn't want them to find out that he's here, would he?'

'I wouldn't think so, no.'

'He'd be stuffed?'

'I think he would.'

'So, it would be beneficial to your little buddy if those Old Country bastards got hounded out of here, wouldn't it?'

'Probably.'

'But here's a question for you, Charlie. How can we drive Old Country out of Little Town? How do you think we can do that, eh?'

HOW THE EFF DO I KNOW?

'I don't know really ...'

'You don't really know?'

'No.'

'I'll tell you then, shall I?'

'OK.'

'You have to speak their lingo, if you know what I mean.'

I didn't.

'You have to learn Old Country lingo?'

'No, you fight fire with fire. It's the only lingo they know.' He held up his gun again.

'Can't our people just speak to their people?'

'That's the thing, Charlie. I wish it were that simple. You see, those bastards don't do speaking; the only speaking they do is with bombs and bullets, not with their tongues. You get me?'

Of course I knew what he meant. I wasn't stupid. I was just lost for words, and thirsty. I wasn't sure if I was signing up for something or being coerced into something that had nothing to do with me.

'It's the only way, Law,' The Big Man said before turning to his men. 'It's the only way, lads, right?'

'Right,' Muscles said.

'The only way,' Square Jaw said.

'But I'm not sure how me and Pav can help though, Big Man.'

'Oh, you can help in many, many ways.'

'But I don't have any muscles,' I said, flexing my left arm to show this. 'I don't have any money either,' I said, tapping my pockets. 'And I don't have any of these,' I said, holding the gun up and waving it around a bit.

'Careful now.'

'So there's nothing I can do,' I said, hoping he'd say something like: *Aw, that's a shame, nice speaking with you anyway. You can make your own way out, can't you? See you around, Charlie.*

'No one can do *nothing*, Law,' he said.

'Pav's the same as me, he can't do anything either,' I said.

'Do you trust him, even though he's Old Country?'

'Yes.'

'You tell him from me that he's got nothing to worry about.'

'Seriously?'

'Of course, seriously. I'm here to look after you both. You tell him that as well.'

'How are you going to look after us?'

'You let me worry about that.'

Of course it was impossible. Old Country was a proper organisation. Wealthy. The Big Man was just some big Rascal in a small pond.

'And what can I do?' I asked, fearing the answer.

'Oh, you've got no idea how brilliant and vital you can be, Charlie. No idea. Do you want Little Town to return to how it was before, or not?' he asked.

Well, to be honest, a part of me did and a part of me didn't.

'Of course I do.'

'I need you to do something for me, for Little Town. Can you do that?'

DEPENDS WHAT IT IS.

'Erm … OK … what is it?'

'How is your mum these days?'

'Erm … she's good,' I said.

'How long will that medicine last her?'

'A couple of weeks, maybe.'

'That's good; a boy needs his mum, doesn't he?'

'Erm … I suppose …'

'And how's your shed coming along?'

'Great. I mean, it looks good with the new chairs. Thanks.'

'Pleasure. And the locks, they work OK? Secure?'

'Very.'

'Who has the keys?'

'Only me and Pav.'

'Not quite.' The Big Man put his finger up teacher style. 'I have one as well.'

'But –'

'My locks, Charlie. My game. Do you think I was going to allow you to lock things away in my town? Come on, you're cleverer than that.'

'I suppose not, no.'

'But the shed is secure?'

'As anything.'

'Good. I need you to take these back to your shed for a bit.'

'The guns?'

'I need you to put them somewhere safe.'

'And do what with them?'

'Keep them for me. Hide them.'

'Why can't you keep them here?'

'I'm The Big Man, Charlie. Do you think Old Country don't have their tabs on me?'

'No, but –'

'Call it security purposes.'

'What if I get caught?'

'You won't.'

'But what if I do? They'll torture me or something terrible like that.'

'Who? Old Country?'

'Yes. They'll torture me to find out who gave me the guns.'

'And you'll not grass. One thing I loathe is a grass. You're not a grass, Charlie, are you?'

'No, but –'

'You're now working for Little Town Security Services. Congratulations.'

Did that mean that I was a junior Rascal now? Not a job I wanted.

'And what do we get?'

The Big Man looked at Muscles and Square Jaw. All three shook their heads.

'Jesus, the youth of today,' The Big Man said to them. 'You get to be in here. You get the stuff you ask for.' The Big Man patted his heart four times. Not much of a gift that was. 'I told you I'd look after you, didn't I?'

'Yes.'

'So, I'll look after you.'

'Right.'

'Now, come on and let's shoot the stuffing out of this Old Country whore.'

Square Jaw positioned the mannequin.

MENTAL MEMO: NOW THE DARK SIDE HAS BEEN ENTERED IT'S VITAL TO FIND THE DOOR THAT LEADS STRAIGHT OUT OF IT. IF NOT, MUM WILL DESTROY ME.

20
Storm Warning

Six bullets make a round. I fired two of them at the target.

Five aims to the head: two hit.

Four aims to the heart: one hit.

Two aims to the lady garden: two hits.

One aim to the gut: miss.

Let's just say if that target had been a real woman she'd have been lying on a slab by now. In all the books I'd read about men blowing someone's brains out, all the movies I'd seen with characters banging away at each other in a final shootout and, all that time, when I think about it now, I never knew how thrilling it would be. I couldn't tell how much fun they were having. I do now. It gave me a massive inside tingle. I didn't tell The Big Man that firing the gun gave me goose-bumps every time I pulled the trigger; I didn't want him to know how much I liked it. And I did. I really did. But you never know what people might do with that information; he could've had me down as this young sharpshooter and before you can say READY-AIM-FIRE I'd be roaming the streets of Little Town in search of legitimate targets.

The drive back from the coal mine was blanket-free. Window open. Front seat. Thankfully my lungs were reintroduced to my body. On that journey I kept telling myself that Pav mustn't know. He mustn't have a clue about any of it. Even though the shed was his domain as well, I knew he'd go ballistic.

Before I dragged one of the chairs to the other side of the shed and pulled a board loose from the floor and placed the steel carefully underneath until I couldn't see it, I held the thing up towards my eye and peered through the aim groove. I so wanted to pull that trigger again. Just one more time. The gun was well hidden now: we had both reached a dark side.

Sheds are great things; they're so versatile. When Erin F comes to the shed there'll be no faffing about. With my fifteenth birthday looming I'm going to have a whopper of a party. It's going to be an animal. It's going to be topper. Erin F and me in a cramped space celebrating my birthday.

Pav will be there too!

My tactic is to play it cool, show her the sharp side of Charlie Law. My sensitive side. Then, maybe ...

Pav will be there too!

Hold hands first … then go for a cuddle … then, maybe …

PAV WILL BE THERE TOO!

I hate having the feeling of wishing Pav would get a bad flu in time for my party.

Maybe just a twenty-four-hour flu would do.

Maybe an obstacle put in place.

It's amazing the things that go through your head in times of stress.

Maybe I could just shoot him?

21
Party People

In spite of the presence of Old Country patrols on our streets, school had finally decided to reopen for the education and enlightenment of Little Town's youth (and Pav). The thought of seeing Erin F again fluttered my heart.

'Charlie! Charlie!' Mum's foghorn yelled. 'You're going to be late for school.'

Late? Erm. Don't think so. I'd been up for ages, preparing myself.

Mentally.

Physically.

Creatively.

'I've got flakes for your breakfast,' she shouted.

Flakes?

Flakes?

Where did she get flakes from?

'And orange juice.'

ORANGE JUICE?

'Do you want me to pour you a glass?'

Orange juice AND flakes?

This was too much.

'You'd better hurry up or your dad will snaffle it all.' Mum's voice sounded clear, as though it'd been put through the washing machine.

A thoroughbred wouldn't have made it to that kitchen faster than I did.

The table was like a Van Gogh painting, or a Picasso, or some other famous artist.

'Where did you get all this stuff, Mum?'

'Don't ask,' Dad said from behind his paper.

'But I don't understand,' I said.

'What's to understand?' Dad muttered.

'I mean, orange juice and flakes. On the same table.'

Dad turned his head to Mum.

'It's the small things in life, Maggie. Eh?'

I'm sure he winked at her.

Mum smiled.

Please tell me he wasn't extracting the urine this early in the morning?

'But how?' I said. I couldn't help wondering whether this new-found breakfast bounty was somehow linked to my own new status as an unofficial employee of Little Town Security Services.

'Just sit and eat, Charlie,' Mum said, pulling a chair out for me. 'Enjoy it, son.' Mum had a spring in her step. A great big bouncy castle more like. She couldn't hide her delight in getting rid of me again. Dad was poker-faced. Normal. But secretly he was glad. I could tell. Back-to-school day was like a holiday for parents.

'Did you buy it from someone?' I asked.

Dad folded his paper on the line – 'Utter rubbish they print these days,' – and looked at me. 'Don't ask questions, Charlie. If you don't want it we can arrange something else for you. Toast and water, perhaps?'

'No, no. This is fine. Totally fine. Promise. I'm just surprised, that's all.'

'Are you going with the Duda boy?' Dad asked.

'You mean Pav?'

'You know who I mean,' Dad said.

'I am indeed. I can't let him go by himself, not on the first day back, can I?' I said.

'You just be careful, Charlie,' Mum said. 'I don't want you getting into any trouble.'

'Why would I be getting into trouble?' They didn't answer. 'Have I ever got into trouble at school?' Dad went back to his *utter rubbish* paper and Mum pottered about doing nothing.

'Just be careful of other people, Charlie, that's all I'm saying,' Mum said.

'People at school?' I said.

'At school, outside school, in the street. Everywhere,' Dad said from behind the paper. He had now reread (or pretended to reread) the same page three times. They were trying to hide it, but I knew their game … and it was up.

'You're scared that something will happen to me because I'm pals with Pav, aren't you?'

They gave each other a snide glance, like they had prepared themselves for this type of breakfast chat, like they had already role-played it.

'Of course we're not,' Mum said.

'Because Pav's from Old Country?' I said.

'Don't be silly, Charlie,' Dad said. Still hiding.

They hadn't role-played with me being there though. Fatal flaw. A chink in the parenting skills armour.

'I'll have you know that Pav can take care of himself. He doesn't need me to stand up for him. He doesn't need me to protect him all the time.'

'That's not what we're saying, Charlie,' Mum said.

'Look, we're just hoping –' Dad tried to offer.

'Pav's more of a victim in all this than any of us, by the way.'

More snide looks.

Game over.

'We're not denying that the Duda boy is a victim in all this, but our concern right now is you,' Dad said.

'You don't need to worry about me,' I said.

'Just keep the head down, Charlie, and don't get mixed up in any unsavoury business or with any unsavoury types.'

I held Dad's eyes for a few seconds more than I should have. Did he know about the apples? The shed furniture? Muscles' visit? Worse, the hidden steel? Did he know about The Big Man? I took a big quenching gulp of the orange juice and was happy to see Dad return to his reading material. What did he know?

Mum took out a huge knife and cut the loaf with it … as well as the atmosphere.

'I thought you'd be late, Charlie,' she said.

'I've been up for ages.'

'I heard you pottering about early doors all right,' Dad said.

'Just getting things ready for today,' I said.

Getting mentally ready for my first day back at school was tough, partly because I didn't know how many of my old classmates would be there. Who'd been hurt in the bombings? Some areas of housing had been hit, but I hadn't heard anything about people I knew. And I still had not actually laid eyes on Erin F. It was also tough because I hadn't spoken about how scared I was going to school with Pav. Scared in case people decided to have a go at battering his Old Country lights in. As his mate, which I am, I'd be expected to play the role of his sidekick wingman and protect him at all costs, lash out if required at anyone who wanted to banjo him or anyone giving him verbals. That's my job. But the thing is, I'm actually petrified of physical violence. I'd rather give someone a good talking-to. I was afraid that people would also see me as the enemy because my mate is the enemy – well, he's not the real enemy; the people from where he's from are the real enemy. He hates the enemy, like me.

Pav stood at my front door looking like a burst couch. His school clothes were shambolic. The shirt collar made his neck appear like a toothpick in a Polo mint. His trousers were almost falling down, undoubtedly to reveal bogging yellow-stained pants. His shoes were the same ones he wore all the time, scuffed and tired. He'd no tie. His eyes looked as if he was saying his last goodbye before embarking on a five-year stretch in the Young Offenders'. I couldn't let him get on the school bus looking like a meth head going to court. He may as well have boarded that bus with a huge target on his back. Action was required.

'Come in for a minute and wait there,' I said, and rushed to my room, leaving Mum and Dad and Pav to stare at each other. It was nice to hear muffled voices when I was in my room. Armed with a spare tie, a belt and a shoe brush, I ushered Pav towards my room.

'What is this?' he said when I produced the goods.

'You can't go to school without a tie; they'll go spare, Pav.'

'I not know about tie.'

'Well, you do now; here, put this on.' I slung the tie around his thin neck. 'And you'd better give these the once-over.' I leaned down and rubbed the shoe brush over his scruffy ones. Fifteen times on each shoe with a bit of spit. Could've probably done with one hundred rubs on each shoe right enough. Afterwards his shoes weren't exactly dinner-eating material but my work made a slight difference. Above me Pav fumbled about awkwardly.

'Come here, let me do it,' I said.

Pav stood upright and allowed me to tie the tie in a perfect knot. A technique learnt from a Scout book.

'Why I must wear tie?'

'It's the rules, Pav. We all do,' I said.

'Rules. Rules. Rules. I hate rules.'

I opened the top button of his shirt so his neck wouldn't look so tiny in the tie; I gave him a big knot to help his case more. Then I made him pull the belt around the loops of his trousers and tug it super tight. He needed another hole punched in the belt. He stood back so I could have a look at him and all I could think about was the Scarecrow from *The Wizard of Oz*. He was presentable. Just. But Pav would have to learn to do it all himself; I couldn't go through this rigmarole every day.

'Where's your mum and dad?'

'Dad work early. Mum in bed.'

'Still upset at seeing your sister?'

'She again cry. She fear we send back.'

'I'm sure it'll get better, Pav.'

'I hope.'

'Pav?'

'What?'

'If you want, we can do some lingo lessons after school. In the shed, maybe.'

Pav didn't even need to think about it.

'What you do, Charlie? You try killing me? One school enough for one day. I learn lingo at school, no?'

One school was enough for one day. For both of us.

My nerves were shattered as we made our way to the bus stop, thinking about what awaited us. What awaited me.

'Charlie?'

'What?'

'You see Big Man yet?'

'I'm going after school,' I lied. I didn't want Pav involved in any of this gun stuff. If truth be known, I wanted that stuff to be mine. I felt like an international spy, or someone important.

'Tell him we no want presents no more.'

'I'll tell him we are done with the presents,' I lied.

'I no want anything from him.'

'I'll speak to him, Pav. Don't worry.'

'I no worry.'

I gave him an everything's-going-to-be-fine nudge.

Shoulder to shoulder.

Mate to mate.

Buddy to buddy.

'Think about it: new school, new times ahead. It'll be good.'

'Look,' Pav said, pointing to an Old Country patrol sat about two hundred yards from where we were waiting for our bus. 'If this new times I no want.' He looked at it for longer than the nerves could take, probably wondering if his sister was on it. Driving it maybe. Looking at him through mega-powerful binoculars.

'But school'll be different, Pav. We won't have any of that there.'

'I rather pick hair from bum than go school,' Pav said.

I didn't know how to react. I wanted to laugh out loud. Thankfully Pav did. I followed. We laughed together. I gave him another shoulder nudge. He did one to me. It felt good to laugh together. When the bus came into view and the laughter slowed down to a stop, my cartwheeling heart took over everything.

Pav stayed close when we got on the bus. So close he was touching me like I was his eyes again. I could tell that he wanted to hide his face, his Old Country features. My insides were going like the clappers. The twenty or so people on the bus stopped what they were doing (looking out of the window, playing with their fingers, scratching their belongings, rummaging through bags, whatever) and stared directly at us. The only two seats together were up the back.

Max Fargo fired the first shot.

'Who's your new bitch, Law?' Max Fargo would be lucky if he got a job collecting supermarket trolleys when he left school. He liked doing two things: training with weights and being a dick pain. I spent all of primary and most of secondary school avoiding him, which was easy to do because I enjoyed going to the library while he enjoyed walking around the yard with sticks in his hand.

'Yeah, who's your new bitch, bitch?' Davis Brown was Max's partner in knob studies; on his own insistence everyone called him Bones because he hated, by all accounts, the name Davis. The mind boggles. This guy made The Big Man's coal mine seem bright.

'Which one of you bitches is on top, Law?' Max said.

I understood this to be a rhetorical question. Pav understood nothing.

'Yeah, what one of you bitches is on top, Law?' Bones said; his brain just wouldn't allow for original thoughts/ideas/abuse. And on the eighth day God gave Max Fargo … Bones.

Pav tightened his grip.

'Nice to see you too, Bones,' I said.

'Will you be sucking teacher cock this year, Law?' Max said.

Mmm, let me think about that for a second, Maxy boy … I really, really – and it was on the tip of my tongue, bursting to get out – wanted to lean down to him and say, *No, I won't be doing that because your mother just won't get out of the way.* But common sense took over and I thought: who wants two jaw punches on their first day back at school, eh? Not me, that's who. I smiled and kept walking to our seats.

'Yeah, teacher sucks your cock,' Bones said, and put an imaginary one in his mouth. This poor sod just deserved pity. What life awaited him, God only knew.

Max clocked straight away that Pav wasn't from Little Town. Bones, on the other hand, believed that the population of the entire world lived in Little Town. No joke. For all he knew Pav could have been born and raised in Little Town; all Bones could see was an unfamiliar face he didn't recognise, so naturally it meant that face was fodder for his bile.

We trudged onwards to the back of the bus. Mercy Lewis threw her eyes up to the ceiling when I sat across from her. She didn't have to say it but I knew inside she was saying something like, *What a couple of twats they are, Charlie. I'm so embarrassed to be sitting on the same bus as them, and even more mortified to be attending the same school.* She smiled at me. I liked Mercy. Not in that way. It was just good to see a friendly face, someone who'd survived the bombing night. You never knew who hadn't.

'Hi, Charlie.'

'Hi, Mercy.'

Like me, Mercy enjoyed a good old-fashioned readathon. Sometimes we'd exchange book ideas or recommend titles. I read some of her suggestions, but not the chick-lit girl-out-shopping-and-being-boyfriend-dumped ones. She wore specs, which made her look clever. She was even cleverer than she looked though.

'How was your summer?' she said.

'Pure mental. Yours?' I said.

'Same.'

'Mad, innit?' I said.

'Same for everyone, I think,' she said. 'At least we don't have to put up with crap TV now.'

'Yeah, that is one consolation.'

Mercy then directed her gaze towards Pav.

Pav flashed Mercy his baby blue blinders.

I'm happy that she was sitting down because those knees of hers would have buckled under the pressure of Pav's eyes. No doubt about that.

I felt part of something special.

She wanted an introduction.

'Oh, sorry, Mercy. This is Pav; he moved into my block at the start of the summer. Before the bombs. We've been hanging around a bit since then.' I felt a little bad in myself for saying *a bit*. There was no *a bit* about it, as we'd barely left each other's sight since his arrival.

'Hi, Pav,' Mercy said, giving him a friendly hand wave across the aisle.

'Pav, this is Mercy. She'll be in our class.'

'Hello, it is pleasing to meet you,' Pav said in his best voice. The poshest one I'd heard. His eyes never left hers. Mercy looked away, more out of awkwardness than rudeness.

> **MENTAL MEMO:** HAVE A WORD WITH PAV ABOUT STARING AT PEOPLE. I KNOW HE DOESN'T MEAN TO BUT IT CAN TURN FOLK TO JELLY AT TIMES. MAYBE EVEN PRACTISE SOME SOFT-STARING TECHNIQUES WHEN YOU HAVE SHED TIME.

'Pav's still learning the lingo, Mercy,' I said.

Pav smiled a bashful one. He even tucked his shirt into his trousers and straightened his tie. My tie.

'Well, I think you're doing quite well, Pav,' Mercy said.

'Thank you. I trying,' he said. 'I studying hard.'

I turned to look at Pav, but didn't blow his cover.

'And where did you used to live, Pav?' Mercy asked.

'I from Old Country,' Pav said.

It wasn't as if the colour drained from her or anything like that; it was the shuffling in her seat, the flicking of her hair, the fiddling with her glasses and the look towards me that gave the game away. She tried to hide her disappointment, but it was there for all to see. At that moment I felt sorry for Pav. Or maybe I was just imagining it all.

'Well, it's nice to have met you, Pav,' Mercy said, and started rifling through her bag, searching for nothing in particular.

Pav gave me his little-boy-lost look. I'm sure his eyes were bluer than they had been two minutes ago. He was urging me to help him. Was this Pav's sledgehammer moment? Had Cupid taken him by the tie and swung him from a great height?

'He came to Little Town before those Old Country bastards arrived here, Mercy.' She looked up from her bag-burrowing. 'They drove him and his family out of Old Country, you see. They're proper refugees.'

'Really?' she said.

'Is true. They violent. We refugee,' Pav said.

'But why?' Mercy asked.

'Because we no believe in bastard country they create,' Pav said.

Mercy nodded.

'They have a different political outlook, Mercy,' I said.

'That must have been terrible, Pav?' she said.

'Yes. It terrible.' His eyes twinkled at her.

'And now you have to put up with those people here as well; that must be hard going? You must feel like they're chasing you?'

'It hard. It very hard.'

Mercy nodded her head in agreement.

'Well, I hope you have a great first day, Pav,' she said.

'Thanking you,' he said, almost bowing his head towards Mercy.

Pav had his first fan. Oh, he was good.

The bus turned a corner and the school came into view. Everyone on it hushed. Stun-gun silence as everyone looked out of the window with mouths gaping. Well, everyone apart from Pav. I couldn't believe my eyes when I saw what was left of our school. Only the vile 'main building' was still standing, erect and strong. This grey square monstrosity, which looked more like a borstal than a place of learning, had somehow escaped the bombs, like one giant brick with a few windows dotted about for good effect. It appeared to be flipping us the middle finger and sniggering as our bus approached. I couldn't believe that not one bomb had hit it. Not even a stray.

Debris from the demolished sports hall, new science block, the art and drama studios and the humanities area had mostly been removed. Only small hills of rubble remained. Cordoned off. Out of bounds. No-go areas. I'd bet my granny that Bones and Max had their murky hearts set on exploring those areas. That bloody main building! Religion, maths. Classics and lingo studies. It would be a tight squeeze in there now. To make it worse the sun never shone in the main building; in winter it was too cold – jackets on in lessons, hard to concentrate – and in spring and early summer it was like a Turkish bathhouse. If ever a bomb should've fallen, why couldn't one have fallen here?

I looked for Erin F among the hordes. No sign.

'Oh, my,' Mercy said.

'Oh shit, more like,' I said.

The bus stopped; its doors snapped open.

'See you two bitches later,' Max shouted up to me and Pav as he jumped off, ready to rock this place up.

'Yeah, bitches, laters,' Bones said, ready to follow Max.

Pav nodded to them in defiance.

I made sure he stayed close.

Mercy, Pav and me entered the huge grey disaster together.

I tried really hard to hold it in, but some people couldn't help themselves. The lump in my throat was like having swollen glands. If at that moment I'd needed to speak, for sure the tears would have poured out of me. Thankfully the news acted like a silencer. The teacher could hardly read out all the names in the register without taking deep breaths between each one. His eyes were like glass. We sat in our registration class looking at some of the empty chairs. Six of them in my class alone, missing, presumed dead. How many in Erin F's class? Mercy's class? God, thinking that Erin F could be an empty chair sent shudders right through me. Of course it was terrible that I wouldn't get to play Capital Cities Quiz again with Taylor Crainey, dodge the fiery tongue of Annette Burns or chat books with Mungo McGhee, but my mind was on Erin F. I could feel my eyes glazing over.

After registration she was all I could think about. From nine until twelve thirty I hadn't clapped eyes on Erin F. My mind was filled with all these images of her lying at the bottom of a pile somewhere, helpless and lifeless. Thinking what her last words and thoughts were. Of all the things I should have told her. I also felt bad for not having more sadness for those who we knew hadn't made it. Some teachers hadn't made it either, as there were lots of new faces to be seen. This wasn't my school. The first day back after summer holidays is always raucous; this time was different: you could hear people's footsteps as they walked through the corridors between lessons.

That first morning I had three classes:

Classics (New Teacher blathered on about how we needed to *put the traumatic events of the summer behind us and focus on what we need to do to pass the big end-of-year exam* … basically start working our socks off NOW. Erin F didn't do Classics this year).

Biology (New Teacher blathered on about how we needed to *put the traumatic events of the summer behind us and focus on how important it is to start working from the outset if we want to pass the big end-of-year exam*. Erin F took chemistry as her science subject).

English (New Teacher blathered on about how we needed to *put the traumatic events of the summer behind us and focus on how imperative it is to hit the ground running* and that we must *hit the books from day one if we want to hit the high grades and pass the big end-of-year exam*. Lots of hitting involved there. Not sure many people understood the word imperative. Erin F's name was called out and she didn't appear. My heart sank).

That first morning was blurry brain melt.

Things change quickly in schools though. Brain melt turned to heart melt.

When I eventually saw her she was like an oasis in the desert, all by herself at the end of a corridor. Books in hand. Hair tied back. Oh, to be a hair bobble. I sped up my walk. All the time I was thinking:

Please don't turn around, Erin F.

Please don't turn around.

Then the little monster appeared with his stupid irritating voice. There he was, perched on my shoulder like butter wouldn't melt. If the nerves weren't bad enough! This pesky percher was the last thing I needed.

Don't say anything too dickish, Charlie.

How could I disagree with him on this?

Please don't say anything too dickish.

I was close. I followed the pendulum of her hair flow. I'd say Erin F's hair could've hypnotised me into submission if I'd followed it for a mile or more. She could've made me do anything she wanted to: eat an onion thinking it was a juicy apple, sing huge serenades to strangers in the street, speak in goblin or elf lingo, or reveal my innermost thoughts to her and hand over my Moleskine when it was complete. Man alive! Imagine.

I was trying to walk in her air, getting the waft of her special smell up my nostrils, that unique blend of sweeties and flowers. An exclusive brand of girly shampoo just for her dome. Top of the range. Collector's item.

I marched in her footsteps.

Left.

Right.

Left.

Right.

So close. There couldn't have been more than a metre between us. My little monster noticed this.

Don't get caught or she'll think you're a mad stalker.

Don't make her think you're a mad stalker, not on the first day back. No turning back. Only one thing to do. My legs were shaking with fear. My back dripping. Only one thing I could do. I knew it. My little monster guy knew it.

So do it then.

A tender tap on the shoulder.

Go on, do it.

DO IT!

I tapped her once on the shoulder.

'I thought I could hear someone breathing down my neck,' Erin F said. It was good to hear her voice again. 'What are you? Some kind of mad stalker?'

'Hi, Erin F,' I said.

'Hi, Charlie Law,' she said. 'Should you not be in the library at this time?'

'I was taking my mate Pav to see his guidance teacher.'

'Who?'

'The guy I told you about when we met at The Bookshop. He's new.' Erin F obviously hadn't remembered our chat about Pav.

'Oh, right. Yes. I remember.' She didn't. 'Shame The Bookshop's gone now, eh?'

'Total shame,' I said. 'Anyway, there isn't a library in this building either.'

She had her what-do-you-want-then face on.

'I didn't see you in English,' I said.

'That's because I wasn't in English.'

'Were you late?'

'I had to see someone about something, Charlie.'

I took this to mean, *It's none of your effing business where I was, Law, so don't ask again.*

'How was the rest of your summer?' I asked.

Erin F took a big deep breath.

'Oh, you know, dodging bombs, hiding from Old Country patrols, trying to eat properly, trying to get life back to normal, trying to keep Mum alive – what can I say? My summer? Couldn't have been better.'

Was this a joke?

Was I supposed to laugh?

I laughed.

Erin F glared.

'Charlie, those Old Country bastards have destroyed our town, our school and our spirit, don't you see that?'

'I do see it, Erin F, but I think you have to remain positive.'

'Remain positive, that's all I hear these days. Remain positive about what?'

'Well, education for starters; it's one way to get out of here.'

'That's if they let you.'

'Of course they'll let us. We can go anytime, can't we?'

'But go where? Some other shit, dangerous place? That's exactly what they want, isn't it? Divide and conquer. It's a classic manoeuvre, Charlie. Classic manoeuvre.'

Erin F was a top-notch history student. Another tick in the box of her modes of attraction.

'So what can we do about it?' I asked.

'Protest? Demonstrate? March? I don't know. I don't have

the answers, do I? I'm just a teenage girl with no influence, no opinions and therefore no voice.' I could see the wheels going around in her head. 'Maybe I should just strap a bomb to my waist and twaddle off into the moonlight.'

This chat was turning serious. It slowed my heart rate down, which was a bit of a relief.

'What? You don't mean, like, a real bomb?'

'Of course I mean a real bomb.'

'And do what?'

'Easy. Just saunter to one of their checkpoints or patrols and press the boom button.'

On the word *boom* she exploded one of her hands in front of my face, widening her stunning eyes.

'But then you'd be ...' I began to say, before it dawned on me. 'You mean, like a suicide bomber?'

'Exactly. It happens to us all one day.'

'But where would you find the bomb to do that?' I asked. It was a vital question because I didn't have a clue where someone would go to find a bomb if they wanted to blow themselves up. I wouldn't know where to start. Maybe The Big Man could sort me out if I asked him.

'Minor problems, Charlie. They can always be sorted out later in the day.'

Now I really wasn't sure if this was a shared joke moment, an extract the urine out of Charlie day or a cheeky yarn.

I neither laughed nor sniggered.

I didn't even grin.

Erin F laughed.

Oh, now I got it!

Erin F looked at me, serious again. 'Do you know what the real problem is, Charlie?'

'No, what?'

'That nobody gives a toss. Everyone in Little Town is happy to just sit back and let all this happen.'

'Not true,' I said, thinking of my mum and dad, then The Big Man's guns flashing through my mind. 'There *are* some people raging about this, Erin F.'

'Who? You?'

'And Pav.'

'Your buddy, he's one of them, is he not?'

'He hates Old Country more than me and you. This is the second time he's been persecuted by them, you know.'

But Erin F had steam coming out of her lugs. This wasn't the Erin F I knew; this was an Erin F with fire in her belly and too much wagging in her fingers.

'I doubt anyone hates them more than me at the moment, Charlie,' she said.

I wanted to ask about her mum's health but didn't wish to send her into a tailspin of fury. 'Does that mean you don't want to meet Pav?'

'I didn't say that.'

'I sent you a message to see if you wanted to come see our

shed,' I said. Erin F stroked her dazzling locks. 'You never replied. I mean, I know the network was down so maybe your phone wasn't working.' She crossed her feet. 'Maybe I took your number down wrongly.'

'You didn't.'

'I didn't?'

'No, my phone got taken off me, Charlie.'

'By your dad?'

The moment I said it I knew that it was a twelve-year-old's question.

'No, not by my dad.'

'Who, then?'

'Some woman from Old Country patrol searched me.'

'A woman?'

'Slimy hands all over me like I was packing twenty kilos of Class A.'

My mind whizzed with the phrase *hands all over me*. I could see it happening; in fact I couldn't stop seeing it happen.

'That's totally terrible,' I said.

'I know. Can you imagine having to do a grubby job like that?'

ABSOLUTELY!

'No way could I imagine that,' I said.

'And from a woman too. God, it's so disgusting and degrading to women all over. A crime against sisterhood.'

This was the best piece of news I'd heard all day. Erin F hadn't rejected me; she hadn't really thought that I was stalking her like a crazy mad fool; she hadn't decided that I wasn't to be the one and only guy for her. I was delighted, but I couldn't show it on my face. The pain of keeping a smile in went all the way down to my toes.

'It's scandalous, Erin F. Scandalous.'

Then I smiled, which turned into a massive chuckle.

'Not funny, Charlie.'

'I know, but I'm just thinking that some Old Country woman has been getting all these texts inviting her to see my shed. She could be there at my shed now for all I know,' I said.

Erin F slapped me on the arm, before howling herself. A real touch on the arm. Human contact. Not-washing-for-a-month contact.

'How many texts did you send?' Erin F asked.

'Eh?'

'How many texts did you send?'

Big giant swear word entered my head. I didn't expect this question.

'Erm … three … maybe four … I don't actually remember,' I lied.

I couldn't really tell her that the figure hit the two-digit mark; if I did she would have definitely thought that I was the king of the stalkers.

'Oh, right,' Erin F said, shifting the weight to her other foot. 'Well, sorry I didn't get them.'

'That's OK, your excuse is watertight,' I said.

'Yes, well ...'

'So do you want to see it then?'

'What?'

'Our shed. Do you want to see it?'

Erin F flicked her hair, a sure sign that she was all flattery and flirty. That's what the so-called brain experts tell us anyway. I was rubbish at reading the signs – the good ones anyway.

'Erm ...' she said, like she'd just been asked if she wanted another bout of root canal.

'It's a cracker! We've furniture and everything in it.'

Time to raise the sail and bail.

'OK,' she said.

'OK?' I said.

'OK.'

'OK, you'll come?'

'Yes, I'll come and see this stupid shed of yours,' Erin F said.

YA BEAUTY! Play it cool, son, play it cool.

I ran my fingers through my hair.

'Really? When? When?' Way too much enthusiasm and very uncool-like behaviour.

'Whenever you like.'

Oh, the pressure. I'd have to go above Pav's head and make an executive decision on this one.

'What about one Saturday?' I said.

'Fine.'

'You don't have anything on?'

'Not unless I drop dead or I decide to blow myself up.'

'Erm … OK …'

'I'm joking, Charlie. I'm doing nothing. There's nothing to do here any more anyway,' she said.

'What about your mum?'

'What about her?'

'Will she be OK without you?'

'I think she'll be fine for a few hours.'

'Is she … ?'

'She's the same, Charlie, but thanks for your concern.'

'Next Saturday then?' I said.

'Not this Saturday?'

'Me and Pav are having a bit of a do next Saturday,' I said.

Erin F's eyes slit up again.

Stop saying his name in front of her.

Stop NOT saying his name in front of her.

'A do for what?'

'It's my birthday and Pav's is a few days later.'

'OK, next Saturday's good,' Erin F said.

'Around two?'

'Two's good.'

'You know where to go?'

'I'll find it, don't worry.'

'Great.'

'So, let me get this right, Charlie.' Erin F's face was confused. 'You're having a party in … your … shed?'

'It's not a party.'

'Who else is going?'

'Just me and Pav.'

'You're having an exclusive party with only two people?'

'Three, now that you're coming. But it's not really a party as such.'

'You're very weird, Charlie Law, do you know that?'

'But you're still coming?' I said with puppy-dog eyes. 'Next Saturday at two?'

'I wouldn't miss it for all the landmines in the world,' she said.

'Me neither, Erin F. Me neither.'

22
Loud Thunder

On the second day back Max Fargo marched towards me as I was waiting to go into my geography class.

'Is it true, Law?'

Max Fargo wasn't in any of my classes. I'd say he was probably the best in the school at wandering the corridors. Most teachers chucked him out after about ten minutes of having him in their lesson, quickly followed by his little lapdog, Bones. Let's say that Max Fargo and Bones weren't your typical pens-out-books-on-the-table-heads-up-teach-me-something students. If Old Country officials ever managed to get their claws into the school system, then clowns like Max and Bones would get their arses rattled big time.

'Yeah, is it true, Law?' Bones said.

'Is what true?' I said.

'That your little girlfriend we met on the bus is from Old Country?' Max said.

For a split second I thought he meant Erin F when he said *girlfriend*. If only!

'Yeah, that Old Country girlfriend,' Bones said.

Bones was a wonder of medical science! He never failed to impress.

'I don't know. Why don't you ask him?' I said.

'We don't need to ask him; we've been told,' Max said.

'Yeah, we've been told,' Bones followed.

'His mob is the reason why loads of our mates are still missing,' Max said.

'Yeah, loads of mates,' Bones added.

I held in a sarcastic laugh. Most of the missing people that I knew would have crossed the road to escape these tossers. Mates? That must have been a joke.

'Who told you?' I asked, because only Mercy and Erin F knew where Pav was from, and surely neither would contemplate sharing the same air with these two tosspots. Any conversation was out of the question.

'Wouldn't you like to know who told us, Flaw, eh?' Bones took to occasionally calling me Flaw; he thought that the entire school would soon catch on to this piece of comedy genius. No one else ever called me it.

'Norman told us,' Max said.

Bones looked offended.

'What does Norman know about anything?' I said.

Norman, bloody mega mouth.

'Wouldn't you like to know, Flaw,' Bones said.

Max piped up.

'He told us his name, where he was from and where he lives now. He told us loads of stuff.'

Bones looked dejected.

'So what,' I said.

'So what?' Bones said.

'Yeah, big deal,' I said.

'Big deal?' Bones said.

I'd lose the will to live if I had to hang with Bones all day.

'Who cares? It's no big deal where he's from, Max,' I said.

'Oh, I think it's a big deal,' Max said.

'Big deal.' By this time nobody was listening to or looking at Bones.

'And I don't like Old Country people anyway,' Max stated.

I hear they speak so highly of you though, Max.

'Yeah ... Old Country people.'

'And neither should you like them, Law,' Max said.

'I don't hate anybody,' I said, which is a bit of a lie because I did hate the people who smithereened our town and school. But I didn't hate just for the sake of hating. That's nuts.

'Well, we know that that little pussy's Old Country,' Max said.

'Little pussy,' Bones said, still floating around in his magical world.

'So what if he is? What's it got to do with me?' I said.

'He's your mate, Law,' Max said.

'Yeah, your mate.'

'That doesn't make me from Old Country, does it?' I said.

'But hanging around with the enemy makes you the enemy too.' Max stepped closer and put his finger on my chest. Jabbed me twice. I didn't move my face muscles. Up until that point I was fine and dandy but now my knees trembled. I think Max had seen far too many violent war movies.

'He's the enemy,' Bones said, taking a step closer as well.

'Pav's not the enemy,' I said, taking a half step back.

Bones guffawed. Max sniggered and shook his head.

'What sort of twat name is that?' Max said.

'Twat name.'

Max gave the eyes to Bones, who stepped back a tad.

'That's his name. I don't see anything funny about it,' I said.

I'm not sure, but I think I might have done a tiny inside snigger myself when I first heard the name Pav.

'Well, you tell Lav or Pav or whatever the hell his stupid name is that he better watch his back,' Max said. 'Or else.'

'Watch his back, or else.'

'What has Pav ever done to you two, eh?'

Max wasn't expecting this. Bones expects nothing from life. Max stared at me.

'I'll tell you what he's done, Law.'

'I'm listening,' I said, puffing out my chest, feeling all high and mighty like I was some sort of top boy. But I wasn't a top boy. I was only little Charlie Law who liked the simple things in life. Shedding, reading, eating and a bit of tomfoolery. Oh, and dreaming about cosy nights in/out with a certain young redhead. I unpuffed my chest and waited for Max's answer.

'He was born, that's what he's done,' Max said. 'He breathes my air, that's what he's done. Look around you: that's what he and his mob have done.'

'We're all born, Max. And we all have to breathe in order to stay alive,' I said.

'Don't get smart with me, Law, or I'll break your pig snout.' Max turned his hand into a fist and lifted it inches from my snout.

Max put his snout closer to my snout. Our snouts were almost touching. Eskimo kissing. His breath reeked of fags and shit.

'Just tell your pal and his skanky Old Country army that he's not welcome here,' Max said. 'That's enough for now.'

Max took his snout and his rank breath back a stride.

I went into geography. Late. Not my style. Sat for an hour bricking it, weighing up my options. I considered The Big Man's guns and how much damage two bullets could do.

23
Bruise

I had no experience of what going to school in a warish zone would be like. I do now. Everyone was edgy and aggressive, including the teachers. You'd be afraid to look at someone the wrong way in case you got an earful. Maybe worse. I lost count of the amount of scraps there were in those first few days.

Because Pav couldn't speak the lingo like a politician under interrogation he was put into some of the thicko classes. They said he'd *catch up much quicker due to the pace being slower* in thicko classes. Now, my brain isn't blessed with the cells of the great thinkers, but this seemed to me like a contradiction, or like some smart-arse was having a laugh at the poor Old Country boy. This meant I didn't see Pav for large chunks of the day, so I couldn't keep an eye on him, protect him, make him laugh, help him with the trauma of a new school. I couldn't be his surrogate teacher. I couldn't plot out a way to Mercy Lewis's heart. All my classes did proper learning. Basically I only saw Pav at break and at lunch, and sometimes I didn't even see him then, as I was studying or doing homework. Keeping on top of it.

It was Mercy Lewis who told me. It was day three. I had my nose in a story. She was out of breath. Her face was chalk, which then made my face go chalk. At first I thought it was due to the hunger; sometimes it made me disoriented and faint. I knew that I looked skinnier and paler. Sure, we all did. But this wasn't hunger Mercy was oozing; sometimes the eyes can tell when something isn't a piss-take. The heart knows right away, and so does the skin colour. Especially when it's Mercy Lewis who's telling the tale; she wasn't exactly renowned for her monkey business and mickey-taking. Mercy had never seen anyone being punched full force in the face or headbutted on the crown before. And it was the first time she'd witnessed one human stamping on another human's head. It left its mark on Mercy, so much so she was struggling to speak. That's why when she tried to tell me what had happened she was shaking like a leaf.

'It's OK, Mercy,' I said. 'Take a deep breath and tell me what's happened.'

Mercy Lewis took a gulp of fresh air. My heart was bursting out of my shirt.

'Charlie, it's Pav.'

'What about him?'

'Max and Bones.'

'What have they done?'

Mercy held her chest. Her oh-my-God moment.

'Mercy, what have Max and Bones done?'

'He was on the ground, Charlie. Blood everywhere. They stamped on him. On his head, again and again.'

'Where is he, Mercy? Where is Pav now?'

'He was lying there,' she said.

'Outside?' I asked. 'Who's with him?'

'I don't know.'

'Teachers?'

'No, I think he's alone.'

As soon as she said the word *alone* I was on my heels. I dropped my book, legged it outside and immediately saw the small gathering. A growing circle had formed. Not one of them doing anything to help. I couldn't hear a kind or sympathetic word being uttered. No warm hand. No words of comfort. What was wrong with these people? Little Town people. My people.

'It's your new mate,' someone said to me as I fought my way through the circle.

'He looks finished,' said another.

'Serves him right,' the first voice said. I didn't even see their faces. My eyes defaulted to tunnel vision mode, exactly the same eyes as when I was inside The Big Man's mine.

Then I saw him.

Little Pav.

My mate, Pav.

Lying in the foetal position.

In a ball.

Tight.

Huddled up.

Trying to protect himself.

Came to Little Town for a better life and here he was lying in a heap, blood trickling out of his ear, nose, mouth and head. Black-and-blue eyes. Swollen. His body shaking. Everyone watching but no one doing a thing. No fingers being lifted. Nothing. All watching the best movie in town. If ever there was a swear moment – not like previous swear moments – this WAS it. I didn't, I couldn't, hold it in.

'Why are you all just fucking standing there? Get some fucking help!' I screamed.

The circle got wider. Less enclosed. People were doing what I'd said. Scared of my voice, my new voice. A voice that shocked even me.

'Go, beat it!' I shouted.

Oh, how I wished The Big Man's guns were tucked inside my trousers. I'd blow them all into next week.

I wiped my eyes and nose and knelt down. I put my hands

on his body. It shook. I picked him up a little, held him close to me.

'Pav, it's me. It's Charlie.'

My hands reached under his head, his blood-matted head. I couldn't see a major cut or laceration. Still.

'Pav, it's Charlie.'

Pav was all over the place: dazed and dizzy. I slid my jacket under his head and tried to keep him warm. I've seen people do that in films. Surely Mum couldn't skelp me for bogging up my jacket in these circumstances?

The circle was no more. Just Mercy standing. Watching. Still chalk-white. Still shaking. Face etched with worry. For Pav.

'You're going to be OK, Pav. Promise,' Mercy said.

'You're going to be fine, mate,' I said.

His eyes had that rabbit stare about them. I looked into them, not in the staring-game way though. I wish. He blinked too much. His trousers were ripped at the knee. He coughed twice.

'You're going to be just fine,' Mercy said.

'Totally fine,' I said.

How did I know for sure? I was no medicine man; I had no qualifications. All I had was my gut. There's no way I should've been telling anyone that they were going to be OK, especially when they were lying in a pile of cuts with a head injury. But I was his mate, his only mate, so it was my duty to tell him that he was going to be fine.

'He's going to be fine, isn't he, Mercy?' I heard my voice rattle.

'You're going to be totally fine, Pav,' she said.

I took out a hanky and wiped the blood from his nose and ear. The blood from his eyebrow had already clotted. Warm water required for that one. When I got him to sit up the colour returned and his eyes seemed to focus. He spat a mouthful of bloody saliva on the ground. We sat there in the yard as if we were fishing. Pav muttered words in his own lingo, words that weren't very nice I'd imagine. I didn't speak. Just sitting with him was enough. I shared a look with Mercy. Pav spat again and tried to pull blood from his nose.

'There you go, Pav,' Mercy said, handing him one of her hankies. A real one that you'd need to wash afterwards. The letters ML embroidered in the corner. Somehow I don't think Mercy wanted it back.

'Thanking you,' Pav said, handing the hanky back to Mercy.

'No. No. You keep it, Pav. Hold on to it; you might need it again,' Mercy said.

'You OK, buddy?' I said.

'I OK. I OK,' he said.

'I can take you to the school nurse if you want?' Mercy said.

'I no need nurse,' Pav said.

'As a precaution,' Mercy said. Pav looked confused. 'Just to be on the safe side.'

'It might be a good idea, mate,' I said.

'You've got some cuts,' Mercy pointed out.

Pav put his hand up to his head.

'Bastards,' Pav muttered, then began to say something again in his lingo.

More spitting on the ground; it wasn't to get rid of the blood this time though.

'We need to get you checked out and cleaned up,' I said.

'That would be my recommendation, Pav,' Mercy said.

'Where is nurse?' Pav asked.

'Just in there.' Mercy pointed to the main doors of the school. We all looked. I had seen neither head nor tail of any nurse since we returned less than a week ago. The old nurse's room had been flattened, but I assumed there would be someone who knew first aid.

'You should really go, Pav,' I said. 'Just in case.'

'I'll go with you,' Mercy said. 'If that's OK with you, Charlie?'

Why wouldn't it have been?

'Of course it's OK,' I said.

'OK, I go,' Pav said.

'I'll give you a hand,' Mercy said.

We helped him to his feet.

I watched them walk towards the school building. Mercy guiding him. Her hand an inch away from Pav's waist. They never touched, but they were almost clinging on to one another.

I remained in the empty yard, looking at the splashes of blood on the ground. Where were the teachers? Where was the concern? Where was all this *protecting the students* crap?

I needed a chat with Norman or The Big Man. Sort this mess out.

24
Psycho

Pav hadn't been back to school since the incident. That day I took him home from school on the bus and helped him to his door. His mum looked like thunder the moment she saw him. And me.

'Thank you, Charlie, for to bring him home,' she said coolly, her eyes flashing blue as Pav's.

She put her hand on his broken face and tenderly led him in, slamming the door in mine. To be fair, he looked like shit – even his baby blue blinders were red and bloodshot, and he might've cracked a rib or two – but I didn't think there was any permanent damage. Through the door I heard his mum speaking in Old Country lingo. Even though I didn't understand a word, her harsh throaty sounds made clear her feelings about Little Town people.

This badly needed sorting out.

Norman didn't see the need to go to school any more. *School is for major losers who just go on to work for the man when they're finished, so what's the point of that, eh, Charlie?* I found this a bit rich coming from Norman, considering that he really did work for The Man. Just a slightly bigger man than your average one. A waste because he could be smart when he put his mind to it. In reality Norman had decided to become a worker for the Regime, a kind of Rascal resistance fighter. He got the message that I needed to see him, though. He turned up on the Saturday after Pav took his beating.

My arse was making buttons when Norman appeared at the shed. I was getting the place shipshape for Erin F's visit the following week, my birthday, and I was worried because she hadn't been in school the previous day (the invasion really seemed to be affecting people's attendance). I was busy scrubbing the floor when the door rattled.

'This place is the bollocks, Charlie.' I was going to invite him to plonk his bum but Norman beat me to it, chucking his chunky frame into one of the chairs and resting his arms on each side like he was testing it out. I looked at his boots to see if he was muck-carrying. He was. Brilliant!

'You like it?' I said.

'I do.' Norman gave the shed the once-over.

'Nice, isn't it?'

'It'd make a brilliant shagging pad.'

Now was not the time to tell him that I saw it as a cross between a study area, a chill-out space and a lads' den. Oh, I almost forgot. It could also be a place to hide full metal jackets. Did Norman know? He was The Big Man's top youngster after all; surely he'd have known.

Keep the trap shut, Charlie.

Norman's eyes scoured the place.

HE KNOWS, DOESN'T HE? THAT'S WHAT HE'S CASING THE PLACE FOR. HE KNOWS.

Ssssshhhhh, he knows shit all.

'Yeah, I'd say you and Pav have done all right with this place, Charlie.'

'We like it,' I said, which didn't sound quite right.

'We *like* it – is it like that?' Norman said with a funny voice and even funnier look in his eye. 'I bet you do *like it.*'

I decided not to be the fish to his bait.

'Erin F's coming round next Saturday.'

'Erin F, eh?' His eyes lit up. Whose didn't when her name was mentioned? 'Are you riding her or something?'

Erin F. Me. Riding. All in the same sentence. In my dreams.

'Erm ... no ... she's a mate, Norman ... It's my birthday. She's just coming round to see the shed and chill and stuff.'

'How's her mum doing? Still knocking on death's door?'

'Erm, I think she's still the same,' I said. 'Erin F doesn't talk about her too much.'

'Aw, well. We all have bad shit going on in our lives,' Mr Insensitive said.

'Yeah …'

'Anyway, hippy happy birthday, mate. If I'd known I'd have brought a prezzie with me.'

God only knows what.

'Aw, no worries, Norman. Even my mum and dad'll barely remember this year.'

Norman shuffled on the chair. The chair that was on top of the floorboard. The floorboard that was on top of the hidden steel. The steel that was on top of my mind. One false move and he'd have no arse left to sit on. The thought of it made me smile.

'Heard about little Pav, by the way.'

The smile flew away.

'Who told you?'

Norman grimaced.

'I mean, since you no longer go to school, Norman. How did you know?'

'Don't be stupid, Charlie. Do you think I'd never have heard?'

'Suppose you would have,' I said.

'I'll tell you what though …'

'What?'

'If you'd asked me I'd have said straight away that it was Max and Bones that done it. No doubt.' Norman shook his head and whispered, 'Couple of fannies,' to himself. I couldn't disagree.

'Yeah, they left him in a pretty bad way.'

'How is he now?'

'He's fine, but he was shaken up by it. I think he's scared to go back to school. He doesn't think it's safe for him any more.'

'Cos he's Old Country?'

'Something like that.'

'But he's decent Old Country, isn't he? Refugee Old Country. He's not like those pricks on patrol. He's not part of any occupation.'

'Try telling the eejits at school that,' I said.

Norman's head spun with thoughts. I knew that look from being in the same class as him for years. It was his I-shouldn't-really-tell-you-this-but-I'm-going-to-anyway face.

'You tell Pav not to worry, Charlie.'

'How?'

'It's been sorted.'

'Sorted?'

'Tell him no more shit will happen to him.'

'What's been sorted exactly?'

Norman hesitated.

'Look, Charlie, just know that Max and Bones have been sorted.'

'Who sorted them?'

'Aw, come on, Charlie, I can't be revealing my sources, now, can I?'

He would reveal them if pushed.

'Did *you* do them in, Norman? Did *you* batter them?'

'Me?'

'Yes.'

'Why in God's name would I batter them?'

He had a point. It wasn't as if we were bosom buddies with Norman. And, after all, Pav *was* Old Country breed. Norman owed us nothing.

'So who sorted it then?'

Norman heaved himself up in the chair. For a minute I thought he was trying to scratch his arse without touching it, attempting to rub his two cheeks together.

'Let's just say someone got wind that Pav took a leathering and did something about it.'

'Someone got wind of it?' I said.

Norman's mouth channel was on mute.

You know who got wind of it, so why are you asking? Blurt it out yourself.

'Come on, Norman, who?'

YOU say it.

'Come on. Spit it out. I won't say a word, not even to Pav. Promise I won't.'

Norman's gub was locked and the key swallowed. Time to throw down the winning hand: 'Was it The Big Man?'

Norman almost vomited the key back up.

Bingo!

'Might have been.'

'Wise up, Norman. You know I know it was The Big Man.'

Norman clicked his feet together, making little nuggets of dirt fall on the floor. More cleaning.

'OK, OK, it was The Big Man,' Norman said, lowering his voice.

MENTAL MEMO: NEVER, EVER TELL NORMAN A SECRET. OR SOMETHING YOU DON'T WANT THE WHOLE OF LITTLE TOWN TO KNOW ABOUT.

'How did The Big Man find out? That's what I want to know,' I said.

'Charlie, he's The Big Man. He knows everything that goes down here. Especially these days.'

'What did he do to get it sorted?'

'That I don't know; all I know is that it's sorted.'

'Sorted how?' I said, not that I was concerned for the welfare of Max or Bones. I was curious. Norman did his face contortion. 'Sorted good or sorted bad?' Very curious.

'It's The Big Man, Charlie. He doesn't tell me these things. If he says it's been sorted then it's been sorted, end of.'

I looked at Norman's boots. Big chunks of mud clung to his heels.

I was going to plonk myself in one of the comfy chairs, but I didn't want him to feel that I was opening the door for a lad-on-lad chat. I remained standing.

'Is that all you came to tell me, Norman?'

'No.'

'Well, what then?'

'The Big Man wants to see you.'

My heart sank. Not again? Not so soon after the last time.

'When?' I asked.

'The day after the day after tomorrow.'

'But that's Tuesday! I have school on Tuesday.'

My mind was awash with images of blankets, air, cars, blindfolds, orders and fear.

'Where?' I asked.

'He's going to come here when you get back.'

'Here? Like, here, to my house?'

NO WAY CAN THAT HAPPEN. Mum would flip her lid if she thought that The Big Man and me were in cahoots. Although, perhaps she wouldn't if she knew it was down to him that her inhaler medicine was still getting to her. She knew the chemist hadn't reopened yet, but not once had she questioned where I was getting the stuff from. She might welcome my *friendship* with The Big Man under the current circumstances. Who was I kidding? If she found out, I'd be consigned to a life of everlasting skelpings.

'Not at your house; he wants to come *here*.'

'Here, where?' I said.

Norman gestured his two index fingers around in little circles. 'Here.'

'The shed?'

'Yes.'

'Why?'

'He wants to speak to you, that's why.'

'No, I get that bit, but why here? Why not at one of his places?'

'He's The Big Man, Charlie. He makes the decisions. Not you. No questions asked.'

'So I've just got to stay in here after school until he arrives?'

'Yes.'

'Does he want to see Pav?'

'No.'

'Why not?'

'How do I know?'

'It's Pav's shed as well, you know.'

'The message is that he wants to see only *you*.' Norman pointed at me.

'Just me?'

'Just you.' Norman made for the door. 'I wish I could stay and talk all day, Charlie, but I've got to see a man about a dog.' He flicked his finger at my zip and laughed. 'And next week you've got to see a dog about a man, know what I mean, eh?' His attempt at being funny was only funny because it wasn't funny.

When Norman left I wiped the muck off the floor and puffed up the chairs, then went up to the house to wash and spray my pits. I was half thinking of going to see how Pav was doing. I got as far as pausing outside his door. I didn't knock. Not sure why. I suppose I didn't want to tell him the good news about Max and Bones getting sorted.

25
You

I hadn't been out on the streets for a while, except getting the bus to and from school. The Old Country patrols were either stopping people for nothing, asking banal questions or simply intimidating everyone by their presence. Erin F told me she'd been hassled before so I was worried about her when she failed to turn up for school on the Monday. That's why, after school, I went in search for her.

In order to get to her section of town I had to go through the park and past the shops area. Climb the big hill. Erin F's section was down the other side of the big hill.

Walking through the park, I noticed that the smell had gone. The air was better. The rubbish had been cleared. There weren't as many troops. Everything was eerily silent. Only half the street lights worked, making this mad humming sound. They flickered and flashed as they hung on to the last breath of electrical life. To keep calm I imagined them saying hello to me as I ambled past. Although I also imagined them warning me about some pending doom. DO NOT ADVANCE, CHARLIE.

The park was different this time round: the see-saw had been fixed. It seed and sawed once again. The roundabout spun again. The six swings swung another day. All the broken glass and booze bottles had been swept off the ground. I put it down to the locals and a collective spirit. I'm pretty sure the Little Town Regime and Rascals would have just left it to ruin. Maybe Old Country troops helped?

Before the bombs Mum and Dad sent me off to the shops to buy things all the time. I'd hated being the house slave, whipped into action to purchase teabags, biscuits, chips, milk, a paper, bread, etc. Nothing ever for myself. Now they told me never to go near the shops area. Old Country had that part of town secured. I needed to go there though; there was no other direction I could have taken. It was the only way I knew how to get to her house. Some of the shops still had their windows panned in. The pavements sparkled with shards of glass. Sharkey's, which was an Aladdin's cave of crap household goods, was an empty shell; just a few lamp-shades and picture frames remained. Tragic. Mum would shed a tear at this. Sharkey's and Mum were magnets. Tommy Tango's, which had row upon row of bright, mouth-watering sweets stacked up in oversized plastic bottles, was our candy shop Mecca, so it was heartbreaking to walk past its shattered windows. Death of the sugar hit. Dad's pub, The Big Tree, had lost its door, its seats, its stools and, by the look of it, its soul; The Big Tree was now a cold empty space, dust and rubble strewn over its bar. Should be renamed The Little Depressed Twig. The shops area was deserted, like a scene from one of Dad's cowboy movies. The sight of the chemist depressed me still.

I couldn't see them, but I heard them in the distance. The chug-chug sound of big trucks growling around, the muffle of voices – probably children shouting and chucking things at the patrol before hightailing it back to the safety of their blocks. Then the worst sound of all. Each crack made my innards shudder. It didn't matter that I couldn't see them. I bet they could see me. I bet they were watching my every move, wondering where this young figure was going to, and why I was out on my own. They might've thought I was a maverick rogue searching for something left to loot. A sewer urchin. I imagined guns pointed at my skull from every direction. Old Country patrol guns. Maybe Little Town Rascal guns too.

Head down, keep walking.

The one good thing about being scared out of my skin was that it took my mind off Erin F for a few minutes. I was no longer racking my brain about why she was failing to show up to school. I couldn't text her since she no longer had her phone. I had a bad feeling – Erin F wasn't the type of person who'd choose to skip school. Even in a war zone.

If I'd known they'd be coming over the top of the hill there's no way I'd have started climbing it. I was about halfway up, heading towards Erin F's block. Puffing hard.

Naturally I heard it before I saw it. The cough of the truck lugging its sad arse up the hill. I always wondered why Old Country hadn't kitted themselves out with spanking new vehicles before they came here. That's what I'd have done if I was trying to wield all the power. If I had occupied somewhere.

The patrol approached me. I stopped walking, gulping for air. They shone their headlights, full beams. There was no reason to do this; they could see me perfectly well. The full beams made me use my hand as a shield, the only weapon I had. The chug got louder. There was an exhaust backfiring noise. I prayed it was only the exhaust. The brakes were worn down; they braked early. I stood rigid. The patrol screeched to a halt beside me. My breathing stopped. There was some hope in my mind that this was The Big Man's mob playing silly buggers. Had they managed to get their paws on an Old Country wagon? No such luck.

Two troops jumped out. One pushed me back with a powerful one-handed shove. I heard my shoulder crack. I bounced off the wall like a wrestler on the ropes. The other troop rammed me again. Same shoulder cracked. I bounced back to them. A third push hit me, but not like the others. I didn't bounce back this time. I was stuck there with a hand on my throat. Gloved hand. He looked into my eyes and I stared at his. No game. They were almond-shaped, like Pav's. Not the blue blinders of Pav's, but blue enough. A clear spring day. I'd give him between twenty-two and twenty-seven years of age. His mate as well. The Throat Crusher didn't say a word.

Keep cool. You've done nothing wrong.

'Where you go?' his mate said.

I could hardly breathe. Speaking was out of the question. The hand squeezed harder. I felt the blood rush to my face. Beetroot chops.

'Where you go?' the mate asked again.

Tighter.

'Where are you go?' the Throat Crusher said, like an iconic horror film character.

'To … see … a … friend,' I managed to force out.

Any tighter and that would be it. Honestly, the blinds were being drawn. I could sense it happening. This was my moment and there was no floating towards the white light, no flying above and looking down on things, no life flashing before my eyes. Disappointing or what? They'd have to leave me lying there. Me, lying there like a dodgy sleeping bag on its knees. They'd have that on their consciences. Did that bother Old Country troops though?

The hand slackened its grip. I fought for air. Rubbed my neck. Loosened my jaw. The two other nuggets stepped back, creating a pathway for the third person to enter. I didn't see the face of the new soldier. I didn't look at it. My eyes were on the concrete. The new soldier was closer, invading my personal space. Boots that were once shiny stopped moving; the baggy khakis tucked into them fluttered in the wind. My head and eyes rose, pinned to the uniform. Rising. Huge brown belt with bronze buckle. Ammo belt. No need to use ammo on me. Surely not? Khaki jacket. Eyes rising. Eyes … STOP! Rising … STOP! My eyes didn't go further than the little strip of fabric on the left breast pocket of the khaki jacket. The name fabric. The name tag. The name leapt out and punched me full force on the cheek. I read it through watery eyes:

CAP DU …

CAPTA DUD …

CAPTAIN DUDA!

There was no mistaking the name. And then those eyes. The same eyes. The same baby blue blinders as Pav's. The exact same. No difference. The same blood. Before me, giving me the mad daggers, was the female Pav. No doubting it, this was the little man's sister. I'd give her the same age as the Throat Crusher. She was the same woman I'd seen at the park's entrance a few days after the bombs came.

It was as if I'd known her for ages. After all, her younger brother was my buddy. I knew her parents. I knew some of her Old Country history. In fact, I knew loads about her. Whereas she knew nothing about me. To her I was nothing more than a sewer urchin.

I'd heard about the things that Old Country troops did to stray teens. Give you a few happy smacks, interrogate you for hours on end until you reached breaking point, leave imprints of their boots on your chest. I'd heard that if they nabbed any Old Country teens they'd ruffle them up good and proper before sending them back to Old Country so they could do their Military Service. Real torture. I could feel the colour draining from me.

I smiled. Her expression stayed the same. Serious and deadly.

'Why you fook smile?' Even the way she swore sounded like Pav. She also had Pav's ability to stare hard at people. I didn't know how to reply but I was about to unleash the tongue when it came. I didn't see it coming. It came from below. Wham! She gave me a little rabbit punch to the gut. No back lift. Just a simple dig. I winced in agony, as anyone with a low pain threshold would have done. Captain Duda bent down and pulled me up by the back of the hair. 'You don't fooking smile at me, little shit. OK?' No more smile.

'OK,' I said.

Thud number two arrived as I was on the way up.

Whack!

A swift dink to the right eye. A sly cowardly jab. Not fair. The pain shot to the back of my throat. My teeth hurt with that punch. I crouched, covered my head and tensed my torso in preparation for a real hammering.

'You smile now, eh,' she said.

Tears filled my eyes, anger tears and anger shaking too. Not once did The Big Man lay his hands on me, not once.

'Get up, you dog.' She said something in Old Country lingo to the other two. They grabbed me and yanked me to my feet. 'ID.'

'I forgot to bring it with me, sorry,' I said, not knowing if I should hold my stomach or my eye.

'You forget?'

'I forgot.'

Her eyes widened, her head nodded, a small grin appeared. 'You have brain inside here?' she said, slapping me on the side of the head with her open hand. ENOUGH!

'Ouch.' How could this be the spawn of Mr and Mrs Duda? These were the precise acts they hated. And now their very own daughter – Captain Duda – was dishing it out with chocolate on top.

Again I put myself into the protective ball position, convinced the rain was about to start, that I was going to be carved a new a-hole right there on the hill. And why? Because of Erin F.

'Stand direct up,' Pav's sister said.

'I'm afraid to,' I said from the position I was in.

Laughing and lingo chat.

'Afraid why?'

'To be hit again.'

'You think we are animals? Do you?' she screamed in my lug, making this animal jump.

'No.'

Yes, I do actually. *Keep those thoughts hidden.*

'Well, stand direct up like human being,' she said.

I did what she asked.

My eye throbbed.

'Name?' she asked.

'Charlie Law.'

'It's Little Town name?'

'I think so.'

'Charlie is stupid name.'

I didn't reply, unsure if it was a question or an opinion.

'Where you go?' Captain Duda asked.

'I was going to my girl– … my friend's house over there,' I said, pointing over the hill. They all looked.

'Where you live?' she asked. I pointed back down the hill, towards the park.

'Over there.'

'You walk all way?'

'Yes.'

'You know this a danger place?' she said. 'Many troubles here?'

'No. I mean, yes. Yes, I knew it was a dangerous place,' I said.

'It danger place. OK?'

'OK.'

Captain Duda said something to the lads. They smirked.

'You very stupid boy,' she said before laying her hands on me for a fourth time. 'I think nothing happen in there, Charlie Law.' She tapped her finger against my temple. Not sore but very BIG GIANT SWEAR WORD annoying. My first experience of seething.

'What is friend's name?' she asked.

Thank God I wasn't going to see Pav. Thank God Pav wasn't with me. Talk about awkward moments in life.

'I ask not two times, Charlie Law,' she said. 'What is friend's name?'

Was that not two times?

'Erin F,' I said. 'My friend is called Erin F.'

More talking in their own lingo, followed by roars of laughter.

Old Country Bastards.

That was the first time that phrase rose from my toes and exploded in my head. That was the moment I saw these people in the same way as many others did: that they were nothing more than Old Country Bastards. Not a nice thought. I didn't want to be like everyone else; I wanted Charlie Law to be different. A thinker. A nice guy. A fighter of wrongs.

It's OK to think this way. Don't sweat it, man.

'What?' I said, severely agitated. 'What are you laughing at?'

Pav's sister, Captain Duda, stepped closer. At my face. She thrust a hand on to my mouth and held it tightly; her nails dug into my cheeks.

'You don't speak in that fook voice to me, OK?'

'OK, yes.'

'Little Town have no respect. You are pigs.'

She released the hand.

'Where are parents?'

'At home.'

'They allow you to walk streets at this time?'

'They don't –'

'Like the rabies dog? They allow, do they?'

'They don't know I'm here.'

'Typical Little Town, no control.'

Further Old Country lingo talking; obviously deciding what to do with me. Decisions. Decisions:

Leave me be with a kindly pat on the dome and a *Sorry for the misunderstanding*?

Send me on my merry way?

Tell me to hop in and they'd make sure I got home safe and sound?

Take me into a dark cell and batter the living crap out of me?

Hand me over to those troops who enjoy a bit of torturing on the side?

What a dilemma.

'Can I go?' I asked.

'Yes. You go. But I will watch for you, Charlie Law. If I see again I will not be so nice,' she said.

Thanks.

'Can I go this way?' I pointed in the direction of where I was going. To Erin F's. I even made my way to go.

'No,' the Throat Crusher said, putting his hand up to obstruct me.

'No?'

'You go that way,' Pav's sister said, pointing to where I'd come from. 'You fook off to home. Now!'

'But ...' Her hand cupped my new shirt's collar and shoved me back down the hill. She was as strong as an ox; must be something in the Duda water. I took three steps before I stumbled and fell. Sniggering from the troops. I always considered myself to be a pretty patient teenager but this was some massive test.

'You get Little Town ass to home,' Captain Duda shouted.

I was going to ask for a ride to my block, but before I could get *Sorry to bother you but I couldn't possibly* ... out of my mouth, they had jumped into the truck and were motoring off down the hill. I watched them drive up the main street, past the deserted shops, hang a right at The Big Tree and disappear into the night. Ready to pull some other poor sod up for doing nothing. Ready to play the world's bully.

I walked with pace, hands in pockets, head bowed, making no eye contact with anyone, which was easy as there wasn't a sinner around. The air smelt toxic. As did my temperament. I could feel my eye swell.

MENTAL MEMO: WHATEVER YOU DO, DON'T TELL PAV YOU HAD AN ENCOUNTER WITH HIS SISTER.

26
Hitting North

When I got home Mum went ballistic. About staying out, my eye, my shirt, how worried sick she and Dad were. Although, to me, Dad didn't seem to be worried or sick.

'All boys need a black eye now and again; it's a rite of passage, Maggie,' Dad said from behind his paper.

'Who did it? Tell me who did it?' Mum shouted in my face. 'Was it one of them?' When she said *them* her head nodded towards our front door, aimed directly at Pav's.

'I told you, I slipped in the shed and banged it against the table.' I couldn't exactly tell her that the Dudas' secret daughter landed a cracker on me, could I? That would be suicide for our friendship.

'Slipped in the shed, my eye!' Mum turned to Dad. 'What do you think, Bert?'

Dad ruffled his paper.

'He must think we're a couple of eejits, Maggie, that's what I'd say.'

'I don't,' I said.

'You'd better not or you'll get another black eye to match,' Mum said.

Dad's paper shuddered. I didn't know if he was laughing at the content within it or what Mum had said. Sometimes Dad just laughed at Mum for no reason.

Mum went on about how money doesn't grow on trees and that I wouldn't be getting any new things for a very long time because I had no respect for money or clothes.

'Go, get up them stairs out of my sight.' Mum puffed at her inhaler as I dutifully got out of her sight.

I didn't think fourteen-year-olds got sent to bed. Guess I was wrong. At least I could keep the light on, unlike when I was younger. I could still read and write. Worry about Erin F.

Lying on my bed, I thought about Pav and found myself getting angry with him. Blaming him for my swollen eye and the dullness in my stomach. I didn't want to see his Old Country face. *Thank god Max and Bones done him like a kipper*. I thought about The Big Man's pending visit and the steel in the shed. I thought about the troops and Captain Duda. How could she and Pav be related? How?

And I thought about Erin F. Oh, Erin F, what will I say

to you at school? How will I explain my swollen eye? My broken heart? My dented ego? It was all for her. All the pain and anger, it was all for her. And even though my heart was broken, I knew it would still go on thumping. She deserved it.

27
Storm Warning II

I didn't go to school on the Tuesday; Mum allowed me time to recuperate. I laid it on thick for her. I spent most of the day in the shed, reading. Doing nothing.

Late afternoon The Big Man came to see me. He walked straight in. No knock. No hello. No *Can I come in, please?* No manners. Barging in bold as brass.

He took time out to look around. Normally when I saw him, nervousness kicked in. Not so much this time; he was flying solo, no big thick-necked henchmen to flank him or run his errands. I don't think the shed could've taken three massive bruisers in any case.

He sat down, puffed his cheeks out as if the weight of the world had been lifted from his shoulders and grinned warmly. His voice was softer. When he spoke, some nice things came out of his mouth. For the first time I felt calm in his company, not like we were mates calm, but I didn't feel that I was going to be buried six feet under in a shallow grave or have a skanky old rag shoved in my gub and set alight. I felt safe.

'Happened your eye?' he said.

'Fell.'

'Best be careful.'

'I will.'

'Here,' he said, throwing a small brown bag at me. 'For your mum.'

'Thanks.' I didn't need to peek inside. I could feel the inhaler.

'Place looks good, Charlie,' The Big Man said.

'Thanks.'

'I mean, for an old shitty shed, that is.'

'It's good to have it comfortable. I spend lots of time here,' I said.

'I bet you do, son. I bet you do.'

'I do.'

'I don't blame you with all this shit happening around us.' He nodded to the outside world. 'Might join you.'

'But you've got loads of places to go, Big Man,' I said. 'The mine, the other block, no?'

'The net's closing in, Charlie. Those Old Country bastards know me now; they know my face and they're doing their damnedest to get me.'

'Really?'

'Anything and everything they're trying.'

'Sorry to hear that,' I said. I wasn't sorry at all. A part of me was wishing that the Old Country net would tangle The Big Man up and protect us all.

'If you want to know the truth, I think there is a rat in the camp,' he said.

'A rat?'

'A rat, a filthy grass.'

WAS I PART OF HIS CAMP?

'Erm ...' My tongue was stuck.

'Some motormouth has been blabbing to those bastards. They've been to the mine, to the block. They won't leave me alone. They want my arse on a spit.'

DON'T COME HERE THEN.

Hello, nerves.

Hi, raging heartbeat.

Howdy, sweaty palms.

How are you, shaky legs?

'I didn't rat, Big Man, honest I didn't.'

'Are you sure?' The Big Man went back to the voice I knew and loathed.

'Yes. I wouldn't do that,' I said, knowing that if pushed I would do exactly that.

'You know what'll happen if I find out it was you, don't you?'

Good afternoon, full body tremble.

'I do, but it wasn't ...'

The Big Man paused, screwed his eyes at me. Sort of smiled. 'Don't worry, Charlie. I know it wasn't you, son. I can trust you, can't I?'

'Yes.'

'You're one of us. One of the real Little Towners.'

'I am.'

I wasn't really.

'And you've got this.' The Big Man tapped his temple with his finger. 'Which is vital; much more important than these.' He flexed his left bicep and pointed to it with the same finger that had been on his temple.

'So who do you think has been ratting?' I asked.

'Norman,' he blurted.

'Norman?'

'The little prick hasn't been seen for days; he hasn't been to see me. I know they've got him and they're squeezing the juice out of him as we speak. It all makes sense.'

'But he was only here on Saturday.'

'All it takes is a few days, Charlie. A few hours, in fact, before a tongue starts to wag,' The Big Man said. 'It's more than his tongue that will be wagging if I get my hands on him.'

'Are you sure it's Norman?' I said. I'd known Norman all my life. We'd been in infant school together. I knew without any doubt that he'd be squealing if an Old Country patrol had picked him up. Anyone with any sense in them would, wouldn't they? I feared for him.

'He's thick enough. He's nowhere to be seen. My warehouse has been raided. Some of the lads have been nabbed off the street. Of course it was Norman. Who else would it have been?'

'Did he tell you about Max and Bones?' I said.

'Who?'

'Two guys who beat up Pav.'

'That scrawny Old Country mate of yours?'

'Yes.'

'Who battered him?'

'Two guys at school. Max and Bones they're called.' I could see in The Big Man's eyes that he knew exactly what I was talking about. 'Norman told me that they'd been sorted. Why would he have done that if he was a rat?'

'Because he doesn't have a brain, that's why.'

'Did *you* sort Max and Bones?' I asked. The Big Man looked at me. Stared. I wasn't frightened.

'I don't keep tabs on everyone I sort out, Charlie.'

'Did you do it because Pav's my mate?'

'Anyone who lays a finger on those in my circle has to pay the consequences. Let's leave it at that, eh?'

The Big Man's eyes didn't move from mine.

'No more questions, Charlie. The more you *don't* know the safer you are. You don't want to end up like Norman now, do you?'

'No.'

'Keep that open and that shut then,' he said, meaning my mind and my mouth in that order. 'Got it?'

'Got it.'

'Good.' He leaned forward in the chair. His chair. 'So, where's the merch?'

'The what?'

'The merch. The merchandise. Where is it?'

'Merchandise?' I said, clearly NOT keeping the brain open.

The guns, Charlie. The guns. Get with the programme, son.

'The steel I gave you to keep an eye on for me?'

'Oh, that.'

'Yes, *that*. Tell me you still have it?'

'I still have it.'

'Well, where is it?'

'Underneath your chair.' I pointed to the ground. 'Under that floorboard there.'

'Oh, I like your style, Charlie, son. I like your style.'

The Big Man lifted the board, took one gun and squashed it into the back of his jeans. He left the other one where it was, shoved another package in there and replaced the wood.

'I've left some more ammo down there,' he said.

'OK.' My chest felt tight, like I might need one of Mum's inhaler puffs.

'Right, ready?' he said, making his way to the door.

'Ready for what?'

'You and I are going on a mission, my old son.'

'Now?'

'No time like the present.'

'But … erm … mission to where?'

'Let me ask you something, Charlie.'

'What?'

'Do you love Little Town?'

LOVE? NOT REALLY.

'Yes,' I said, out of fear more than anything.

'And are you willing to do things to protect it?'

NO.

'Erm … depends.'

'What if it's a *them* or *us* situation?' He waited for an answer, which I didn't have. 'You'd pick us, right?' he said.

'Erm … right … I guess.'

'Well, that's the shitstorm we now find ourselves in. It's *them* or *us*, Charlie. *Us* or *them*. So you've got to ask yourself: which side are you on?' This was a massive question. The Big Man demanded an answer. The correct one.

'I suppose I'm on the *us* side,' I said.

'Thought so. OK, let's go.'

He allowed me to exit the shed first.

'They'll never get near me on this,' The Big Man said as he handed me a spare helmet. I didn't show it but it was exciting. The helmet made me look like a giant Martian. It crushed my cheeks together and puckered up my lips. If only Erin F could have seen this cool rider. Well, cool, but terrified at the same time.

We zoomed through the park. Whizzed past the shops. Zipped over the big hill. It was the first time I'd ever been on a motorbike. The Big Man rode it fast. All throttle and bottle. I enjoyed hiding behind his back and feeling the wind in my face. Mum and Dad would never sanction a motorbike for me. Nothing to do with safety; it would be a case of where would they get the cash from? No chance of a motorbike in this life.

We pulled in behind some concrete rubble near the bottom of the hill, about seventy yards from where Old Country patrol had duffed me up. He switched the engine off.

'What are we doing here?' I said. I didn't like the feel of the place. This was Old Country territory, near their main base. Far too near to where Pav's sister took her potshots for my liking. The Big Man was packing some nifty metal as well. We'd get more than a few potshots if he got nabbed with that gun tucked down his arse. 'I don't think it's safe here, Big Man.'

'Don't worry, Charlie.'

'But what are we here for?'

'You'll see.'

We waited.

The patrol truck's engine hummed and hawed in the distance.

'Here it comes now,' The Big Man said. 'Hear it?'

'I hear it,' I said.

'Down, keep down.' We both went on to our hunkers. The patrol stuttered over the top of the hill.

'See it?' The Big Man asked.

'I see it.' I didn't tell him that not only did I see it but I'd seen it once before.

'Right, watch now. Watch what they do.'

The truck stammered down the hill before coming to a stop midway down. Near to where they sprung me.

'They've stopped,' I said.

'That's what they do, like clockwork. They put the brakes on halfway down, hop out for a little gander about, two minutes max, then jump back in and piss off again.'

It *was* the very same crew who rattled my cage: Pav's sister and the thick necks.

It happened exactly like The Big Man had described. We watched the truck saunter down the hill, turn the corner at the battered Big Tree pub and disappear.

'How did you know?' I said.

'I've been watching these bastards just as much as they've been watching me. I know their every move.'

He might have seen you getting roughed up, Charlie. Ssshhh.

'Why them?'

'This mob are responsible for the rack and ruin of the shops, my shops. I mean, look at them. Nothing left. Place is a mess. And these aren't your everyday ground troops. One of them has a rank. A top rank. You know what that means?'

'Not really.'

'Well, you should. It means, don't mess with us.'

'Oh, OK.'

'See, these bastards terrorise and hound everyone that comes into their path, Charlie.'

AND YOU DON'T?

Terrorise and hound, was it? Probably wasn't the time to teach The Big Man about the wonderful world of irony, or throw the words pot and kettle at him.

'It's not on, Charlie, not on my patch, know what I mean? They are interfering with my business. They keep pulling my associates and stopping us trading. They're out to get me and I'm not going to let them win. The future of Little Town is in our hands, Charlie, understand?'

'I think so.'

'They're the ones who nabbed Norman.' The Big Man's smirk suggested he didn't believe what he was saying. As if it was for my benefit.

'You think so?'

'Dead serious I think so. I'd say they chucked him in the back of that truck, kicked the stuffing out of him, drove him to their headquarters and made his little rat tongue flap.'

'Wow!' I said. It was all I could think of adding.

'Which buggered up our plan.'

WHAT PLAN?

'Erm … plan?'

'Norman had been lined up to do a job on them.'

'A job?'

'Before he turned rat, that is.'

'What kind of job?'

'Left me up shit creek, Charlie. Norman would have been perfect as well.'

'I bet he –'

'But you know who would be better though?' The Big Man winked.

'Who?'

YOU KNOW EXACTLY WHO. STUPID.

The Big Man pointed his leather-gloved finger my way.

'You've got brains in there, Charlie. A bit of savvy. You're clever. I've no doubt that you could do what Norman couldn't. Even better, in fact.'

I was genuinely afraid. I kept my eyes on the hill.

'I should've asked you to do it right from the start,' The Big Man said.

'What sort of job?'

'We have to get this town back on its feet, Charlie. Do you not agree?'

'I do.'

'And people like that are stopping us doing it.'

'The patrol?' I said.

'They're hindering us.'

'Those three?'

'It starts with those three. Hit them hard and fast. And if we get some top rank that'll send a firm warning.'

'But it's only three people, Big Man. We're fighting a losing battle.'

'But we have to fight regardless, right?'

'Suppose.'

'And it starts with them.' He nodded to the hill. 'Well, not all three, just the ringleader, the rank; take down the rank and the rest will buckle like a donkey with a broken knee. It'll get them off the streets for a while at least.'

'Who's the ringleader?' I said, still pretending that these people were all new to me.

'The doll.'

'What doll?'

'The bird, the chick, the girl. She's the ranking officer, the one who makes the decisions. The two monkeys with her wouldn't have a clue without her. She's the one. This is Little Town fighting back, Charlie. Standing up to these Old Country invaders.'

'And what can I do about it?' I asked.

'You're clean. They have nothing on you, nothing to suspect you of; you'd be perfect.'

'For what?'

'To take her down.'

'Eh?'

'Take her out,' The Big Man said.

'Take her out?'

'You mean … ?'

'You've got the merch. You've got ammo. You know how to use it now. In this position here you've got a clean shot. It's a simple aim-pull-fire-dead gig. Then you bolt to where I'll be and that's it. Job done. A quick in and out number.'

Everything in my mind slowed down to a WHA WHA WHA pace. The Big Man's voice sounded muffled, like his voice had been distorted. I couldn't hear it clearly. My eyes watered. My stomach churned. One minute it's the start of the summer and I'm flapping thoughts and dreams about being a lawyer or a doctor or a teacher, dating Erin F, and the next I'm faced with lugging the title of murderer around with me. My shoulders couldn't take it. How does one minute change so dramatically like that? Pav's sister skelped me good and hard; she battered my pride. I was raging with her; I wanted revenge. Revenge. Not death.

'Charlie?'

'I don't really want to do it, Big Man,' I heard myself saying.

'Oh, I don't think you have a choice.'

'Why can't you do it?' I said.

'Two reasons. One, they know me – I'm hot. Two, you have to earn your stripes.'

'But I don't want any stripes.'

'You're now part of the crew, part of the fellowship. Think

of this as a kind of initiation. Doing something positive for our Regime.'

'I don't want to shoot anyone, honestly I don't.'

'Tough,' he said, returning to the intimidating Big Man I saw in my sleep. 'You're doing it. End of.' He slapped my chest with the back of his hand. 'You're either with me or against me, and if you're against me the consequences are massive. Think of all the things I've done for you, Charlie Law. Your shed. Your mummy's medicine. I even let you nick my apples.'

He looked at me as if his eyes were bullets.

'Tell me, who else will get that medicine for your mum? She'll be the one who might suffer the most out of all this.' He put his giant hand on my chin and squeezed my cheeks together. Tight. Sore. 'I'd think about that before you make your decision.'

'But …'

'And you want to see that little scrawny pal of yours again, don't you?'

'Pav?'

'That's the one. He's Old Country. You wouldn't want them to find him, would you? Christ, the things they would do to that pretty mother of his. So if you want to keep things safe your end, you'll listen to me.'

'What if I get caught?' I said, not recognising my own voice.

'Use this and you won't.' His hand released my chin and he tapped my head yet again. Only harder this time.

My throat lump was about to explode, about to let the rivers flow.

Don't cry. Keep the taps off.

'Please don't make me do it.'

'Let's put it this way, Law. It's them who are making you do this, not me. And let's put it another way: in my town you're either loyal or you're not loyal, and if you're not loyal then what good are you to anyone? Know what I mean?'

'But ...'

'Just ask Norman and those other two bozos who beat up your Old Country buddy. Ask yourself if they were loyal.'

My world spun, but I could hardly make it out due to the blanket of water covering my eyes.

The Big Man looked thoughtfully into the sky.

'What I'm offering is a take it or *take* it deal.' Not one tear fell. I held it in. I didn't want to give The Big Man the satisfaction. The bully must NEVER win and all that jazz. 'I guarantee you'll feel much better about it afterwards; you'll feel like a man, like you've done something important, something to be proud of. You'll have given something back to Little Town.'

'I can't even use a gun; what if I miss?'

'I saw you shoot down the coal mine. You can handle it.

The target's easy to hit. Get yourself down behind a boulder, steady aim, steady hand, steady fire. More importantly, steady head. You'll do it, no bother.'

'When?' I asked.

'Next week.'

'Next week?'

'One week from today,' The Big Man said.

'Next Tuesday?'

'Exactly. Next Tuesday afternoon. Two o'clock on the button.'

'What, I just come back here then and do it?'

'Don't be a tosspot, Law. Remember to use the head, son. At *all times*.' The Big Man took out a pen and a piece of paper from his inside pocket. He scribbled something. Handed me the note. 'This is where and when we meet, after. Don't be late, don't make me come looking for you and don't mess me about on this, OK?'

'OK,' I said.

'Remember that medicine for your mummy, and your Old Country buddy.'

'I will.'

'Right, hop on and I'll drop you off.'

I hopped on.

I didn't enjoy the return trip. I didn't enjoy being so close to The Big Man, having my hands around his waist, having my face inches from his back. His metal was there, above his bum, no more than a swipe away. I could have done it; I could have done to him what he wanted me to do to Pav's sister. Reach. Swipe. Fire. Done. No aim required. The only thing that stopped me was that his bike would fall and I'd end up with a broken something. Or worse, the metal might not have been loaded. Then I'm sure I'd have ended up with a broken limb.

Something else stopped me: I wasn't a cold-blooded killer.

I needed to see Pav. I was worried. I didn't know whether I should tell him about The Big Man's plans.

It was agony not knowing what to do.

28
A Message

After The Big Man dropped me off I went straight to Pav's house. His mum answered; she swung the door open and waited. Waited for me to say something first, stared at my bruised eye; she didn't tut outwardly, but that's what she wanted to do, I'd bet. She'd lost weight since the last time I saw her. The daggers she gave me could have punctured lungs. No more nice smiles and warm gestures. Who did she think I was? Could she see through me? Did she know I had a mission to shoot her daughter? A mission to save her son? And maybe even her?

'Hello, Mrs Duda, is Pav in?'

There was a pause.

No *Hello, Charlie.*

No *Come away in, son.*

Nothing.

Just two piercing eyes. Nightmare stuff. My legs jiggled inside my trousers.

'Is Pav in?' I said again. Mrs Duda swallowed her saliva. Perhaps I should have brought a present – grapes or a book. No, not a book. Some apples?

The seconds seemed like minutes. It wasn't a lingo thing. Mrs Duda knew perfectly well what I wanted. Maybe she thought that I was just like the rest of the Little Towners. Maybe she blamed me for not protecting her son better at school. No point in asking again. I turned to leave. My left leg was about to make its move when the door swung open. Mrs Duda shifted her body and allowed me to walk past.

'In there,' she said, nodding to the living room door, which was closed. I could hear the faint sound of the telly from the other side. Their house was exactly the same as ours. Well, almost. Ours smelt different. Very different. The smell in Pav's house smashed me in the face as soon as Mrs Duda let me in. It was a combined mix of fustiness, dampness and cabbage. An Old Country speciality? It was exciting and scary to be in Pav's house for the first time. I think he was embarrassed about inviting me in. I can understand why.

'Maybe you make him smile, Charlie,' she whispered.

'I'll try,' I said.

'He not happy.'

'I know.'

'He want go back.'

'To school?'

'To Old Country.'

'Old Country? Why?'

'You talk with him, you see,' she said.

Pav obviously heard us chatting in the hallway and shouted something in his lingo to his mum, who shouted something in return. We did lots of shouting through doors in our block.

'Go, go,' Mrs Duda said, ushering me in.

Pav was lying spreadeagle on the couch, a minging brown velvety couch that looked as though it had taken the weight of an army over the years. An army who'd also trampled over the carpet, which made it appear bare in places. So much so that leather bits were splattered on the floor where carpet should have been. A star-shaped mirror hung over the fireplace. Pav was watching an old telly. I'm not sure it had a remote. There was a pink haze over the image. It didn't seem to bother him; he just lay there glued to the screen. He must have thought I was his mum.

'All right, Pav?' I said.

'Charlie, what you do here?'

Pav's face was still bruised and swollen. There was still crusty blood on his top lip and right eye. He winced when he sat up. Boots to the ribs and jabs to the kidneys will do that. My shiner was nothing in comparison. I wanted to tell him the news. To share with him the craziness of it. For him to help me get out of the situation. For us to work it out together. I wanted him to know that I held his destiny in the palm of my hand. I said nothing.

'What happen your face?' Pav asked.

'Oh, this,' I said, touching the bruise. 'I only slipped in the shed, didn't I? Banged it off the desk. Idiot.' I could tell Pav didn't believe me.

'Idiot numpty,' he said. 'Why you here?'

'I just popped in to see if you were OK.'

'I OK. I OK,' he said.

'You haven't been at school since the incident last week,' I said.

If I'd been a better mate I'd have brought some work home from school so he wouldn't be playing catch-up when he returned. Saying that, he'd have probably launched it at me or out the window.

'I no go back.'

'Maybe next week,' I said.

'I never return, Charlie.'

'To school?'

'Yes. I no go back.'

'You can't just not return, Pav.'

'I do what I want. I no go back.'

'But Max and Bones –' I almost told him that The Big Man had intervened – 'haven't been at school since it happened.'

'I don't care of Max and Bones. School shit for me.' Pav lay back down on the couch and put his eyes on the screen in front of him. I was half thinking of asking him what he was watching, but I couldn't give two hoots.

I took a chunk of air into my lungs.

'It's been sorted, Pav. Max and Bones, they've been sorted,' I said.

'What mean sorted?'

'Taken care of, been dealt with.'

'You mean they dead?' Pav said.

'What? No. No, Pav. I didn't say that. I'd say they were probably given a good talking-to, a verbal warning. Know what I mean? Not dead. I didn't say dead. I didn't mean dead.'

'If not dead I no care.'

'At least they won't be bothering you again,' I said. 'They won't be giving you any more shit at school.'

'Not so true,' Pav said, reaching around to his back pocket and pulling out a white piece of paper. He held it up to me. 'Take.'

I snatched the paper from his hand.

'What is this?' I asked, opening up the four small square folds.

'Read.'

I read the note.

Twice.

The sick litany of abuse and threats didn't get any better the second time around. It made my bones boil.

'It come few days ago.'

'From who?'

'We not know.'

'Are you sure you've no idea who sent this, Pav?'

'No idea.'

'Has your mum or dad read this?'

'No. Just me.'

'Do you not think they should?'

'No. This won't happen, Charlie.'

'But this is ...' I held the note up towards Pav.

'Our life in Little Town,' he said.

'No, I mean, it's dangerous. Maybe you could give it to someone in a position of authority?' I said.

Pav laughed, scrunched up his face and rubbed his ribs. 'You funny guy, Charlie. Yes, let's take to police here,' he said sarcastically.

'Do you think this was Max and Bones?' I said, holding aloft the note.

'I not know; could be.'

'I don't think so, Pav. Too advanced for those two.' I laughed, trying to lighten the mood. Pav kept it gloomy. 'I mean, the level of words in it is way too advanced and the spelling is spot on, so probably not them,' I said. 'Any ideas?'

'Maybe The Big Man. Maybe Norman. Everybody hate people like us, so could be anyone. Could be Old Country patrol.' Pav's eyes fixed on mine.

'It wasn't me, Pav. Do you think it was me?'

'No.'

'Jeez, for a minute I thought that you thought that ...'

'You good guy, Charlie. I know you.'

'I don't think it was The Big Man; he likes you.'

Pav shook his head and sniggered.

'He hate all things Old Country.'

I was going to say *Not true* but thought better of it.

'Want me to hang on to it?' I said, holding the note up. 'I could do some detective work, try to see who did it.'

'What is point?'

'Well ...' I didn't really have a point.

'I want get hell out of Little Town, so no point.'

'Get out? Where?'

'I not yet know.'

'But out of Little Town is dangerous, Pav.'

'For you. Not me. This place dangerous for me.'

'What about your mum and dad?'

'They stay here; they say same as you.'

'What about ... ?' It was on the tip of my tongue to say something about his sister, how I'd seen her, how she could maybe help him, make all their lives a lot better here, but Pav beat me to it.

'They want stay for my sister. They think she can help them in Little Town.'

'Have they been talking to her?'

'No, but Mum want to find her. They speak about all time. All day. Sister. Sister. Sister. My nut is done, Charlie.'

'And you? Do you want to meet with her again?'

'I say she still bastard like she was in Old Country. I want go different place. Far away from here.'

Pav stared at the floor, ran his hands through his growing, unwashed hair, put them over his face like he was trying to hold in a huge sneeze. They stayed on his face for ages. His shoulders went up and down. His knees shook. He sniffed loudly. Then this huge howl came. Just one. His shoulders began to move quicker. Galloping pace. If you didn't know better you'd have thought he was suffering a shivering spell. I didn't know what to do. If I should sit next to him, put my arm around his shaking bones, pull him close and tightly hug the life out of him. I didn't know what the hell's fire to do. I froze. I did nothing. I didn't even have a hanky in my pocket. Once more I read the note that he'd given me. I folded up the squares and put it back in my pocket. Then I took the bull by the horns.

'It'll be OK, Pav.'

'No, it not.' He sounded like a baby.

'Come on, little man. It will get better soon, you'll see.'

'I no see.'

I put one hand on his back. His sniffs were louder, harder.

'Everything will blow over. Give it a week or so.'

'I want leave, Charlie. I hate here.'

'Life's slowly getting better; the school will be rebuilt soon and some of the shops are reopening, so there'll be food. Proper food.'

'No more school. No more Little Town. I go now.'

My thoughts shifted to Pav's mum. Was she listening? Did she know her son was in bits? Was this normal behaviour? Everyday stuff? Was Pav having some sort of breakdown? What does someone having a breakdown even look like?

'It'll be OK, Pav. Honestly. If we stick together it'll be OK,' I said.

'It never be OK here.'

'I'll look after you, Pav. Promise I will.'

Pav looked up at me. His baby blue blinders were surrounded by an explosion of red spiderwebs. I felt a wave of guilt wash over me for knowing what I knew. Knowing what I was capable of doing. Knowing that The Big Man really did have me by the short and curlies.

'No!' He was deadly serious.

'No?'

'You need look after you, Charlie. This is dodgy place.'

'But we're mates,' I said.

'You must to forget me.'

'Don't be …' I was about to say stupid, but I stopped myself, knowing how much Pav hated to be called stupid. And that's one thing he wasn't.

'I serious, Charlie. Forget all.'

'Don't talk like that, Pav.'

'It what I want.'

'What about school?'

'I say before. I no go there again.'

'What about the shed, our shed; can we keep going there?'

'You go, Charlie. I leave.'

'But you can't just leave.'

'I can to leave.' Pav thudded himself in the chest. Each word got its own beat.

I stood up, removed the note yet again and held it out.

'What about this? Want me to see if anyone knows anything?'

'You keep. I no care.'

Pav smiled. He held out his hand for me to take it. Our hands met. Both our hands were so clammy that they slipped as we went up and down two times.

'Good to meet, Charlie. You top guy, no numpty or dick-head person.'

'Erm … thanks, Pav,' I said.

He shouted something in his lingo and before you could say *See you later* the door was swung open and his mum was waiting to escort me out. It was like I had been in a dream as

I headed for the front door. A bad dream. Was I really saying goodbye to Pav?

When I went into my room I sat on the bed and played the bad dream over and over in my mind. But it wasn't a dream because I still had Pav's note buried deep in my pocket. I read it another time. Unbelievable. I never wanted to read that note again, those awful threats. I needed to erase it from my memory. Tell no one about its contents, and I mean NO ONE. The Big Man's note was in my other pocket. I didn't need to read that again either.

I'd give Pav a few days before seeing if he'd settled down any. My thinking was that once all the bruises had disappeared he would. I was glad I didn't mention anything about The Big Man's plan. That might have sent him over the edge. He'd have joined me in peeking over it, at the least.

The following day, Wednesday, I awoke from a rubbish sleep and wished I'd told Pav everything. Grassed. Ratted. Squealed. I think Pav could have done something to help me; he was the only chance left.

I didn't want to get out of bed, but school awaited me. I couldn't face it. I hated taking days off, but really, I couldn't face it.

29
New Sun

'Good God in heaven, Charlie.' Mercy Lewis's mouth nearly hit the deck of the bus. Her hand rose up to the gap she'd left. 'Don't tell me that was Max and Bones as well?'

Mum didn't let me stay at home on the Wednesday – and, as much as I didn't have the stomach for it, it was back to school. By the Wednesday morning the shiner had gone down a bit, yet it was still eye-catching.

'No, Mercy, it wasn't Max and Bones.'

'Did someone smack you?'

'No.'

'It looks as if someone smacked you, Charlie.'

'No one smacked me, Mercy. I slipped in my shed and fell into a table. No big deal,' I said.

'You slipped in your shed?'

'Crazy, isn't it?'

'Who slips in a shed?' I could tell that she wasn't buying it.

'Well, me for a start. Totally stupid thing to do, eh?'

'Very.'

'Is it really noticeable?' I asked.

'Is that a trick question, Charlie?'

'No, I was just –'

'How's Pav?'

I was glad of the deflection. But I couldn't tell her the truth – that Pav was broken and desperate to escape our horrible town.

'Still majorly peed off about what happened to him.'

'I'd say he is.'

'And he's still a bit battered and bruised.'

'Poor thing,' she said.

'I can't believe those two eejits got away with it.'

'Don't worry, Mercy. They didn't,' I said.

This was a case of the tongue wagging before the brain engaged. Of course Mercy picked up on my big-mouth moment.

'What do you mean?' She sat herself upright in her seat. 'Has something happened to them? Did they get suspended or anything like that? I haven't seen them in school.'

'No … I mean … they probably won't get away with it. I think Pav's parents have been on to the school and they've said that they're going to do something about it,' I lied.

'I bet the school'll probably side with Max and Bones,' Mercy said.

'You think?'

'Well, it's obvious, isn't it?'

'I don't know. Is it?'

'Two reasons why …'

'Which are?'

'One, Pav is Old Country, and two, his mum and dad are Old Country,' Mercy said.

I looked at the rubble outside the window. 'Yeah, you might be right.'

'People here are beginning to really hate Old Country folk, Charlie.'

'You think?' I said.

'Haven't you noticed?'

'It's hard *not* to notice, Mercy.'

'And what about you?' she asked.

'What about me?'

'Do you hate them?'

'Old Country people?'

'Yes. Do you hate them, Charlie?'

It was an important question. A vital one. I thought hard about it. In the depths of my innards I had good cause to hate them. Mum and Dad had good cause too. Even Max and Bones had cause. The blasted buildings that surrounded us had their cause too. Time to play the cards close to my chest.

'Do you hate them, Mercy?' I asked.

'Ah, I see what you're doing, Charlie Law. Answering a question with a question. Very clever. Very clever indeed.'

'Well, do you?' I asked.

Mercy turned away to gaze out of her window. Thinking time.

'It's complicated, Charlie. But the short answer is, no, I don't. I think it's counterproductive to hate. It blurs the real issues and distorts an understanding of the possibility of progress.' Last year Mercy was in the school debating team. She was its youngest member. Always a straight-A student. Some of us needed to scrap like dogs to get As, but for others, like Mercy Lewis, it was a breeze.

'Which are?' I asked.

'Which are what?'

'The real issues?'

'Well, people have got to ask themselves if the life they had under the Regime was better for them than the one they could have in the future under Old Country rule. Say, in five years' time.'

'Look around you, Mercy. What do you think?'

'Yes, Charlie, but one day all this rubble will be swept away to reveal some kind of future. What future did we have under the old Regime? Tell me that, eh?'

'You call this a future?' I said, pointing out at the piles of brick hills.

'Sometimes you have to take major steps backwards in order to take a giant leap forward.'

'This is a leap forward for you, Mercy? This is progress?'

Mercy placed her bag on her lap, slapped her two hands on it and shook her head as if she was disappointed in me.

'Charlie,' she said, in her teacher voice. This was a girl destined for a job that required tons of speaking.

'Mercy.'

'What are we doing?'

'When?'

'Now, what are we doing now?'

'Erm … talking?'

'Exactly, Charlie.'

'And?'

'And what are we *talking* about?'

'Life. Old Country haters. Pav. Max and Bones. I don't know. You tell me, Mercy. What are we talking about?'

'We're talking about politics.'

'Oh, is that what you call it?'

'We're basically talking about understanding our life, our surroundings, our environment.' She indicated towards the world outside the window. 'And what our place in all this means to us.'

'Are we?'

'Yes, we are.'

'OK, I'll take your word for it then.'

She slapped her two hands down on the bag.

'And *where* are we?' she said.

'Eh, hello, we're on the school bus. At least I think we are.'

'Right. So here we are on the school bus, which is a public place, right?'

'Right.'

'And we're having a chat about politics and other stuff, agreed?'

'Agreed,' I said.

'Let me ask you something then, Charlie,' she said.

'Go ahead, Mercy.'

'Could we ever do that under the old Regime?' I tightened my lips. 'Think about it, could we? It was only a few months ago. Could we sit on a bus and chat openly about how good or bad life was?'

'I guess not, no.'

'No guessing required. We categorically couldn't.'

'OK, we couldn't then.'

'And why was that?'

'Too dangerous, maybe,' I said.

'Far too dangerous, Charlie. Far too dangerous. For you. For your parents. For people who knew you. Everyone was scared out of their wits to open their mouth in case someone's lugs heard something they didn't like and ran off to blabber it to the Regime or their Rascal lackeys. We spent our time in silence or looking over our shoulders.'

'I know, Mercy. I was there.'

'Yes, you *were* there, you experienced it. You lived it.'

'Don't remind me.'

'But now look at us sitting here chatting about things we actually decided to chat about. It's great, isn't it?'

'Yeah, terrific,' I said.

Sorry, Mercy, but I don't remember ever getting a black eye from the Regime or any Rascal, or being gubbed in the stomach for the deadly crime of WALKING. I don't remember that bit at all. She didn't need to know any of this.

'So there you have it.' Mercy rested her hands on her bag like she was a hotshot lawyer (she probably would be one day ... maybe we could be partners). Case closed.

'There you have what?' I said.

'Progress.'

'Progress?'

'We are the embodiment of Little Town's progression in action, Charlie.'

For the rest of the journey I thought about what Mercy had said. I tried to see her point of view, I really did. It seemed like she was beginning to enjoy our new Old Country existence. Maybe I was down to shoot the wrong person? Erin F would've had a fit if she'd been part of this chat.

When the bus pulled into school Mercy turned to me and said, 'Have a nice day, Charlie, and do tell Pav that I said hello and that I'm thinking about him.'

'Will do, Mercy. Will do.'

'I really am, you know,' she said, then disappeared into the crowd.

Ever since Pav got done for, it seemed that folk were dropping off the face of the earth.

Pav had holed himself up and hadn't returned to school. And after our chat the day of The Big Man's plan, I doubted he would ever return.

Erin F hadn't been to school for almost a week. To say I was worried was an understatement. My body shuddered at the thought of her being face down in a ditch somewhere. I couldn't get her out of my mind. What's new?

Max and Bones hadn't been to school since using Pav as a human trampoline. I didn't want to think about how Norman or The Big Man had sorted them.

Then Norman hadn't surfaced for days. I really feared for Norman. The Big Man now considered him to be a rat. I feared big time for him.

30
Guns

Time gathered apace. Everything sped up, pushing me towards the day. D-Day. I didn't know what the D in D-Day meant though. My D meant death. My D-Day was next Tuesday. Next Tuesday! The words reverberated around my head.

I couldn't think about much else. All I could do was plan, imagine, visualise and persuade myself that this was for the best. At times I'd catch a glimpse of my bruised face and be convinced that this was the right thing to do. That if I could just eliminate a rank, a captain, then they'd get the message that Little Town wouldn't be taking this occupation lying down. Old Country couldn't throw their weight around willy-nilly without there being consequences. Punishment.

I had to do it.

All I needed to do was make friends with the thing. Get better acquainted.

On the Thursday evening I went to the shed, making sure no one was on my tail or watching me. I took it out of its hiding place and carefully removed the bullets – one by one. I held it outstretched for as long as I could. Twenty-two seconds. My arm ached. I sat back in one of the chairs for a breather and thought about my next move, how I'd do it. I held it up again, looked through the aimer. Aimed. Licked my lips. Squeezed the trigger. You have to pull really hard. It's definitely not like the movies where it's all bang-bang-bang stuff. You'd need a finger of granite to do that. I'd have to practise the routine of aim, squeeze and fire. It needed to be rapid. Lightning speed. No hovering about to admire the work afterwards.

There in the shed I tried out a few technical moves. I bent down behind one of the chairs, jumped up: pulled the trigger. I walked three paces, swivelled sharply: pulled the trigger. I lay face down, dived up: pulled the trigger. It became more comfortable, less heavy. I practised standing up, kneeling down and lying in the sniper position. The Big Man suggested kneeling down; it'd be easier to make a sprint for it.

After I replaced the bullets and fed it under the floor-boards I didn't want to touch it again. My mouth became dry.

I didn't want to do it.

But,
I needed to do it.
Mum needed me to do it.
Pav needed me to do it.
The Big Man was making me do it.
But,
I didn't want to do it.

31
War

I was glad when Friday arrived. School was rough. Everyone gawking at my eye. Asking awkward questions about Bones, Max, Pav and Erin F. Such a drag. In reality I wasn't *glad* about anything. I was wandering around in a daze, thinking: this time next week I'll have blood on my hands, death on my soul. Those guns sat heavily on my shoulders, weighing me down with all their firepower. The shed was the only place I could go to think. The only place that could provide sanctuary. That's where I went after school.

'Just passing and thought I'd pop in.' I almost hit the shed roof with terror when I opened the door and saw The Big Man perched on the chair, staring ahead at me. 'See how you were doing; see how the plans were coming along …'

'Erm … well …'

'See if you still remembered our little deal, what to do and whatnot.'

'Yeah, yeah,' I said all enthusiastically because I didn't want him to know that I was so consumed by fear. That it was all I could think about.

'Can't have you running scared on me, can I?' he said.

'No … no way.'

'Your mate's family don't want any heat on them, do they now?'

'Erm … don't think so, Big Man.'

'Don't think so? Have you any idea what would happen to them if those Old Country bastards knew refugees were hiding guns in their garden? Some of their own turning on them? Have you a scintilla of an idea what would happen, Charlie?'

'Erm … I think that –'

'And imagine if some of our boys found out that info as well.' The Big Man licked his lips, looked up. 'She's a fine-looking woman, that Duda woman. Shame!'

'They're not the ones hiding the guns,' I said.

The Big Man laughed. I could hear the phlegm rattling in his big chest.

If anyone came for Pav and his fine-looking mum and brainbox dad, would I tell them that the shed was mine? That I was the one hiding the guns? Would I admit that to Old Country troops? Would it matter if they believed me or not?

'I'd start thinking about it if I were you. Get your head in the game.'

'Right.'

'Start thinking about the most unimaginable torture techniques known to civilisation.'

'Well … OK.'

'Have you any idea what a starved and ravished rat will do to an exposed arsehole?'

'I hadn't really thought about it, Big Man,' I said.

'Don't get smart, Charlie. This shit is serious. All it will take is a little word in some Old Country bastard's shell and they'll be round here in blink time. All heavy-handed and tooled up. They won't care if it wasn't the Dudas keeping guns, Charlie. There's nothing those bastards like more than a traitor. Everyone saves the worst for traitors. That's what I'm talking about … so are we clear?'

I didn't know how to reply because I didn't know what we were being *clear* about. Was he threatening me or Pav? Don't be stupid, Charlie, of course he was.

'I said *are we clear*?'

'Yes, we're clear.'

'Good. I know I can count on you, Charlie. You've got something the others never had.' He tapped his temple with his finger, like he'd done previously. 'That's why they didn't make it.'

DIDN'T MAKE WHAT?

I was too afraid to ask, not because I was interested in the plight of his rascal cronies, but in case he informed me that it was now just me and him against Old Country. I thought about what Mercy had said on the bus, about not looking over my shoulder any longer and how things could be in the future. I didn't want to return to the days of curfews, searches and patrols. I didn't want to return to the ineffectual Regime and bullying Rascals. I wanted to walk freely, to study, to learn, to work and be who I wanted to be within the law. I wanted to have mates from inside the border and from outside the border. I also wanted Erin F, but that was a different issue altogether.

If it were just me and The Big Man then we'd be fooked, as Pav would say.

'How's your mum, by the way?'

'OK, good.'

'Still on these?' he said, pulling out a brown paper bag from inside his leather jacket. He shook the bag. 'I'd say all this debris dust doesn't help with her breathing.'

'It doesn't, no.'

He reached inside the bag, took out an inhaler and waved it at me.

'She must be going through these like they're water now, eh?'

'Erm …'

'Pity that chemist is still not operating.'

I kept my eyes on the bag. It was bulging; must have been at least six months' supply in there, enough to see her through to the birth of a new chemist. Things were happening in Little Town; shops were slowly getting fixed and services were being resumed. Even my dad said so. Although I'd know it was fully repaired when my stomach didn't rumble as often.

I switched between looking at The Big Man's hand, the bag and his eyes. He kept his eyes on mine, twiddling the little plastic inhaler in his fingers.

'So, Charlie, do we have a deal?'

I didn't blink.

'Do we understand one another?'

I didn't speak.

My head nodded instead.

'We're on?' he said.

I nodded again.

'I want to hear you say it.'

He glanced at the inhaler and the brown bag.

'Be a shame to burn all this … I want to hear you say it.'

My mouth was dry. I opened it.

'We're on,' I whispered.

'Sorry, can't hear you, Charlie. Speak up a bit.'

'We're on,' I said.

'Sure about that?'

'Yes. Sure I'm sure.'

'Excellent!' he said, rising from the chair. He walked towards me and put his face close to mine. Close enough to kiss. 'Rats and arseholes, Charlie. Rats and arseholes. Not a good combination, know what I mean?'

'Think so.'

'Good, so you enjoy the weekend and I'll see you Tuesday.'

I glanced at the bag.

'And you'll get this inhaler swag when the job's done, OK?'

'Can I just have one now though, Big Man?'

'When it's done. When it's done.' He patted me on the shoulder and left the shed.

I flopped down in the chair The Big Man had vacated. It was still hot. I gritted my teeth and tried everything to hold in my tears. I sat in silence. Wished that I'd never laid eyes on Pav. That I didn't live in Little Town. That I hadn't asked Norman to get some crap chairs. That I was not here. That I could just escape. Maybe escape with Pav.

I stared at the floorboard.

I guess I needed some practice.

32
Kissed

I hardly slept. On the Monday morning I felt exhausted. All I wanted to do was curl up, not think about the future and try to get some sleep. All weekend I thought about possibilities of escape: feigning illness, wandering the streets or running away. To where though? Anyway, the streets were still off limits. And that would do nothing to help Pav's family or my mum's breathing.

'Charlie, get up, you're going to be late,' Mum whispered. Each day her voice was losing its penetrating power.

I wasn't going to be late. I was never late. Mum just wanted those who lived in the same house as her not to be getting under her feet. I knew her game by this stage. There wasn't a hope in hell that I'd ever be allowed to stay off again. Maybe if my head had been dangling from a slither of ligament I would be allowed to stay in bed. But my black eye had cleared up so there was no chance. I had to get up, shake life into myself and get on with it. Leave the thoughts of the weekend behind. Put that head in a drawer for a few hours.

I placed Pav's note and The Big Man's note into my Moleskine, left without saying goodbye.

I thought people were staring at me, that they somehow knew what I was about to do. What I was about to become. Who I really was. I convinced myself they were all whispering behind my back; someone would definitely grass me up, go running to Old Country troops and blurt out what they'd heard. Their reward was to watch me being frogmarched out of school … never to return … never to be seen again.

Stop being paranoid. No one knows jack!

Mercy Lewis continued to ask about Pav; it made me slightly jealous that someone wasn't showing the same level of concern about me. Maybe if I lived in a place where they spoke a different lingo, someone would see the pain in my face and the isolation in my heart too and take pity on me. Or just plain fancy me.

Dream on, Charlie.

There's always a positive in a negative. Bones and Max seemed like a bad memory, as their seats on the bus were now filled with other bums. I didn't mention to anyone what had happened to Bones and Max, or what I thought had happened to them. I'd a fair idea.

When the bus dropped us off at school, people still mingled and spoke about very little, shouted into each other's faces, made wild gestures. That's school for you. The empty chairs in the classrooms remained empty. Those people weren't coming back. Nothing changed.

Well, not quite.

I spied her in the crowd. That hair. That stance. That movement of her head. I saw her. And she knew it because she spied me too. That awkwardness. That grimace. That foot shuffle. It was all I could offer. Our eyes met, and when I say met I mean we locked them together for more than a few seconds. Five, easy. After the look she was on the hoof, heading my way. Towards me. She wasn't sheep-walking nor striding either. She walked slower. Where had she been? Her hair appeared injured; it didn't have the same fullness about it. But still cracking nevertheless. Thankfully she couldn't see the car crash that was occurring inside my body, things piling up on top of each other, everything careering out of control. Sheer carnage. My face was the same as someone who'd just seen a ghost. Her mouth shifted position. As she got closer to me, a tiny unsure smile appeared on her face. I followed her lead. I sucked in as much oxygen as my lungs could take. This was it. Any worry I had for her evaporated in that instant. I was delighted that she wasn't lying face down in some manky ditch somewhere. I really was.

Keep cool, my old son. Stand up straight, shoulders back.

'Hi, Charlie,' Erin F said.

'Hi, Erin F,' I said, trying to sound cool and indifferent. I sounded more like a doe-eyed dope though.

'Sorry I missed you in school last week.'

What? She missed me? Like actually missed me?

'Was everything OK, Erin F?'

'Yes, well …'

SHE missed ME!

'I was worried when you didn't show up,' I said.

'Aw, that's nice, Charlie. Really it is.' Her hand brushed my wrist as if I needed consoling. I thought my throat was going to burst out of my mouth and scud Erin F full force in the kisser.

'I thought something terrible had happened to you,' I said.

'You did?'

'Yes.'

'That's sweet.'

'I thought that maybe Old Country nabbed you or something like that.'

Erin F chuckled. 'No, it wasn't quite like that. I wish it had been; that sounds exciting.'

'I even came to look for you, you know.'

'Really?' Her eyes widened. *Wow* was the only word. She was impressed with my brave man action.

'Yes, but they stopped me on the hill and … and … anyway, that's boring now. How are –'

'I was in hospital, Charlie. With Mum. She was in a bad way last week and badly needed hospital treatment.'

'What, like proper hospital in Little Town?'

'Yes, proper hospital, but far away from Little Town. In Old Country actually. They were the ones who took us there.'

'Old Country did?'

Erin F's mum was lucky to have avoided treatment in Little Town hospital, which was a health hazard itself.

'So, wait,' I said. 'You went to Old Country last week. To hospital in Old Country?'

'Yes, in a helicopter.'

'No way, an actual helicopter?'

'They're massive inside, not what you'd think,' Erin F said.

'God, sorry to hear that, Erin F.'

'Don't be.'

'I hope she's going to be OK.'

Erin F squeezed her lips tightly together, as if she didn't know how to answer. I'd seen that look in class as well. Even though it was a travesty for humanity that Erin F's mum had been sick enough for an actual helicopter hospital visit, I was delighted inside because it meant that Erin F hadn't been snatched off the street. Progress.

'She is going to be OK, isn't she?'

'I hope so, Charlie. I really hope so.'

'I hope so too, Erin F.'

'I'd still like to visit that shed of yours, you know.'

'Anytime you want. It would be great to show you it. You'd think it was brilliant.'

'I'm sure I would.'

Erin F blew her nose with a real hanky, similar to the one Mercy Lewis gave Pav. I shifted my bag from shoulder to shoulder. Erin F coughed. Then again, harder.

Say something! Don't just stand there like a fart in a trance.

'It was good of Old Country to allow you to use their hospital.'

NOT THAT!

'Amazing.'

'What was it like?'

'Different … clean … nice.'

'If they had a decent hospital here, not like the manky one we have now, your mum wouldn't need to travel,' I said.

'I heard that they might build a brand spanking new one here,' she said.

'Really?'

'Apparently.'

'God, that would be great.'

Erin F smiled. I returned it. We shared a raised eyebrow. The bell rang to save an awkward moment.

'I'd better get going, Charlie. Double geography. I've missed a lot already.'

'Yeah, double Classics for me.'

'I best rush.'

'OK, see you later,' I said. 'Maybe at break?'

'Good plan.'

Erin F went to go, but before she did she made a little ballet dance move to pivot back to me. I smelt her. Her fresh woman smell shot up my nose.

'Happy birthday,' she said.

'It's this Saturday,' I said.

'Well, happy birthday for this Saturday then.'

Then came the best thing that had happened to me in my life so far, and that's no exaggeration: Erin F leaned up and pecked me on the cheek. Not a wet, sloppy one, but a real, genuine kiss. Pucker-lipped. The best moment ever.

'Have a good morning, Charlie,' she said.

'You too, Erin F.' At least I think that's what I said.

You hear about those crazy people not wanting to wash their hands or face after someone kisses them; well, I'd just joined their ranks. I was hovering on cloud nine. No, cloud ninety-nine. The monster didn't like being that high up though. There's always someone to put a damper on life's delights.

Don't forget you have a job to do, Charlie. Don't forget what happened on Friday. Don't forget about your responsibilities. Remember The Big Man? Remember rats and arseholes?

I dropped a few clouds.

33
Bang! Bang!

On the bus home I felt my cheek, stroked the part where her lips had touched me. God, what a sensation. I stood up to get off near the bottom of the hill.

'This isn't your stop, Charlie,' Mercy Lewis said.

'I know, I've just –'

'Where are you going?' She caught me off guard. I didn't know what to say. There was no reason for anyone to get off the bus at the bottom of the hill. All the shops were damaged; it was seen as the injured part of town. Old Country troops driving up and down, day and night. I had no need to be there.

'I'm going to see if the chemist is open,' I said.

'Charlie, you know the chemist isn't open, so …'

'No, I mean, I'm going to see when it will reopen.'

Mercy wasn't buying it. Her eyes tightened.

'You're up to something, Charlie Law, I can tell,' she said, pointing her finger at me.

'I'm not, seriously.' I was going to say *promise* at the end, but then she'd have known for certain that I was up to something.

'Mmm, we'll see.'

Once off the bus, I made my way to the place, constantly looking over my shoulder in case any eyes were on me. Looking left and right to see if I was being followed. Keeping my ears open for the sound of the chugging vehicles. I could make out the sun glistening off some of the shops in the distance, meaning that new glass had been put in. Progress was being made. I picked up a stick, six inches long. Perfect size.

I arrived without anyone spying me. There I was again, huddled behind some boulders, out of sight, hidden. On my hunkers waiting until the chug sound arrived from the other side of the hill. A few cars drove over it, two buses – one from school and one with clean-up workers aboard. I put my school bag down at my feet and held on to the stick tightly.

MENTAL MEMO: ON THE DAY OF THE DEED MAKE SURE YOU'RE NOT CARRYING A BAG. PUT THE MERCH INSIDE A BACKPACK. EASIER TO RUN WITH THAT ON.

About seven cigarette butts surrounded my bag. Maybe a day old. Hours old? One by one I flicked them away with the stick.

I didn't check the time. My focus was too strong. I concentrated on being as still as concrete. I even tried not to blink and regulated my breathing. Deep breaths through the nose, slowly exhaling out of the mouth, helps the heart rate normalise itself. It didn't work; it was as if there was a massive bass drum beating away inside me. My hands were sweating so much I had to rub them dry on my thighs. I didn't look but I knew there was a palm mark on my trousers afterwards. I didn't dare look away.

Hunkered down waiting for the chug of the Old Country Patrol, nightmarish images flashed through my mind. Too nightmarish to even consider.

And then I heard it.

It stopped at the exact same place where they had slapped me around. Three of them got out. My breathing felt shallow. The drum inside got louder. *This is it, my old son. This is it. Just hold the nerve and do what you have to do.* The three of them huddled together. Far too close. I couldn't get a clear view. I held the thing tight, ready to lift it up to my eye level. Ready to make my move. A cigarette was lit. I saw the smoke rising from Captain Duda's lips. The two men held binoculars up to their faces. They began scanning. I ducked, just in case. They walked four, maybe five, paces away from the huddle. A gap appeared. Captain Duda was free. I could see her. As clear as day I could see her. She dragged on her cigarette. Make no mistake, this was definitely the same one who duffed me up, the same one who was at the park's entrance, the same blue eyes, the same blood as Pav had. The one The Big Man wanted gone.

I closed one eye and squeezed her into the line of vision with the other eye. I lifted up the thing shaking in my hand. I heard Mercy's voice saying, *You're up to something* Charlie *Law.* If only she knew. I heard, *Do it!* Captain Duda's head was squashed into my eye's line. Clear head shot. The two others started to walk back, dropping their binoculars around their necks. This was the moment. It had to be quick. It had to be now. Now? *NOW!*

My left hand was needed to steady the right. The stick wasn't even heavy. Imagine what the real thing would be like. Instead of a proper bang after the trigger had been pulled I voiced the sound. POP! Just one would do it. One pop and she'd fall like a wet sack of spuds. I'd be on the hoof before the other two noticed anything. I'd be on the back of The Big Man's bike before they even knew what direction it came from. Hugging him tightly. This would be easy street. A doddle. The hindrance was my shaking hands and sweating brow.

I watched them return to their vehicle and drive down the hill. I watched them turn right at The Big Tree. I stood and shook my legs back to life.

Captain Duda didn't realise how close she'd come. But she would.

I kept the stick in my hand until I was walking through the park; it reverted into being a stick again. As soon as I chucked it away the little monster piped up. *Think about this, Charlie. There's no going back if you do it. Think about your future. The chemist will be back in business soon.*

But what about Pav's family? I said to myself.

34
Alone Again

After my reconnaissance mission I went directly to the shed. I needed the peace, some place to take deep breaths. I needed a place to sit and think about Erin F's touch, to stroke my cheek. I needed to think about what I thought I knew about the two notes. What I'd discovered when I looked at them closely. I needed a place to go through pending events and practise my moves. Visualise my getaway. Mum could tell when I had something on my mind; to her my face was an open book, so it was vital to find a place where I could get all my fear out.

When I opened the shed door everything drained from me. It felt like being picked up and driven into a huge vice. All thoughts of my mission were sucked right out of me in a flash. The more I stared at what was facing me the tighter the vice twisted. The crushing was similar to being kicked senseless in the stomach; new fear replaced old fear. I couldn't bring myself to fully enter. The new fear forced me to stand at the door. I couldn't take my eyes off of it: a rope. A sleeping snake curled around the roof's jutting wood. The chair had been moved slightly underneath it.

The monster inside urged me to go in and touch it. Yank it down. Do a Tarzan on it. A greater power – terror – rooted me to the spot. My eyes watched it dangling. The looped part for the head to fit inside was expertly formed. He must have made that himself. If I wanted to pack it all in I wouldn't even know how to make a loop.

For a fleeting moment a shocking realisation entered my head, a thing that shamed me: it might be a lot easier to rub out Pav's sister if he wasn't here. He could be doing me a favour. There would be no need for any painful confrontation between us.

– *Why you kill sister?*
– *The Big Man made me do it, Pav.*
– *But this my sister.*
– *He said he was going to torture you and your family and make my mum suffer.*
– *This not good, Charlie.*
– *Sorry, what else could I have done?*
– *Come speak with me?*
– *He had me by the short and curlies, Pav.*

– *OK, but I still no happy.*

– *Sorry again. Want to look for some bees?*

– *OK.*

I was always having these worst-case-scenario thoughts. I felt shame about my friendship flaws with Pav. I mean, how can one mate not recognise when another mate is going through a trauma? In the course of a few days our shed had become a place of death. Death by rope and death by gun. My dream for a place of peace scorched.

I decided to wait in the shed for Pav to arrive. Wait until he came back to do whatever he was planning on doing. And when he returned I'd be there to save him. I took a deep breath and entered, sat on the chair directly underneath the noose. I didn't touch the rope; I didn't want my fingers on it. I left it floating in air.

When Pav returned I could tell he was surprised to see me sitting there, as if I'd just scuppered his master plan.

'Charlie, what you here?'

'Pav, what the hell is that thing hanging there for?' I said, pointing to the rope.

'It is rope.'

'I know it's a rope. What's it doing there, in here? In our shed?'

'I hang it,' he said.

'Pav, are you saying what I think you're saying?'

'What you saying?'

'I'm saying, why is that rope hanging in our shed?'

'You ask already.'

'So tell me.'

'Because I not want to do it in house.'

'So you thought it was better to do it here, knowing that I'd be the one to find you. I'd be the one to have to tell your parents?' I paced the shed. Ran my hand through my hair. 'Why didn't you talk to me? I could've helped.'

'Help with what?'

'This,' I said, pointing to the noose.

'You thinking … you thinking that I want …'

'What?'

'That I want put neck in that,' he said, pointing to the rope.

'Yes.'

'I no want to do that. You crazy guy, Charlie. You funny.'

'I don't find that funny at all. I almost had a heart attack when I saw it. I thought … I thought …' I couldn't get out what I wanted to say. I could feel the tears trying to ease themselves out of me. Did he not understand all the things I had going on in my head? His expression changed.

'I sorry, Charlie. But it was letter note.'

'The note you gave me?'

'Yes.'

'What's that got to do with this?' I said, pointing to the rope.

'It say we all hang in house.'

'I know. I read it, remember?'

'So I take rope from house and put here.'

Did he not realise that whoever sent that note could've quite easily brought their own rope?

'And you made a noose for them … why?'

Pav frowned. 'I want see –' He fell silent and shrugged. I guess stress makes everyone a bit loopy.

'I no want die, Charlie.'

'Me neither, Pav.'

'I no want die in Old Country Military.'

'Well, if you return there that might happen, Pav.' He glared at me. 'It might!'

'And I no want Little Town Rascals to take us away for beating and raping either.'

'I doubt that would happen, Pav.'

'But letter note say so.'

'It's just bullying, Pav. Nothing else.'

Pav paused.

Now wasn't the time to reveal my discovery about the notes; this was all about Pav.

'Maybe,' he said. 'I need much think about.'

'It might be best to do normal things again,' I said.

'What normal things?'

'Well, getting back to school would be a good start.' Pav didn't tut me away or swat my words back at me. 'You don't want to fall too far behind.'

'This what Mercy say too.'

'Mercy Lewis?' I said in my high-pitched voice.

'Yes.'

'When were you speaking to her, Pav?'

'She come to house for visit.'

'*Your* house?'

'Yes, Mum made Old Country tea.'

'Tea? For you and Mercy?' I asked.

What about you?

WHAT ABOUT ME?

'Yes, and Mum,' he said.

'What did Mercy want?'

'For say hello and see if bruises go away.'

'I take it you had a good chat with Mercy then?'

'She nice girl.'

'She *is* very nice. I think you two would –'

'She say no point thinking in past.'

'She has a point, Pav.'

'She say think about tomorrow.'

'Mercy is full of wise words.'

'She wiser lady, Charlie. She say our mind is powerful muscle.'

'You bet it is ...'

'She say my mind should be like balloon.'

'A balloon?'

'On broken string.'

Pav looked upwards, as though he was watching a balloon floating off in the sky.

'A balloon on a broken string, eh?' I took a few seconds to ponder this. I could see Mercy's point. 'That's deep, Pav. Do you know what she means by that?'

'She explain.'

'It's good to have your mind as a balloon, don't you think?'

'Flying up, up away. Here, there, everywhere.' Pav was in his own world.

'Did Mercy teach you that?'

'Yes, she teached.'

Perhaps Mercy was better at being Pav's teacher than I was.

'So you feel happier now? More optimistic about things?'

'I feel this.'

'So, Mercy Lewis came to visit you then,' I said, raising my eyebrow.

'She visit.'

'And do you like Mercy?'

'Shut trap, Charlie.'

'I think she likes you.'

'Don't be dickman.'

'She must do if she came to our block to see you.'

Pav's face was getting redder.

'Zip mouth. We pals, like you and me.'

'Yeah, pals who do the …' I smacked my lips three times. Pav leant over in his chair and gave me a belter of a dead arm.

It felt good to be back in the shed cracking jokes and extracting the urine. I had a warm feeling inside, until it returned:

My task.

The Big Man.

Captain Duda, Pav's sister.

Tell him. You can't hide it.

I wanted to tell him. A problem shared and all that! My mouth even opened to allow the words time and space to get out. But nothing. Just air and dread. Pav sensed something was wrong.

'You OK, Charlie?'

'Yes, yes. Just tired, I think. And hungry.'

See, I'm just Charlie Law, from Little Town. I'm not a Regime supporter. I'm not a Rascal. I'm not much of a fighter, unless you can fight with words on paper. I don't have enemies, even if they've invaded my country. I don't want to kill anyone. But there are two guns and a load of bullets in my shed, and tomorrow I'm going to shoot my best friend's sister right between her baby blue blinders ... which I didn't want to do. However, with Mum's breath on my mind and Pav's family's life, I knew there was no place for *didn't want* any longer. Time was fast running out. What my after-school spying mission told me was that I could do it. I could. Couldn't I?

'Maybe you go get food, Charlie,' Pav said.

'I think that's a good idea.'

35
Airwaves

That night – the night before my mission – Mum was in a bad way. Ever since the bombs came Dad had been saying that a new chemist would open up in no time, but still there was nothing. No questions were asked when I got those inhalers for Mum. But that supply had dried up and she was struggling. Dad rubbed her back, his newspaper untouched. The television was switched off. This was serious.

'Breathe, Maggie,' he said as he rubbed her back. 'Don't talk, sweetheart; just concentrate on taking short breaths.'

Every so often he pecked her on the side of the head. It was Dad's turn to have little red spiderweb lines in his eyes. I'd seen those eyes before. Dad was scared again. I thought back to us hiding under the duvet that night the bombs came, how the duvet seemed to protect us. How it was those bombs that brought us together. I guess the last place Mum wanted to be now was somewhere airless.

'It's going to be OK, Dad. Promise,' I told him.

'I hope you're right, son. I hope you're right.'

'I think I can get my hands on some inhaler medicine in the next couple of days.'

No time for doubts, Charlie. You've got to do this now.

It needed to be now.

'I don't think we can wait a couple of days, Charlie,' Dad said.

Mum's face was pale and sweaty; her coughing prevented her from talking. Her chest wheezed as the pains intensified.

'I think we need something *now*,' Dad said, his mouth shuddering. He kissed Mum again and rubbed her back.

'What about the hospital?' I said.

'Little Town hospital?' Dad said.

'Yes.'

'Your mum can't go anywhere in this state. If we get stopped at a checkpoint or by one of the patrols we could be there for hours. By the time we get there and by the time we're processed it could be too late. And there's no guarantee they'll have the right medicine anyway – they've got serious shortages, Charlie.'

'What about Old Country hospital?'

'Old Country hospital?'

'Yes, they can take Mum there in a helicopter.'

Dad looked at me like I was the biggest idiot in Little Town.

'It's too hard to organise something like that at short notice; she needs help fast. She needs help now.'

Any fool could tell that she needed help now. Here's the stupid thing: all she required was a few deep puffs of her inhaler. That would sort her out and get her back on her feet. Before she knew it she'd be nagging at me to do some menial chore.

I missed her nagging.

You know what you have to do, Charlie.

BUGGER IT!

There was little time to think or explain.

'Right, I'll be back soon,' I said, and bolted for the door. I didn't wait for Dad's response. All I heard was 'Charlie' as I slammed the front door behind me.

When I got to his block, I made my way up to the second floor. Thankfully there were no guards around. No muscle watching over the door. No sign of protection anywhere. My breathing was heavy. I put my hands on my knees to steady myself, get everything back on an even keel. Then I hammered and pounded the door.

'Hey! Hey! Hey!' the voice came from behind.

'Open,' I said.

'Who the hell is this?'

'Big Man, it's Charlie. Please open.'

He unclicked the lock and pulled the door towards him, leaving a gap of six inches or so. All I could see was the middle part of his face.

'What is it, Charlie?'

'I need –'

'You better not have come here to pull out of our agreement now.'

'No, I just need –'

'You better not be playing the shitbag on me. It's far too late for that. You know what'll happen.'

'I'm not. I need a favour, Big Man.'

'Another bloody favour?'

'Please,' I pleaded.

'All I do is hand out favours to you, Charlie.'

'This is serious, Big Man.'

He opened the door wide. I entered, making sure I wasn't being followed.

'Get in.'

The house stank of cheap booze, fag smoke and fast food.

WHERE DID HE GET THAT FROM?

'This better be good,' he said.

'It's my mum …'

'What about her?'

'She's in a bad way, Big Man, she can hardly breathe.'

'And that has *what* to do with me?'

'You're our only hope tonight.'

'Tell her to stick her head out the window.'

'She's really sick. All I need is one inhaler.'

'I told you, didn't I? I told you you'd get the stuff when the job was done.'

'I know you did, and I'm definitely going to –'

'And not a minute before.'

'I know, Big Man, and I will. I am going to do the job, honest I am, but I just need a little something before tomorrow.'

'No chance; she'll have to wait.'

'But if she waits she won't make it; then if Mum doesn't make tonight I won't make it tomorrow, if you know what I mean?'

The Big Man's eyes softened. He blew air out of his nose. He sank into his leather chair. Thinking time. Staring at me.

'You know what this means, don't you?' he said.

'What?'

'You've compromised me.'

'I ... erm ... didn't ... mean ...'

'And I don't like being compromised, Charlie.'

'Sorry, but it's an emergency, Big Man.'

'We live in a goddamn *emergency*, Law, don't you see that?'

'I do.'

'And we're going to do something about that, aren't we?'

'Yes.' I did not hesitate.

'Just as long as you know that.'

'I do.'

'Because we don't want to live in an emergency any longer, isn't that right?'

The pain was similar to badly needing to pee.

'Big Man, I'm in a real hurry here. Can you please –'

It hit me on the chest.

His throw was strong. The inhaler bounced off me and on to the floor. We looked at it.

'Well, pick it up, Charlie.'

'Thanks, Big Man. Thanks a lot.'

'Now get the hell out of here.'

'OK, I will,' I said, heading for my escape.

'And Charlie?'

'Yes.'

'If you're a no-show tomorrow it will be more than your mother's air I will cut off. Get me?'

'Get you,' I said.

When I handed over the inhaler I went straight to bed. I lay trying not to think about it, telling myself that I was part of some sick joke. An elaborate hoax that Pav and his family, including his sister, were all in on. Or that this trip with The Big Man on his motorbike was nothing more than a great illusion I'd created. I popped my head under the covers, closed my eyes and attempted to run away from it. Scarper. Bolt. Skedaddle. Eventually I fell asleep. But I kept waking up. Suddenly I was back to square one again. My choice was simple: either I killed Captain Duda or The Big Man would bring untold pain down on my world. I think they call this a catch-22.

An effing living hell is what I called it.

Earlier, when Pav was sitting on the chair above the steel, I'd wanted to tell him everything. The lot. I had one day to go before the shooting; he needed to know the plan.

Did I say something?

Yes.

I did tell Pav.

'Maybe you go get food, Charlie,' Pav had said to me.

'I think that's a good idea,' I'd said, and made to leave. But then the monster stopped me in my tracks. *HE'S YOUR ONLY HOPE, YOU CLOWN*. So I had turned to him and in all seriousness I said: 'Pav, I've something I have to tell you. Something very important.'

'What you tell, Charlie?'

'I want you to listen and not get angry. Just listen, OK?'

'I listen. I listen good,' Pav had said, shifting himself into a comfortable position.

I cleared my throat.

'Tomorrow …'

And I told him everything.

What I'd discovered about the two notes.

Everything.

36
Bag of Hammers

On the morning of the shooting I left the house to go to school as normal. And so did Pav. Playing everything cool. Not drawing suspicion. Instead, we met at the bottom of our block before rushing to the hill. Time was against us. Against me. Pav had agreed with my hurried plan. Shoddy and ludicrous as it was.

We crouched down behind the boulders, giving us a good view when the truck chugged down the hill.

'They drive up and down here all the time,' I said. 'Then they stop halfway down to see if there's anything going on.'

'And what I have to do again, Charlie?'

'Walk towards that big hill.'

'This hill?'

'Yes, all you have to do is go up the hill and wait for them to come around once again.'

'What if shoot at me?'

'They won't shoot you, Pav.'

'What if don't stop?'

'They will stop, believe me.'

'What if no stop though?'

'Pav, your sister will surely spot her little brother standing all alone on the hill; believe me, they'll stop.'

'OK, I go,' Pav said.

'You have the two notes?'

'Yes.'

'And you know what you're going to say?'

'I know.'

'And how you're going to say it?'

'I know. I know.'

'Right, I'll be here watching everything.'

'OK, I back soon.'

'Good luck, Pav.'

Pav rose, pulled up his trousers, fixed his school tie (strange) and began walking.

'And Pav?' I called to him.

'What?'

'Thanks, mate. Thanks for doing this. For helping me.'

'We pals. You and me, Charlie Law. Pals always help, no?'

'Yes.'

I watched the little figure of Pav get smaller as he walked away. On the hill he seemed positively tiny, like a lost boy looking for his mammy.

He paced. Back and forth. Again and again. No sign of the truck. He must've been twenty minutes on the hill and still no sign. More pacing. Back and forth. The Big Man would need patience waiting for me if this was how it was going to play out. Pav looked in my direction, put his arms out like a bird as if to say, *What the eff?* And just at that moment, that's when I heard it: the sound of the stuttering engine, the wheels turning, slowly grinding its way up the hill. Pav obviously heard it too. He stood to attention. Like, really stood to attention. He fixed his clothes, pulled up his trousers. He put his hands in front of him, in the praying position.

Maybe because it was morning time the truck didn't come to a sudden jolting stop. No, it came to slow retrospective halt. For sure someone in that truck knew who it was stopping for.

One of the thick necks came out and pushed Pav back with one hand. Pav returned the push. WHAT ARE YOU DOING, PAV? They played word tennis. The thick neck went for him again until the woman put an end to it. Chat was exchanged with the woman. His sister. Their lingo. The thick neck returned to the truck. Pav and his sister stood facing each other. Pav produced the notes from his pocket. I made out the small flecks of white paper. Pav's sister read them. More speaking. Pav pointed towards me.

No!

I took out the steel.

I had a clear shot.

Two clear shots.

Bang! Bang!

Job done.

I could have done it then. The sister looked my way. Why didn't she use the binoculars? Captain Duda returned to the truck, leaving Pav alone. A minute passed. Maybe two. The door swung open; she returned to her little brother. Further talk. Then came the thing that made my eyes widen and water. Captain Duda reached out and pulled Pav, her little brother, towards her. They hugged. They stopped hugging. More chat. *COME ON. DO IT. COME ON.* The sister jumped into the front of the truck. Pav jumped into the back. The truck hopped down the hill. It didn't take its usual right at The Big Tree. This time it drove in the opposite direction.

I waited for about two more minutes before scarpering. Knowing that I'd have to return later in the day. Pav knew where to find me.

At two o'clock on the dot it wasn't raining hard, just spitting. I was worried that my canvas backpack would weigh me down, hindering my escape. I had some books (why did I bring books?) and the steel inside. I felt that I had the load of the world in that backpack, that I was carrying a bag of hammers around with me. The last thing I needed was the additional weight of a rain-soaked load.

As I walked, the steel constantly bounced off my lower back. Thankfully the safety was on, otherwise imagine! There's no point talking about nerves. I was beyond nerves; my body had shifted to another stage, way past anything I'd ever experienced. Past what the bombs did to me or The Big Man's threats or Erin F's tender kiss. It was as if my body and mind weren't my own any longer.

The rain's spit plastered my face and the front part of my clothes.

I knew The Big Man would be watching my every move. Every step I took he'd have taken with me. No doubt about it. I got to the boulders just before two on the button. The rain drizzled down, my clothes soaked, hair matted. The constant sound of my sniffing echoed around my body. My back ached. This was not the best physical condition to be in. I dropped my bag of hammers to the ground and stretched out my back as best I could.

Not long to go.

I shuffled into my favourite position, on hunkers. Steadied my body, eyes peeled, ears adjusted. Listened to the rats scurrying around in my head. Rubbed Mum's back in my mind, opening all the windows to allow the fresh air to circulate around her. I took deep breaths. Sniffed, wiped the rain away from my head. A mixture of sweat and rain really. I unzipped the backpack and drew open the flaps like two miniature curtains. There it was. Lying on its side. Clean and ready to go. Loaded for action. No more mannequins; this was the real deal now. No more games. This time it was flesh, bone, blood, guts, brains. All I had to do was decide whose it was going to be.

Not long to go.

What if he'd planned it all? What if *he* was the one, you know, the grass, on the payroll of Old Country? *His* job to rid Little Town of all potential junior Rascals, to set me up. *Of course it was. Think about it. Think about Norman. Think about Max and Bones. You forgot about all them, didn't you?*

> **MENTAL MEMO:** ASK MORE PERTINENT QUESTIONS IN FUTURE. DON'T ALWAYS TAKE WHAT PEOPLE TELL YOU AS TRUTH.

Not long to go.

I took the thing out of the bag and positioned it comfortably in my hand. Dried my trigger finger as best I could. Stroked the trigger. *You'd better steady that thing, son. That's not a bloody toy you have there.* I peeked through the V-shaped aimer. Everything was in place. Ears now waiting for the chug chug of the vehicle. That's all I had left to do … apart from squeeze.

Not long to go.

Hunkered. Waiting. Wiping tears.

Just a matter of minutes.

Hunkered. Waiting. Holding tightly. Holding steady. Hand on the steel.

Anytime now.

Hunkered. Waiting. Aiming. Ready. Two hands on the steel.

Just a matter of …

The chug sound arrived. I watched it move up to the top of the hill and saunter down. Like clockwork. It stopped. Like clockwork. I waited. Aimed. Finger on the trigger. All set. Nothing happened. Shit! The rain. Please get out of the truck. *Please stay inside, you mean?* The rain. My breathing became short, loud spurts. It was an age until one of the thick necks exited. Not her. Then another thick neck came out. Still not her. I wiped snot away from my lip. Then it was her time. She appeared. Captain Duda. Into my view. No huddling for a chat this time. She was free. A target. A legitimate target. Pull! Get it over with. I blinked some water out of my aim eye. Not sure if it was tears or rain. I waited. The thick necks did their binocular routine, leaving her alone. I placed my wet finger on that trigger …

'What are you waiting for, Charlie?' The voice behind made me jump. I turned to see The Big Man standing ten feet behind me, all leather-clad and dripping wet hair hanging from him like an irritated apostle. Nostrils roaring. He was different, more menacing. Where was his motorbike? Why was he on foot? This wasn't part of the plan. Where was Pav? Where was everyone else? Where was the help? What had happened to the bloody plan?

'Surprised?' he said. I didn't answer. He held his arms out in the crucifix position like he had that first time we met.

'Big Man!' I said.

'What's the delay, Charlie?'

'Nothing, I was –'

'I'd be thinking about that mummy of yours.' The Big Man coughed, trying to imitate Mum's chest struggle. 'Think about that little mate of yours' family. Oh, I know what they'll do to them. To her.' He smirked. 'Think about that.'

'Big Man, I was just –'

'Think about that rat grass, Norman. Think about his bulging eyes with my hands squeezing the life out of him.' He gritted his teeth and stepped closer. 'So before you betray The Big Man, think carefully, Charlie Law.' The bag of hammers was now inside my body, attacking my every bone, every muscle and every blood cell I had. The pain of hearing his words was excruciating. He nodded towards Captain Duda on the hill.

'Go on, do it,' he snarled.

'Do it!' he barked.

I couldn't see properly; everything was a blur. The wind blew strong against my face. It felt like I was actually dying.

'FUCKING DO IT!' he screamed. 'Do –'

BANG!

Both hands immediately reached for my ears. The sound was much louder than I'd imagined.

And it was done.

It was done.

37
War Masters

Blood isn't as red as, say, the colour red is. It's deeper. Darker. Thicker. Like a stickier version of wine. The wine that Mum and Dad like to drink. I couldn't keep my eyes off the blood. How it flowed from the nose and trickled out of the ear like hot gummy lava. I didn't know that eyes could bleed. Of course I knew about the nose and mouth, but not the eyes. It looked like The Big Man was actually crying blood. And I watched that blood stream, gush, flood and spurt from every possible opening. I was mesmerised by this torrent, this river of red. It hypnotised me.

I wasn't aware of where the bullet had hit. After hearing the loud bang, all I saw was The Big Man falling. Everything happened in slow motion. The thud when he rattled the ground was long and dull. He bounced once or twice before rolling on to his back. Momentum taking him there.

I stood over him. I remember feeling calm and, I hate to say it, relief also. As if a tiny bullet had lifted a ton weight from my shoulders. And it had. I was no longer a killer, a murderer, nor a criminal. I was no Rascal. I was Charlie Law, schoolboy. I was Charlie Law, witness to a death in a war zone.

I heard The Big Man exhale his final breath on earth. Saw his eyes take their final flicker. The blood seeping from the wounded area formed a type of halo at the back of his head. I might've smiled at this, who knows?

My arm hung down by my side, still clutching the gun. When I realised this, and all that had befallen me, shock set in. Severe shock. My body caved to the intensity of the moment. My shaking was uncontrollable, my lungs ached with the rapid intakes of air I was trying to pour into them and my brain trembled at the realisation that I might be next. Next to get a bullet in the back of the head. I opened my mouth and howled. Not like a wolf, but like an abandoned child. I couldn't move my legs. I suppose real terror does that: it renders you immobile. That's what I was. A statue. Just waiting for a bullet that would force me to join The Big Man. I closed my eyes. Waited.

'Drop gun!' a voice bellowed. An Old Country voice.

I opened my hand. The gun fell.

And I waited.

'You can move now, boy,' the voice said. I remained in my position. 'You can move now.' I was stuck.

'It OK, you safe.' The voice had his hand on my shoulder. 'You safe with us now, boy.'

And when I opened my eyes, safe was exactly what I felt.

38
Confessions

WHY I TOLD PAV ABOUT BUMPING OFF HIS SISTER

- His mum was at the end of her tether with the desire to find her only daughter. *There's no way I was adding to her misery, especially since I knew how and where to find her.*
- I was terrified of becoming a murderer, terrified I'd have to spend fifty years in solitary, terrified I'd have to spend the rest of my life guilt-ridden and regretful. *Even though at the time the freedoms we had were rubbish, I was convinced that things could get better. I needed my freedom if I wanted to have dreams.*
- Pav was my mate. My best mate. It was a duty of one mate to inform the other whenever the chips were

down. *And at that time my chips were so down that they'd need a gravedigger to get them up.*

- I think deep down Pav wanted his sister back in his family's life. *I could help him do that, with a brilliant plan, however ill-conceived.*
- It was those notes. Something wasn't right. Something was amiss, but I cracked it. *That's when the plan was put into action.*

WHAT HAPPENED WHEN I TOLD PAV I'D BEEN ASSIGNED TO BUMP OFF HIS SISTER

(And how he was going to help me get out of this sticky wicket)

- Not long after the words came out of my mouth, Pav wanted to wring my neck.
- After I explained what The Big Man had asked me to do, and what it meant for me, he didn't want to throttle me any longer.
- I cried.
- He cried.
- We cried.
- He slumped on the chair and said nothing for a while. His sobs weren't as bad as mine.
- Our little cry made things seem better and brighter.
- He grilled me for ages about his sister, what happened when she and her cohorts duffed me up and just how

she was causing eruptions in The Big Man's camp by hassling their daily dealings and stopping them ripping off everyone in Little Town. We agreed that she was actually doing a good thing.

- He proclaimed that he was going to bump The Big Man off himself in order to save my and his sister's arse. I put a stop to such mental talk and informed him of my master plan.
- I produced the notes and explained the master plan idea.
- Pav wasn't exactly ecstatic but decided to go along with it, for the sake of his buddy and Captain Duda.
- Tears turned to smiles; he was eager to get the plan into action.

MENTAL MEMO: IF I EVER GET MARRIED TO ERIN F (OH, YES, PLEASE), PAV WILL BE MY BEST MAN. I'D HELP HIM WITH THE SPEECH!

39
Fire Setting

It was during that weekend before the 'next Tuesday' that I had read and reread those notes more closely. Two and two made four on the Sunday night. Hit me like an Old Country bomb. I couldn't believe how stupid I'd been in not noticing anything. Some detective I'd make.

Pav's note read:

Dear Scum … blah blah … you lot better … and then … blah blah … strong rope … mother and father will be … blah … you all will wish that … blah … now … or else …

No signature. No goodbyes. No see you later.

I sat on my bed with Pav's note beside me. Trying to figure it out. On the floor, in the back pocket of my crumpled-up school trousers, the note given to me by The Big Man bulged. My eyes closed in on themselves. I pictured the content of The Big Man's note alongside the one sitting on my bed.

I pictured hard.

The words leapt off the paper.

I had watched him write that note to me.

The one with 'next Tuesday' *when* and *where* details in it.

The death note.

My mouth was dry.

My lips parted.

I wetted them with my tongue.

Opened my mouth wider.

I knew exactly why I was doing this.

I was waiting, waiting for it to cement itself, waiting for it to smack me good and hard, uppercut style, on the chin. The knockout blow.

Then it arrived.

WHOOSH!

How utterly thick had I been? This was a brainless schoolboy error on my part. How could I not have seen this sooner? How could someone who reads tons of books and listens intently in class have missed this glaring piece of evidence?

I produced the notes the night before the mission. The night I told Pav everything. Right before The Big Man had given me the emergency inhaler. Right before he threatened me, us, again.

'Look at both of them,' I said, handing Pav the two notes.

'What I look for?'

'Look, closely.'

I so hoped he would see exactly what I'd seen, that I wasn't slowly going demented.

'Do you see anything?' I said. 'Any similarity? Anything at all?'

'What similarity?'

'Look at the paper, feel it.' Pav rubbed the two notes between each set of fingers.

'They same, no?' he said.

'Exactly. They're the same.'

'They same paper, Charlie.'

'Look at the writing.' I pointed at the words on each note, trying to direct his eye.

'What I see?'

'Look at the letter *i*; there are loads of them. Look how the dots at the top are similar.'

'I see. I see.'

'Now look at the letters *g*, *d* and *b*.'

Pav scanned.

'Same loops, eh?' I said.

'It is same. I think yes.'

'And the style of the writing leans to the right.' I illustrated this with my hand.

'Yes. It true, Charlie. It go right.'

'Now look at the colour of the ink.'

'Also same?'

'Pav?'

'What?'

'If it's the same paper, the same writing style and the same bloody pen … You know what that means, don't you?'

'Same person,' Pav said.

'Spot on, Pav. It is the same person.'

'Big Man?'

'The Big Man himself.'

'Fook me, Charlie.'

'That's who sent that note to you.'

'Big Man bastard! But why?'

'To put the fear of God into you,' I said.

'But I no threat to Big Man, Charlie. I no understand.'

'It's easy. The Big Man does want to get rid of you and your mum and dad. He wants to drive all Old Country people out of Little Town. But really, he wants to get at me. He wants to control me. He wants me to know that you're genuinely scared.'

Pav glared at me. He was seething. I think he growled.

'This not happen, Charlie. I have to make this not happen.'

'I think I know how, Pav.'

'How we make?'

'First you have to go to your sister and show her the notes. Tell her everything.'

'My sister? No ways.' He shook his head. 'I no do.'

'It's our only hope, Pav. You have to.'

Pav's baby blue blinders controlled mine. He sat down.

'Speak,' he said. 'I listen.'

'Look, I know how to find your sister. I know where she patrols. The plan is simple. You go to her, show her the notes, explain to her what is supposed to be happening. Where and when.'

'Simple for you,' Pav said. 'My sister is not the good person, Charlie.'

'Do it for your mum. Do it for your sister. You don't want any harm to come to her, do you?' I looked at my shoes. 'Do it for me, Pav. I can't kill anyone. I don't want to be a killer. But if I don't, The Big Man will sort me out. And your family. He owns me, and in some way he owns you too.'

'Short and curlies, right?' Pav said.

'Short and curlies, and then some,' I said.

Pav looked at his shoes. He snorted.

'Then what?' he said.

'Maybe your sister can stop The Big Man doing all this bad shit. Before it all gets out of hand.'

'Put Big Man in jail maybe?'

'Hopefully,' I said. There was a silence while Pav swirled the idea around. 'It'll be worth it, Pav.'

'Promise?'

'I promise.'

'OK, I do it for this reasons.'

'You will?'

'I do it.'

'Brilliant.'

'When we do?'

'Tomorrow morning, Pav.'

'Tomorrow morning?'

'Time is running out; we have no other days.'

'OK, we go tomorrow morning.'

'So, we'll meet at the bottom of the block as if we're going to school. We'll go to the hill and you wait until Captain … er … your sister's patrol passes. They'll stop no bother. Then you simply explain to her what is about to happen that afternoon. Easy!'

'For you easy! What if no stop truck?'

'You'll have to wave your arms around.'

'I can do,' Pav said. 'I can do.'

And he did. Only they didn't arrest The Big Man that morning. They couldn't find him in his skanky flat or in any of his regular hangouts. So Captain Duda decided that *I* was the one who'd bring *him* to *them*. Charlie Law, The Big Man's little lap dog. Knowing that The Big Man had me by the short and curlies, they gathered that he wouldn't be too far away when I brought *his* gun to the hill at two o'clock in the rain to kill Pav's sister. And they were right.

40
You and I

We made the list together. I wrote it out in my best handwriting, but then I ripped it up and told Pav to write it instead. He should practise. He needed the practice. It was time to be ruthless with him. A no-mercy approach was my new philosophy. No more Mr Nice Guy teacher.

The list wasn't very extensive:

Mineral water, still and sparkling (my choice)
Orange juice (Pav's)
Four chocolate bars (both)
Dried fruit and nut selection (my choice)
Bunch of flowers (Pav's)
Plastic cups (both)
Paper plates (both)

Crisps (Pav's)
Assorted finger snacks (my choice)

Both our mums and dads gave us money to buy the stuff. I think Pav's sister gave him a cheeky backhander too. It'd be good having a big sis or bro to hand me money from time to time. Think Mum and Dad are too old for that nonsense now. Who knows? We'll see.

We went to the shops in the morning to get the gear. It was the first time I'd ever shopped for my own stuff that wasn't a book. When we walked past The New Bookshop I tried to drag Pav inside for a quick browse, but he was having none of it.

'Don't be crazy academic, Charlie. We have the ton work to do.' Trying to get Pav inside the bookshop was a bit like asking the old Regime to vote for free elections. Things were about to get rougher for Pav though, you see; we had made a pact to drag his scrawny arse in there, and the school library, as much as possible. He would have no choice other than to learn the lingo properly.

When the shed was all set we sat in the chairs and tried to slow our heartbeats down. My backside was flapping. Pav's was crawling in ants. We constantly hopped off the chairs to arrange or rearrange things. Fluff up the flowers. Anything other than sitting and waiting.

'Oh, shitting hells,' Pav said, 'I forget something.'

'What?'

'I back in minute.'

'Don't leave me here alone, Pav,' I said. 'What if they come and you're not …'

But it was too late; he was out of there like a blue-arsed fly. While Pav was off doing God knows what, I considered painting the shed the following summer. They sold cheap paint and brushes at the new DIY store. It could be a summer activity the four of us could partake in. Man, imagine having a television in here? What a dream that would be. I'm sure it wouldn't be too hard to rig up electricity.

I looked at the stuff we'd bought: the lovely flowers, the bright orange juice, the reds, maroons and yellows of the dried fruit and the allure of the chocolate. All these colours were the same as my outlook. My eyes floated to the once loose floorboard. I was glad that Pav had borrowed his dad's hammer and nailed it down.

'God, I thought you were never coming back, Pav,' I said, which wasn't true.

'I forget this.' From a bag Pav produced a Moleskine notebook and a pen. The pen with the four different colour choices. *The* Moleskine notebook and pen.

'Is that the one given to you by The Big … ?' I said.

'Yes. I save it in room, but I give as a gift today,' Pav said. He opened the Moleskine and removed – o*h, not another blinking note* – a pristine white handkerchief. Not one of your throwaways; this was the real deal. One hundred per cent cotton.

'You forgot that as well?' I said.

'Yes.'

'I could've given you one, Pav.'

'Not this one.'

'Why? What's so special about that one?'

'It not mine. Look.' He showed the hanky. The letters ML were positioned in one of the top corners.

'ML, that's …' Then I remembered.

'Mercy Lewis,' Pav said. 'She give me when dickhead numpties batter lights in of me. Today I return to Mercy with notebook and big thank you.'

'Nice move, Pav. Nice move.' I wished then that I had something to give to Erin F. All I had was myself. I really hoped that it would be good enough.

Pav took Mercy Lewis up to say hello to his mum and dad. All that was left over from the feast were a few crisps, sparkling water and some dried fruit. And me and Erin F. She dazzled.

In unity with her mum, Erin F had shaved her hair off. I didn't want to go on about how much I missed her stunning locks. Hair comes. Hair goes. But her amazing gesture would remain in many people's hearts forever. I couldn't wait to run my hands through it when it did grow back though.

'Sorry it's taken ages for me to come see this place, Charlie,' Erin F said.

'Don't worry, you're here now.'

'It's cool.'

'Really?'

There you go, Charlie. You're now cool.

'Yes, it would be a brilliant study area as well.'

'Eh, hello. That's what I keep telling Pav.'

'Want some help clearing up?' she said.

'That's OK, you just sit and relax, Erin F.'

'Don't talk crap, Charlie. I don't buy into all that chivalry rubbish.'

We got on our feet at the same time, almost touching bodies. Erin F looked at me. I looked at her. I loved looking at her, not only because she was so utterly beautiful, but because she made me feel so utterly special. So utterly wanted. I'm sure nerves could be heard shattering all over my body.

What do I do now?

Who makes the move?

Am I supposed to?

I don't know.

I, Charlie Law, haven't a clue about such things.

Go on. Kiss her. She wants you to do it, daft arse.

I closed my eyes, drew nearer to her, put out my lips and let myself float away. And I floated and floated, and kept floating until it was as if we were a part of the same body.

You know, I've often wondered: would we all have been together if the bombs hadn't come to Little Town? I mean: was it *only* the bombs that brought us together?

Who knows?

Who knows?